TUCKER
AND
HMS LION

TUCKER
AND
HMS LION

THE EXPLOITS OF LIEUTENANT REGINALD
TUCKER IN THE GRAND FLEET

JOHN HINTON

Library of Congress Control Number:		2014910500
ISBN:	Hardcover	978-1-4990-8697-3
	Softcover	978-1-4990-8698-0
	eBook	978-1-4990-8699-7

Apart from Lieutenant Tucker, some of the characters in this book are real, others are wholly fictional, and almost all of what occurs, at least in some form, actually happened in real life.

This book was printed in the United States of America.

Rev. date: 06/23/2014

To order additional copies of this book, contact:
Xlibris LLC
0-800-056-3182
www.xlibrispublishing.co.uk
Orders@xlibrispublishing.co.uk
617510

INTRODUCTION

THE EXTRAORDINARY EXPLOITS of a young officer in the British Grand Fleet during the first two years of World War I are described in this journal. Lieutenant Reginald Tucker's account of his life in the Royal Navy a century ago was discovered by relatives in his seaside retirement cottage in Hampshire. Also found was his Distinguished Service Cross, granted for exceptional services to his country, along with his dress uniform and sword.

The journal begins with the first serious clash between British and German battlecruisers at the Battle of Dogger Bank in January 1915, the first fight ever between these fast new warships with their long-range guns.

Tucker joins HMS *Lion*, flagship of the legendary First Battlecruiser Squadron under the command of the dashing Vice Admiral David Beatty just before the visit by the squadron to Russia prior to the outbreak of hostilities in 1914. They were welcomed by Tsar Nicholas II and his daughters in St Petersburg, where they hosted one of the last great parties of the belle époque.

Tucker's subsequent adventures are linked with his encounters with the eccentric First Sea Lord, Jacky Fisher, who in many ways becomes his mentor, giving him chances to advance his career. Jacky decides to send him as his envoy on a testing mission which could alter the course of the war. As part of that mission, Tucker has further romantic encounters with

Grand Duchess Tatiana, meets friends in the Royal Flying Corps and the First Lord of the Admiralty, Winston Churchill.

Never intended expressly for publication, the journal is remarkably candid about the sometimes deadly yet often hilarious reality of life aboard a warship of the period.

SIGNAL

FROM THE ADMIRALTY'S top-secret Room 40 to the First Lord of the Admiralty, Winston Churchill, on 23 January, 1915: 'Those fellows are coming out again. Four German battlecruisers, six light cruisers, and 22 destroyers will sail this evening.'

From the journal of Lieutenant Reginald Tucker, of the First Battlecruiser Squadron, on board HMS *Lion*: 'On the face of it, we were the superior force. Yet no one knew what to expect when these big ships met. It certainly wasn't going to be a duck shoot.'

CHAPTER 1

I AWOKE BEFORE dawn in my cabin on *Lion*, too tense to sleep soundly. As I drew back the curtains over the porthole and looked out, the eastern horizon was showing a gleam of first light over the sullen, icy grey of the North Sea. I switched on the light, glanced at my wristwatch—6.45 a.m.—and pressed the bell for my servant, Haddock, who brought a strong black coffee.

"Good morning, Lieutenant," he said brightly enough as I scrambled into my uniform. A quick fried breakfast followed in the wardroom. Then just after seven, the bugles sounded Action Stations. Jacky Fisher's fast new battlecruisers were about to be baptised in battle with ships of the same class. More than a century after Trafalgar, had their captains, officers, and men still got the "Nelson touch"?

Just after 7.45 a.m., the light cruiser *Southampton* signalled: "Enemy sighted." Thanks to the decoders of German signals in the Admiralty's top-secret Room 40, we met as predicted at Dogger Bank. Importantly, we had the element of surprise.

Three of Admiral Franz Hipper's battlecruiser squadron, including his flagship, *Seydlitz*, had 25 knots and eight 11-inch guns. His fourth ship, *Blucher*, was older, with only 23 knots and 8-inch guns.

Vice Admiral Sir David Beatty's battlecruiser force—the Splendid Cats—led by his flagship, *Lion*, each had 28 knots and eight 13.5-inch guns. It was five against four. Daylight was now spreading, a light breeze causing only a slight swell on the sea. Conditions were perfect apart from the squadron's billowing black funnel smoke.

I was scared, exhilarated. As I came up on the weather deck in my greatcoat, my teeth were soon chattering, my eyes watering in the freezing wind created by *Lion*'s slipstream. Then I ran forward 100 yards up to the signal bridge, getting showered with sparks and soot billowing from the funnels, the stokers below slaving to feed the furnaces with tons of coal per hour to raise steam for the roaring turbines.

And here on the open bridge of the 26,000-ton giant was Beatty and his team. The New Nelson of popular imagination appeared to be enjoying himself. He gave me his usual keen glance, a quick smile.

"Ah, Lieutenant Tucker, right on time. It should be quite a scrap. Fireworks any minute." And he pointed to the eastern horizon and the enemy's heavy ships: four wedges perched on the horizon as the wan winter sun rose. Behind them, clouds of smoke rose from their destroyers.

"Can't wait, sir," I shouted back with more conviction than I felt.

Lion's bows dug into the sea, the salt spray vaulting up, the spindrift lashing our faces. We were closing fast. Then at 22,000 yards—twelve miles—two muzzle flashes of white flame followed by a faint rumble came from one of the enemy ships. After a flight of 30 seconds, two great columns of water rose more than half a mile off, blossomed into a crescendo of spray, then majestically fell back into the sea.

"He'll have to do a bloody sight better than that," growled Chatfield, the Flag Captain. It was a sobering sight. I had been at Heligoland Bight back in August, an unequal contest when we sank three enemy light cruisers. But our opponents this morning were heavy ships.

If *Lion* started taking punishment, some would inevitably face horrors worse than the jagged wooden splinters punched out by the solid shot of Nelson's day. You could get turned into a wind-blown crisp by the blue flame of a direct hit, flayed alive by escaping steam, sliced like ham by razor-sharp shell splinters, killed by cordite flash which left you eerily untouched before you blew up like a balloon, or trapped by buckled steel hatches and drowned in the cold North Sea. Just thinking about it was bad enough.

At 8.25 a.m., at 20,000 yards, Beatty snapped: "Sighting shot."

One of the forward B Turret 13.5s roared out, the blast of cordite smoke blowing back from the muzzle and smudging our faces. One sailor too near the turret was bowled over by the blast as if hit by a typhoon. My ears cracked. A little fountain in the distance showed our shot too was short. Behind their shield, the crew of one of the 4-inch guns were singing, strangely consoling as we moved into the killing zone of around 17,500 yards.

At 8.55 a.m., now steaming at 26 knots, Beatty ordered maximum speed. As the speed signal hoist was hauled down to execute, *Lion* appeared to surge forward.

Ten minutes later, the range now effective for accurate fire, Beatty signalled: "Open fire and engage the enemy." The sea was becoming alive with shell splashes and splinters, some big enough to cut a man in half. I had a perfect view of the forward, midships, and stern turrets belching smoke and flame and their 1,400 lb shells. The gun flashes were temporarily blinding, the noise indescribable.

At 9.35, Beatty signalled the battlecruisers by flag: "Engage corresponding ship in the enemy line." *Lion* and *Tiger* were to target the *Seydlitz* and *Moltke* respectively while *Princess Royal* and *New Zealand* took on *Derfflinger* and *Blucher*. But aboard *Tiger*, Pelly foolishly joined fire on *Seydlitz*—not hitting her once by all reports, but dangerously leaving the unmolested *Moltke* to punch holes in *Lion* at her leisure. The clouds of black funnel smoke swirling over the scene might have obscured the signal—but it was a fatal mistake.

Spray from near misses was now drenching the decks. Then one of the lookouts cried out; a shell splinter had laid his cheek open to the bone. Under heavy fire, senior officers were supposed to crowd into the armoured conning tower. Detesting its slit-like views, Beatty stayed on the open bridge despite the danger. As did I, joined by Filson Young, RNVR, a writer, on board to observe life with the battlecruisers. He had been waiting for this moment and grinned.

Chatfield approached. "Man of the phone at the foretop has caught one. Anyway, he isn't talking on the navy phone. Get up there, Tucker, and do your best. And watch it, it's starting to get a bit nasty." He looked at Filson. Chatfield didn't like scribblers. "And take Lieutenant Young with you—good views from there. Now go and get your gear."

We met at the bottom of the 60-foot-long steel ladder to the foretop, encumbered by thick clothing, oilskins, swimming waistcoats (you'd be dead in this temperature of water in about three minutes), and binoculars. Rubber hoses were strewn all over the deck in case of fire, and some damage control crews lurked about. The cold steel rungs of the terrific ladder were icing up nicely, and the ship's slipstream did everything possible to loosen our grip. A big ricocheting shell painted in yellow stripes passed very close, cartwheeling over and over in the air.

Its engines generating 80,000 h.p., *Lion* vibrated quite violently at top speed—28 knots is going some in a 700-foot-long ship—and Beatty was now zigzagging to avoid the salvoes from *Moltke*. We needed the combined skills of a trapeze artiste and a mountaineer. My buttocks were tightening; I was dizzy with fright. To make matters worse, as we were halfway up the ladder, clinging on with gloved hands, a blow from a shell hitting the hull nearly shook us off.

I looked down at Filson. "Okay?" I shouted.

He looked up, grinned, and nodded. I'd got to know him better in more peaceful days. How he'd wheedled his way on to a ship at a time when Jellicoe, the Commander-in-Chief, treated journalists like lepers was nothing short of miraculous. Bet he was thinking: "Wouldn't miss this for the world." Gave me heart, really. Mind you, I did have responsibilities— keeping us both alive, for instance.

Above us, the mast still seemed to reach the sky. And stretching over a halyard and stained with funnel and gun smoke was the White Ensign, the Navy's battle flag, blowing flat-out in the wind—the *Victory's* flag.

My wristwatch read 9.25 a.m. when, after a dreadful heart-stopping reach across to the trapdoor on the underside of the foretop platform, we were there. Then we had to throw the dead marine unceremoniously off to make room, his body landing on the deck far below.

It was impossible to stand up in the box-like foretop because of the freezing wind, so we knelt uncomfortably on the rivet heads of the steel floor, rested our elbows on the rim, and poked our glasses over the edge to witness the battle a giddy, swaying 90 feet above the sea.

The oldest German ship, the *Blucher*, had a bad list, several fires but was still shooting, and the concentration of our squadron seemed to be on completing her destruction. With her puny 8-inch guns, she should not have been there at all.

The other Germans were shooting well. We were in a perfect position to see the shells coming; making a rushing sound, they took about 23 seconds to travel to the target. You widened your eyes until it seemed they would explode inside your head. Some exploded in the sea, shown by the 100-foot-high waterfalls of spray and the splinters, which we could often see coming. Put a finger out beyond the thin steel screen, and it would be cut off in seconds. Some of the salvoes whizzed over. Some hit. Below, the teak deck was battered and littered with fragments of steel and yawning gashes where heavy shells had burst or large fragments had penetrated.

At 9.50 a.m., *Lion* dealt a blow to *Seydlitz*. Hits on two turrets produced gouts of flame that reached 200 high. They must have instantly killed both turret crews. But Hipper's flagship was not crippled. As if to prove it, just after 10 a.m. *Seydlitz* hit *Lion*, knocking out two dynamos. It was a bloody nuisance, but not crippling.

Ten minutes later, the German destroyers and light cruisers laid down a thick smoke screen, behind which their heavy ships attempted to open the range. Their light craft then massed to attack but met a violent curtain of fire from *Lion* and *Tiger's* 4-inch secondary armament and turned away.

Then at 10.15 a.m. we thought we would be tossed from our perch. A gigantic hammer blow—two simultaneous shots from the *Derfflinger*—drove into the 9-inch waterline armour plate and allowed in seawater, which soon crippled our port engine. Members of the fire control parties were washed along the deck like cockles on a beach.

We started to list and fall back. The rolling of the ship and the hail of splinters kept us alert, but there seemed little we could do except wish for some steel helmets. The huge volumes of funnel and gun smoke drifting across the range made visibility patchy at best, and then the navy phone rang.

"Foretop? Thought you'd got hit. Can't see much at gun level at the moment. How's your vision?"

"All right. Bit patchy."

"We've got a target, 11 o'clock. See our splashes. Let me know." The 13.5-inchers boomed out.

"You're over. She's stern on. Hold it, hold it. Shoot! Straddle. Wait now . . . a hit!"

"Good. Rapid. Thanks . . . er."

"Tucker. She's making 24 knots, I would guess, so keep upping your rate. I think she's trying to go home. Look at that!"

"Missed it—bloody smoke again."

"You've just hit her forward funnel. Flames all over the place. Good shooting. Keep it up."

"Yes, we can see her now. Thanks, Tucker."

"Glad to help." Damn it, that felt better. Done something at last. The dull red glows from the target indicated other successful hits. I had started to lose track, the mind beginning to reject the continuous commotion. Then the navy phone rang again from the bridge.

"The Admiral's spotted a periscope track. Seen anything?"

"No, not a thing." How could any submarines be around given their slow underwater speed?

"Well, start looking. And if you spot anything, let us know."

I swept carefully with my glasses, but all I could see was bodies, bits of smashed lifeboats, and shoals of dead fish floating belly up in the sea.

Blutcher was finished. But she was still being punished. We learned later from a surviving officer of the impact of seventy heavy shells. In the terrific air pressure of explosions in confined spaces, men were whirled around like dead leaves in a winter blast, tossed into the machinery; explosives mixed with oil and sprayed around causing dreadful burns and scarring. Below, there were gasping shouts and moans as the shells plunged through the decks—a nightmare of flesh versus steel and explosives.

In a small lull between salvoes, Beatty soothingly hailed us from the signal bridge, his cap at its usual jaunty angle, unflustered by the risk of being hit by splinters at any moment.

"Enjoying yourselves?" he shouted, munching a sandwich and generally exhibiting a stupefying amount of sangfroid. He might have been at Ascot, his wife beside him wearing—knowing Ethel—a hat which would probably have cost more than I earned in a year.

"Yes, sir," I shouted, lying through my chattering teeth, "jolly good view from here," as though I too were at the races.

"Bloody good, copy, eh, Filson? You've been blooded!"

"Yes, sir!" said Filson, waving.

Beatty waved back encouragingly. But then came the split-second grimace I had got to know, a flicker of discontent. *Lion* was badly wounded and was still being battered by *Seydlitz's* remaining turrets and by *Moltke*. The last dynamo had died, so had the wireless. I could see only two flag halyards that hadn't been shot away.

Our knees were bleeding from the rivets in the steel floor—the designer ought to be shot. The drenching spray was starting to ice up on us. Filson's cap was winged away by a splinter into the long ribbon of foam astern, and we were going deaf from the thunder of the guns.

There were 1,000 men below us on *Lion*. I prayed for them all: navigators, signalmen, the telephonists, clerks, the engineers, the gunners, the medics. Would they survive? Would I survive? And how in hell's name did I get here in the first place?

Soaking, freezing, battle-stained, concussed, but still intact, I fell into my battlecruiser dreams of only two or three years ago. The *Lion*, still ostensibly in command, was losing ground. First by one mile . . . then two.

As for me, I too was drifting away . . .

CHAPTER 2

APART FROM THE dashing Beatty, my schoolboy ambition to join the Senior Service was fired by admiring articles about the man responsible for lashing us into the lead in the naval race—the amazing First Sea Lord, Jacky Fisher.

Explosively energetic according to one account, Jacky began each day with a dawn prayer about smiting the Philistines, then went down the slipway of rectitude into a cold bath containing his toy dreadnoughts. "Shoot!" I imagined him saying, holding one of the tiny ships above the surface, then "Down among the dead men let them lie," gleefully plunging his opponent under the water and biffing him with the soap. I also read the hit novel *The Riddle of the Sands* about German warships being prepared for invasion among the Frisian sandbanks. This young interest—virtually an obsession—was not unusual by early 1912, when everyone had caught war fever in spades.

And there was another reason.

I grew up in Birkenhead, which last time I saw it looked about as interesting as Sunderland on a wet and windy Tuesday in February, but was then making battleships in John Laird's shipyard, which was the town's raison d'être. Humming with class distinction and driving ambition, it had a town hall full of pot-bellied aldermen, hundreds of damp slums crammed with underfed shipyard workers, and docks crammed with freighters and navy ships—even some magnificent old windjammers.

It had a splendid park—used as the model for Central Park in New York—where I had the pleasure of fondling Margaret's tits for the first time in the bushes beside the mock-Chinese pagoda and the ornamental pond. She may have been the daughter of a primitive Methodist preacher, but by God, the sap was rising in that girl even though she would invariably submit to God's will, declare "What we have done is very wrong," button up her blouse, purse her lips, and look at me as though I was something in an advanced state of decomposition.

Margaret herself fell for the Navy in the shape of my older cousin Hugh. Of course there was no comparison between a no-hoper still at Liverpool Institute and a young officer and gentleman in His Majesty's Royal Navy, splendid in his new uniform with its stiff white collar, jaunty cap, and gold flashes on the sleeves.

Less to do with the tailor than what it signified. This was, after all, the uniform of the Royal Navy—not pipsqueaks like the Russian Navy or the French Navy, but the British Navy, the world's biggest maritime force with its long grey lines of battleships and cruisers stretching in awful menace back over the bowl of the horizon. As the press saw it, the Grand Master of these thousands of tons of firepower provided by Jacky Fisher's genius was Beatty with his matinee idol features, his cap at a rakish angle, and his distinctive monkey jacket with six buttons instead of the regulation eight. He was casual, debonair but highly dangerous in the best British tradition—just what I yearned to be. "Look here, Johnny Foreigner, play the game by our rules, or we'll breeze along with some of the lads and blow your socks off."

I did fear, perhaps unduly, that I had one major disadvantage. Hugh's father was a kind of executive at Laird's, hardly high-ranking yet clearly respectable within an industry vital for the security of the nation. But the Tuckers didn't make defective artillery shells, .303 rounds, and go to Ascot. We made sausages, delivered all over the place, and ran a high-class butcher's emporium for the rich Liverpool merchants and toffs who lived in big houses on the hill delivered by bicycle boys or prize-winning ponies and traps. And when we did go to the races, it would be no further than Chester. Even if we did make pots of money, we were in—hem—trade or, stretching the point because of the sausage "factory," commerce. Naval officer recruits generally came from fractionally higher up the social scale.

Before Jacky got going, the Royal Navy was virtually a gentleman's club, with gunnery practice frowned upon because it dirtied uniforms and gleaming paintwork.

I could have done with some contacts, but not Hugh, whom I found dull and annoying. I would do it though, anything but help father strangle the entire North of England with Tucker's Famous Beef and Tomato Sausages.

"Hugh looks so handsome in his uniform," said Margaret after he'd returned to his ship. She straightened her skirt and gazed sideways at me in mute disapproval after the heavy necking session at the pagoda.

Margaret was not only a tease; she was also a prize cow—loved every minute of it too.

"He may look handsome in his uniform," I scoffed, "but so would the Hunchback of Notre Dame. It's all about personality. You've got to impress with more than brass buttons, or you'll end up paddling a rusty old gunboat around the East Indies. Those fellows don't see their families for years on end."

She'd started to redden in the face; I was getting to her. "And," I added, "you know as well as I do that Hugh hasn't an original thought in his head. You'll get no poems to make your head reel from Hugh's distant outpost. Wait till I'm in uniform."

"You? You'll be lucky to get a rowing boat," said the randy little trollop.

That did it. Decision time—time to make clear my intentions. Father wasn't in the best of moods at dinner. The mad lady halfway up the hill had been at the sherry again and had decided to hold another of her doggy parties. His brow wrinkled in agitation above his fearsome beard.

"I don't mind selling her tripe and whale meat for her dreadful hounds, but those little poodles and terriers—far better off under the wheels of a car, in my view—get best sirloin! Think of that. Some of the people down in the town have never tasted a decent piece of beef in their lives!" He glared and savaged his plate of lamb chops as though taking revenge on the effete little pouches that were even now nibbling prime cuts.

Still, no time like the present.

"Father?" I said suddenly. "I've been thinking about the future." My earnest confession that I wanted to join the Navy and had thought about the subject deeply stopped him in his tracks. Slowly his scowl lifted, and a smile twitched the ends of his moustache. He had twigged that I was an ambitious rogue some time back, perhaps in the nursery, but being secretly one himself, we were quite close. His smile broadened.

"Reginald, it's my fondest hope that you will join me in the business and blaze the name of Tucker's sausages throughout the North. You know our sausages are irresistible, Reginald—you've had enough of them!" I had indeed.

Mother was looking distinctly apprehensive.

"Don't worry, mother," I said.

"But," said father, "there's time for you to spend in the Navy first if that's what you've set your heart on." He frowned and added: "But judging by your reports, you'll have to crack on at that expensive school of yours."

"You won't come to any harm, will you, Reg?" echoed mother. The sun was starting to kiss the tide at day's end, and it streamed into the dining room, turning us into pale shadows. Father picked up a cutlet and gnawed it down to the bone. "Some of the new ships can fire shells up to twenty miles. That's from here to Chester. And they've got to hit something, haven't they, Reg? Well, just make damned sure it isn't you."

"Father, you're on my wavelength," I said heartily.

"Wave what, Reg? Wave a flag?" asked mother apprehensively. "Those German boys who came on an exchange last summer seemed very nice. Do you want to put on the phonograph, Reg?"

"No, thanks, mother." Much more talk of huge shells heading in my direction to the accompaniment of Handel's *Largo*, mother's mournful favourite, and I might get second thoughts.

"I think, just this once, this calls for a glass of sherry. Like one, Reg?" said father, reaching for the key to the liquor cabinet.

"Rather," I said brightly.

Between us, we finished the bottle. I have never been so close to my father before or since.

CHAPTER 3

ACROSS THE MERSEY river, I wasn't exactly the star pupil at Liverpool Institute. "Fair" dominated my half-term reports for the spring term of '12, and only literature was "good." Geometry and mathematics were "poor," which didn't augur well for the important navigational abilities needed on HM ships. But the headmaster summed up with one comment I was pleased with. "Lots of go!" he wrote. Encouraged, I resolved to climb the mountain of despair called Matriculation in earnest.

Unfortunately, my enthusiasm lacked the murderous elan of father chasing a stray poodle in his Studebaker, which he had imported at considerable expense from America. My natural reluctance to study somehow had to be overcome. Also, pulling in the wrong direction was the school bully, a sadistic German maths teacher, and two tearaways called Chips and Ian. They came with me by train through the new Mersey Tunnel each morning, lounging around with their feet on the seats, smoking like chimneys, and laughing like crows at anyone they thought looked funny, which was nearly everyone—particularly unfortunates with goitres, cross eyes, and club feet. Cruel lot, the Merseysiders.

The bully was an oversized brute called Senior, who was chauffeur-driven to school—his father was making a fortune out of cinemas. "What's that blood on your shirt, Tucker?" he'd ask as we unloaded our stuff in the locker room before assembly. "Been doing some butcherin' again on the way to school? Chopped up a few dogs for the stew, eh, Tucker?"

And minutes later, Schmidt, the German maths tutor, would be at me with his lazy, take-no-prisoners Prussian drawl.

"You seem to have missed the point again, Tucker. Stay behind for half an hour, won't you?"

But somehow I kept grinning and bearing it and hacking away at the intellectual coalface until Easter, when Hugh came back on leave and dazzled Margaret with an invitation to a cocktail party aboard an American cruiser which was paying a courtesy call to Liverpool.

"I know how much you'd like to go," said Margaret, trying successfully to make me mad. "But only ship's officers are allowed to accompany a young lady, not schoolboys. So sorry, Reginald."

Bitch.

And that was the start of it. Down the slipway of devil-may-care I launched, letting loose the first broadside in chemistry class. I chose to ignore Senior's mutterings and "accidently" jabbed a piece of armature wire into his neck.

He howled.

This led to a showdown in the changing rooms when I went berserk and nearly brained him with a cricket bat; it missed by half an inch and then split in two. He backed away after this murderous assault and never bothered me again.

One problem solved.

This was the new me: bold, assured, taking no nonsense. Next time I saw Chips and Ian on the train, I hauled a packet of strong Capstan Navy Cut cigarettes out of my pocket and lit up.

"I'm fed up with bloody Liverpool Institute," I announced grandly with evident sincerity, my head spinning with the unaccustomed nicotine. An old lad next to me was puffing on a briar; Ian and Chips were exhaling Senior Service—all rather fitting with the talk in the papers about war clouds looming. We were making as much smoke as a flotilla of destroyers.

"And I'm fed up with trying for Matriculation with sadistic krauts like Schmidt. And girls—all girls."

"Well, that's a change of tune." Chips grinned through the smoke. "I don't know about Schmidt, but you should take your mind off things and meet some girls we know."

"Make you feel better in no time," said Ian, flicking his cigarette ash into a passing shopping basket.

"I don't want girlfriends. They're fickle. They let you down."

"We don't exactly mean girlfriends," Ian said wickedly. "More like young lady companions."

"With an educational bent," said Chips.

"Oh, I see—like personal instructors," I ventured, puffing away with my head reeling and not the faintest idea what they were talking about. If the train didn't reach Central Station very soon, I was going to throw up in the gangway, which would do nothing to burnish my reputation as an apprentice rake.

"That's one way of putting it," Ian said. "Others call them ladies of the night."

"Blimey." I grinned, finally twigging and rather appalled and excited at the same time.

My tempters conferred in whispers for a moment.

"You can come with us tomorrow night," Chips said. "Oysters and a steak and a few drinks at Ma Boyle's and then on to Maggie's place. We'll introduce you to Greta, a lovely girl who's got a special place in her heart for boys from the Institute. Oh, and bring a few quid if you can manage that."

I had been trying to enjoy smoking as I awaited what was to be one of my first "adult" nights on the town. And you can hardly be a rakish aspiring member of the Senior Service without a fag in your mouth. I persevered—waking up during that night and dragging away at one, leaving a dizzy feeling which was not too bad.

But of course the big thing with cigarettes was the nonchalant opening of the packet and the extraction of the fag, the practised concentration as you lit up and took the first long draw so that the tip glowed like a furnace, then lifting the chin and exhaling and looking around with a knowing smile.

I had a good opportunity to try this out the following evening perched on a bar stool at Ma Boyle's Oyster Bar in Liverpool, waiting for the lads to arrive—and dressed to kill in my three-piece light-grey suit, starched white shirt, and bright-red tie. There were two remarkably pretty office girls glancing in my direction from a corner table, and I thought the sophisticated sight of me lighting up would be just the ticket for them.

Unfortunately, I had just reached the bit where you raise your chin when a stray whiff of smoke got caught at the back of my throat, and as I exhaled, I exploded at the same time. Then I got more smoke in my eyes, and they started watering. And I went as red in the face as if I'd farted in the middle of one of Margaret's father's sermons. I tried a watery man-of-the-world smile, but by this time, one of the girls was laughing so much her tits nearly fell out of her blouse.

There was a great big list of drinks chalked up on a board, and the most expensive was Black Velvet at eleven pence a pint, which was going a bit.

"I'll have a pint of Black Velvet, please," I said, catching Ma Boyle's eye.

"Celebrating, are we?" she asked, looking at me knowingly.

She probably guessed I was under the limit for imbibing, but they didn't worry too much about things like that in those days. She uncorked a bottle of champagne, poured half a pint into the glass, then topped it up with draught Guinness, leaving a snowy-white head as thick as whipped cream.

There was only one way to drink the stuff apart from asking for a straw, and that was to dive in. This I did, and it tasted fit for a King. But then I heard the girls tittering again, and I realised they could see my reflection in the mirror behind the bar with a big handlebar moustache of foam on my upper lip and a big blob at the end of my nose.

"Do you think he's brought his shaving tackle?" one of the jezebels said in a loud whisper, cracking up and nearly spilling her drink.

"I don't think he's old enough . . . to shave," said the other.

And they both giggled like schoolgirls. And once those Liverpool girls get going, there is no stopping them. In fact, they became so hysterical that Ma Boyle had to go over to their table and calm them down, giving me a chance to have a few more gulps of the foaming Black Velvet. It was so wonderful that I finished the pint in no time and ordered another. And by the time I'd finished that, I was winking at the girls and not caring how much they laughed. And by the time Chips and Ian arrived, I was well in control of the situation.

More Black Velvet followed, and by the time we'd each had a plate of oysters, steak, and chips and shared a bottle of claret, I was ready for anything.

"Time for Maggie's," said Chips. And we piled into a taxi which chugged up the hill past the art gallery, then in and out of the trams on Lime Street. At St George's Hall, there was a great civic event going on with carriages and motors drawing up and doors being opened for men in toppers and tails and women with fantastic headwear and long evening gowns. Just further on, we ran into the usual hubbub of porters wheeling luggage to the new Adelphi Hotel, where the nobs stayed overnight before taking their berths on the big liners bound for New York.

But we weren't going anywhere—not far anyhow—as the taxi rattled up the cobbles of Mount Pleasant and came to a halt in a side street.

Maggie's place was mock-Chicago, raffish with red-and-cream flock wallpaper, and reeking of cigar smoke. Maggie looked as though she's had a few, beaming at us after we'd been let in by a big Irish ruffian in an ill-fitting suit. She must have been over forty and enjoyed her wine, but she was still a looker with a firm figure, an ample pair of tits, and cobalt-blue eyes that sparkled with a genuine welcome.

She insisted on being introduced to me, pulling me close, and kissing me on the cheek. Then she whispered in my ear and ruffled my black hair: "You'll do, Reginald."

Others in the salon included a couple tinkling the piano and trying to sing, a whiskery old gent fondling one of the girls on the settee, and two ship's officers with heavy foreign accents flirting with their partners at the bar.

"Right, boys," said Maggie, all businesslike after we'd helped ourselves to some wine. "Who'll it be tonight?" I lit a cigarette and tried to look nonchalant, but my heart was hammering away like the reciprocating engine on the Mersey Ferry.

"Molly's for me," said Ian, smiling with assurance.

"Down in five minutes."

"And Chinese Sue's for me," said Chips, expectantly combing his tangle of blond hair.

"Ten minutes."

"And," said Ian, "we thought Reginald here would love to meet Greta."

"Excellent choice, boys!" Maggie chortled. "And what's more, she's free right away. Clean as a whistle and with those unusual little touches of hers. So off you go, Reg, up the stairs and first on your right. And enjoy yourself!"

"Come," commanded the voice as I knocked on the door. And I took a deep breath and entered.

I thought I'd come to the wrong place at first. Greta was all girl, with lovely full lips and jet-black hair—but the hair was done in a rather severe bun. She had a pair of steel-rimmed specs clipped to the end of her nose and was wearing a full-length white smock. And a stethoscope round her neck.

"I'm the doctor, and you're my patient," she said in broad Scouse with not a hint of German. "An' you make an appointment to come and see me, and I use me skills at doctorin' and find out wha's wrong. S'all right? And I say, 'What is required is a full examination, young man. Take off your clothes down to your underpants and stretch out on the bed.' And you take your clothes off and gerron de bed. All right, lah?"

"Thanks, Doctor," I said, entering into the spirit of things. Margaret had never played games like this in the park. "I'm aches and pains all over. I think it might be my adenoids."

"Don't come your lah-di-dah with me, pet. I'm the expert around 'ere."

"Yes, doctor." And I flapped about undoing my collar stud, braces, and cufflinks and stretched out on the bed.

"And I use my instrument here to listen to your heart, and as I'm doing that, you're a naughty boy and reach out and undo me hair, and it all falls down, like." And I did, and the long black hair flowed down and started to tickle my chest.

"Then I say, 'What did you do that for? Me hair will get in the way. What you need is some medicine to quieten you down a bit.'"

The "medicine" turned out to be fortified Australian wine, which tasted like burnt mince pies. Doctor Greta administered it in true Florence Nightingale fashion, holding the back of my head as though I'd got shell shock. Coming on top of the Black Velvet and the wine, this much made the bed sway as though we were rolling around at the Mersey Bar Light, waiting for a berth.

"Enough," I gurgled.

"How about a light ale, then—bit more refreshing, like? And a nice piece of pork pie."

"No thanks—I'm fine."

"Got to eat enough and grow up to be a big boy, don't we?" Her hands brushed lightly in the vicinity of the main magazine, which was well on fire by now. "I could eat a scabby horse, know what I mean?"

"I feel faint, doctor."

"Yes, but then you take me glasses off and bring up your head and kiss me. And I say, 'Wha's this? I am a professional person, and you are abusing me. Kindly allow me to continue unhindered.' And I start to feel around and carry out an expert examination."

Very expert indeed. She started prodding me and peering at me closely and listening through the stethoscope.

"Can you hear anything, doctor?"

"You're a bit thin."

"I sound a bit thin?"

"I can hear your bones rattlin'."

And she tapped away and pinched me on the arms with her long fingers and explored my ribcage.

"Is that where it hurts?" she said, working down towards my middle.

"Um," said I, getting carried away.

"I think the doctor's getting warmer, don't you?"

"Oh yes, doctor."

"And then I say, 'What's this? We'll need to take your underpants off to take a closer look at this, won't we? C'mon, gerrem down. Now, let's give it a little rub and see if it feels better. All right?'"

"Um." I was fit to burst.

"Does it feel better when the doctor rubs it?"

"I think so, doctor."

"Let's rub it a bit harder then. All right?"

"Um."

"Then you reach behind me and undo me smock—like that—and then you start feeling me and kissing me. And all of a sudden, I don't mind—know what I mean, like?"

She had a figure like an angel's. I felt her tits and stroked her thighs, and she said, "Oh, what a terrible boy—what are we going to do with you?" And by the time we started the serious business, the pleasure was too keen to last. I tried to prolong it, but all those agonies of unrequited lust with Margaret were lying in store, and the magazine soon exploded in a highly pleasurable way.

Greta had a whole wardrobe of outfits to add zest to her meetings with clients. But the medical examination routine seemed the most fun to me—probably because it was my first time. I'll never forget Greta.

"Well . . . ?" inquired Chips and Ian as I bounced down the stairs, grinning.

"Couldn't be better," I said with as much sangfroid as I could muster, though the fellows must have strongly suspected that it had been my first time. The huge grin, the sheer joy of discovery gave me away.

The pubs were still open as we sauntered down to Lime Street, so we decided a refreshing pint would be in order at the American Bar. There were some jack tars and soldiers from a Scottish regiment enjoying themselves. But we were just taking our first sips of ale when trouble arrived in the shape of a dozen American ratings with a young lieutenant, all tanned and dressed in white, making our lot look like scarecrows.

They paused in the doorway rather theatrically, and above the noise of the trams and the bar's shrill gramophone, the lieutenant spread out his arms and shouted: "Hoy, hoy, hoy-hoy-hoy!" He bared his ivory-white teeth.

"Hoy, hoy, hoy-hoy-hoy!" chanted the squad in reply.

This all went on a bit and didn't go down at all well with the British tars and the two kilted Queen's Own Highlanders.

"You Yankees wanna drink, or are you just getting your breath back?" asked Dora, the barmaid, toying with the silver police whistle tied loosely round her neck.

"You got Kentucky whiskey, miss?" asked the lieutenant.

"Clean out of it, luv."

"Call this an American Bar? Well, I guess Scotch will have to do."

"It'll mair than do, laddie," growled one of the Queen's Own. "It's a vastly superior drink."

"Anything you say, soldier. By golly, it must be hot today in that woolly skirt."

Then Chips piped up: "Know what we've got, Yankee Doodles? A new type of shell designed for the American Fleet. Beats anything you've got so far."

"Oh, yeah?" came the chorus from the Yanks.

"Suit you lot down to the ground," said Chips. "It's made of rubber. When you fire it, it gives the target a good biff and then comes back up your bum."

This led to great jollity among the British contingent. But sure enough, after one of our American cousins had dubbed the Liver Building "that undersized office with the buzzards on the roof," the fists started flying. I got a bloody nose, and it could have got worse if Dora hadn't run out and blown her police whistle. In no time at all, we were in the station house in front of the desk sergeant.

Explanations, excuses—all fell astern like scraps from the galley. The following morning, we duly attended Liverpool Magistrates Court, got fined £2 each, and thought we'd got off quite lightly. What we didn't realise was that the spotty youth in court jotting in a notebook wasn't an inky clerk but a reporter from the *Liverpool Echo*. And there's nothing quite as powerfully flatulent as a thoroughly rotten story in the local paper.

At least that's what father thought.

"'Liverpool Institute boys in drunken brawl,'" he said, reading the headline as he strode up and down the living room, tugging his beard. "That's it, Reginald, you've brought the Tucker name—and that includes the business—into disrepute. And to think how you connived us into thinking you were resolved to do well. What an exercise in insincerity to inflict upon your own parents! There's only one thing for it—" He was interrupted by a ring at the doorbell.

Mother, her eyes averted, brought in a telegram. Father tore it open.

"As I feared," he said. "From Liverpool Institute—they don't waste any time on miscreants. 'This is to inform you that Reginald Tucker is expelled from the school with immediate effect. His personal effects will be delivered in due course.'"

"A disgrace, Reginald," echoed mother. "Just look at your nose. And we had such high hopes for you."

I expected that Ian and Chips would also be getting a dose of the same medicine, but as both their fathers were faintly important—a solicitor and a member of the dock board—they'd be relatively comfortable as clerks, which was decidedly better than cutting up acres of tripe, probably severing my thumb with a cleaver, and becoming Tucker's delivery boy—the boy who'd disgraced himself.

So it was a welcome diversion from all this gloom and disappointment (mother had put *Largo* on full tilt, enough to make even a wealthy pools winner reach for the revolver) when father phoned home a little later and asked me to put on a clean shirt for a delivery of sirloin up to the shipyard owner, Laird's, grand house on Bidston Hill, using our best pair of trotting ponies, Matilda and Doris. I hopped down to the shop gloomily and helped load the meat on to the spotless white cloths within the big wicker baskets that sat behind the driver.

Matilda and Doris were already hitched up to the rig, looking as they did when they won first prize for Trotting Ponies at Birkenhead Carnival. Not having read of my stark calumny in the early edition of the *Echo*, they were as friendly as ever, whinnying and giving me a nuzzle before starting to trot up the hill past the ladies' golf club and on to the Lairds' mansion.

Call it cheerful imbecility if you want, but I have always subscribed to the notion that when things seem at their very worst, some great hand on the tiller has already started to turn the situation around. "For suddenly the worst turns the best," as Browning had written. And so strangely, my heart started to lift as I lightly flicked the reins.

Something was going to happen. But what?

CHAPTER 4

MATILDA AND DORIS knew the way to the shipbuilding magnate's villa pretty well by heart, and we swung into the left-hand entrance of the house in fine style—only to meet a very large Alvis rumbling in from the right.

The chauffeur wasn't to know that both mares were averse to cars being driven towards them. And to make things worse, he sounded a particularly guttural klaxon, which goaded the girls on so that when his passenger decided to alight from the car, they crowded towards him, threatening to knock him down—or worse. In a day of disasters, I could have done without the murder of Mr Laird's guest, so I leaped athletically out of the driver's seat, got between the violent nags and the visitor, and grabbed them by the bridles. Luckily, it was enough to stop the chap being squashed flat against the side of his car, caving in a few ribs at the very least.

By this time, old Laird and half his household had appeared. A groom calmed down Matilda and Doris, a kitchen maid struggled in with the meat, and the visitor—only slightly ruffled by the incident—took a long look at me. I was expecting five bob and on-your-way-lad but instead met the warmth of a long-lost friend.

"Best fun I've had all day," he said approvingly, his Mandarin features—strangely familiar—creasing into a delighted smile. "Young man, if you had had to endure several hours in a train from London reading interminable Admiralty memos about what can't be done, re-organised or delivered in the time available, you'd understand what I mean. Anyway, thank you for saving me from your flashing hooves. Biffed your nose too [*one benefit of the fight*, thought I]. Ah well, that'll mend. I'm all at sea with horses, prefer trains and ships myself."

Laird looked a little taken aback by the incident but was obviously relieved because, like the other shipyard men, preparations for war had brought him riches beyond compare. But Laird and Co. could look after themselves. My mind meanwhile was racing. I touched my nose and winced and affected a slight limp as I turned towards our distinguished guest and tried a salute. I was sure I had seen him in the newspapers and periodicals. Here goes.

"Reginald Tucker, sir, at your service. My cousin Hugh is in the Navy, sir, and I'm rather hoping to join up myself." I got my eye to tick a few times to underline my sincerity, bloody but unbowed.

"Well, Tucker, I'm Lord Fisher, the First Sea Lord as was and will be again, and I'm impressed by the way you staved off disaster. Would you have any objection to joining me for a drink? I'm as dry as old bones. And we'll fix up that nose of yours—damn good show."

The surge of unscrupulousness was in me. Here was a chance to leapfrog over all my difficulties. The articles came back to me now: Jacky Fisher didn't give a hang for red tape—he hacked and slashed at it with ferocious loathing—and didn't give a hoot about preferment either. Those officers who ranked polished brass work over gunnery were likely to be consigned to shore establishments and depots of fantastic boredom and inconsequence.

I limped into the house with one arm on the great man's broad shoulders and was left alone, whisky and soda at my elbow, while Fisher and Laird had a row about the costs of converting from coal to oil in the study. A maid tiptoed in and dabbed my nose with hot water and offered to bandage my ankle, but I shooed her away after asking for another drink.

Jacky's bellowing could be heard coming through the wall, but when he entered the room ten minutes later—Laird was making some phone calls to the yard—he was all smiles.

"Three months to build a light cruiser? A good yard should be able to put together a pipsqueak cruiser in two weeks, a weekend. They should be able to turn 'em out like tins of beans. *Nil Sine Labore*, what?"

He rolled over to the decanter and poured himself a modest snort.

"Now, young fella, what can I do for you, what? And don't hold back. Whatever you do, remember that. I have a high enough opinion of myself to know that without your quick thinking, I'd have been squashed flat by those bucking broncos of yours—squashed flat, sunk, kaput! Quite a few people would welcome that—Beresford and Keyes and all those skunks and my countless other critics! But I wouldn't! Never forget, a good idea will always attract critics, but a very good idea will attract derision in spadefuls!"

Jacky spoke as he wrote—or was it the other way round? His handwritten and typewritten letters, I was to learn, exploded off the page in red and black ink, laced with block capitals and exclamation marks. He regarded language as something to be imbibed, drunk in great draughts of metaphor and incantation. He thumped the table for emphasis and, against critics, would employ the shaken fist like a battering ram until he saw the white flag of surrender when he would suddenly beam and be as sweet as honey. Yet fiery hearts could also be sympathetic—I hoped.

"Well, I'm in a bit of a spot, sir. Some friends and I got caught up in a fight between some lower-deck lads and some visiting Yankee sailors in Liverpool . . ."

"Hope you gave the Yanks a damned good hiding. Upstarts."

"Well, it was quite a good brawl, sir. But unfortunately, the police arrived, and I'm afraid we got hauled up before the beak, and to make matters worse, it got in the *Liverpool Echo*."

Jacky's eyes were twinkling with enjoyment. He was certainly enjoying the tale. "Damned rags," he said. "Always poking their poxy noses into other people's business."

"And then I got expelled from the Institute. And I think that was a bit rich because I'd been working very hard and was looking forward to completing my studies there and going on to Dartmouth." This sounded so goody-goody that I manufactured a wince from my "sprained" ankle to ground the sentiment in a little pain. "And now," I added, "it seems a perfectly harmless fist fight has done me in for good. What a dull fate, sir."

"And all that lies in store is delivering the meat, eh?"

I sipped my Scotch and nodded, my head swimming with the strength of the liquor, though I twigged that Jacky's pale grey eyes were staring right through the back of my head. He was a fearful bully, was Jacky, but was also a man of enormous sympathy. I had, it seems, got it right. And so I piled on the steam.

"My dear father is a very good businessman and wants me to open more factories making sausages. But what I really want, sir, is to be on the bridge of a ship, getting to grips with the enemy." This involved, in my mind, nothing more heroic than closing in on the enemy, showering it with shells made by the ingenious Mr Brock, then watching it sink.

"Good!" Jacky beamed. "Fast and hard-hitting. Who wants to make sausages when you could be running circles round the enemy, smiting him to smithereens? You should be with the battlecruisers. You know what a battlecruiser is?"

"It's a fast battleship, sir," I ventured.

"Exactly! Get among the enemy with one of those, and it's like an armadillo licking up ants. Speed and hitting power. As Napoleon said, 'Without celerity—failure.' Do you know what *celerity* means, my boy?"

"Speed, sir," I said, thinking fast; things seemed to be on the up and up. "Striking fast and then getting away before the other side's battleships have time to engage." It seemed to me then that Jacky's ideas made perfect sense, though I was to worry about them more when gentleman journalist Filson Young and I were crammed into the foretop of *Lion* during the Battle of Dogger Bank. "It would be an honour to serve with the battlecruisers, sir. I'd give ten sausage factories to do that."

"Well, I'm bound to tell you, Tucker, that the navy can be a hard master, and as to finances, you might save as hard as you like, but on a lieutenant's eleven shillings and sixpence a day, you would only be able to afford a very small sausage factory. Still want to enlist, and if so, what do you know about the sea?"

"I do, sir. And actually, I know quite a lot about the sea." What I knew about the sea largely concerned daydreams about shipping to New York and opening a gaudy bordello, but never mind; the half-truths were shuffling along quite nicely. "My uncle works at Laird's, and my cousin Hugh is on the *Duke of York* . . ."

"And you're distantly related to Nelson." Jacky smiled.

But I think he liked me all the same. When you lack social preferment (which he had lacked in his day), you have to make up for it with guile.

"Right, Mr Tucker," he said, moving his chair closer and using his cane as a pointer. "Your light cruiser screen on the port beam has reported submarine activity, the enemy destroyers are making smoke and massing for a torpedo attack, you are making 22 knots with the light right in your face, and the opposing battlecruisers have turned away. The range is about 20,000 yards. What do you do?"

There was only one thing which commended itself to Jacky. And that was aggression. I was later to learn that the Grand Fleet Battle Orders called for a prudent turn-away from torpedo attacks—Jellicoe's careful drafting left little room for aggression—but the hell with it.

"I'd ask for 28 knots from the battlecruisers, Sir. Then I'd tell our light cruisers to see off their destroyers, and I'd chase the enemy's heavy ships on both flanks, keeping up rapid fire until they were sunk. In other words, 'move closer to the enemy.'" I hadn't the faintest clue what to do in reality, but this last Nelsonian touch—what schoolboy didn't know that one?—did the trick.

"And if you saw one of those Zeppelin things?"

"Well, if it was low enough for the guns to bear, I'd shoot a shrapnel at it from one of the big guns. That would give it something to think about."

"Excellent," said the great man. "Right, Mister Tucker, can you move fast?"

"How do you mean, Sir?"

"Well, I think you ought to get started right away, don't you? We need aggression like yours. I haven't built the most powerful navy the world has ever seen for it to be manned by namby-pamby theorists. Caution won't do. What I want is fighting spirit. So take those murderous nags of yours back to your base and report to my train at Lime Street at noon tomorrow. There'll be a chit waiting for you. But first . . ." He got up, stretched, and finished his drink.

"Mr Tucker," said the saviour of the fleet, walking over to the gramophone—a new-fangled electric one—and putting on a record. "How's your ankle? Let's have a whirl!" And opening his arms, he caught me in a bear-like embrace. He was no Nancy Boy, Jacky; he just liked to dance with great leaping steps and bugger anything that got in the way.

He led of course, and it was quite a caper. First, we bumped into the gramophone, which made a terrible screech but kept playing, then we demolished a fragile table and its vase of dried flowers. Next to be dismasted was a tall standard lamp, which landed noisily on the drinks trolley. The music was ragtime but not a tune I knew, and I had no sense in which the great man would steer next. Age—he must have been seventy—had brought no loss of speed or incaution. Then we cannoned into the grand piano keyboard, making an amusing discord. And we ended after too many twirls, with Jacky skidding on the tiger skin hearthrug and scattering the fire irons all over the place. "Blood and sand!" he exclaimed, picking himself up and dusting himself down, then bursting into peals of laughter just as old man Laird returned to see what all the fuss was about. He didn't seem unduly pleased with the rearrangement of his living room, but as it was Jacky's caprice, he pretended to think it was a great joke while secretly wishing he could set the dogs on us.

By means of a thoughtful note scribbled by Jacky on Admiralty notepaper, I had little difficulty persuading my parents of the luck which had greeted me on the hill that afternoon. "If you ever harboured any doubts about your son, please cast them aside," he wrote, "for he has already done his country a great service by saving my life and will do more yet as Reginald Tucker, RN. I am sorry to rush him away like this, but we need young men of his calibre. I trust we will meet one day. Yours ever, John Fisher, First Sea Lord."

"Good grief," cried father after reading the missive aloud and brimming over with relief and pride, "it's an Act of God. I'll take you over to the train, Reg. Let me help you get ready." He laughed, and our eyes met warmly, celebrating luck and success. "Your lapse will soon be forgotten when I tell people what's happened. It certainly is by me. Fisher's a great man—better keep your wits about you!"

"Gracious, Reg," said mother, "what a nice gentleman he sounds." Whether the feeble *nice* could ever describe Jacky Fisher is a matter for debate.

I hadn't an earthly what to pack, never having been far away before, but mother got our girl Gladys to haul a trunk down from the attic, which looked to me as if it would hold enough clothes for Nelson and all his captains. I had a brush-and-comb set, along with bottles of cologne and tins of tooth powder magically provided from my father's stores along with a pair of binoculars and nifty Colt .38 revolver, which he insisted me having, along with a box or two of bullets. "If ever you need it, son." And also a wallet containing £100, which was enough to get into—or out of—serious trouble in those days. My heart was already starting to beat faster. There was no turning back now, no escape from the fruits of my misfortune.

I slung in a copy of *The Riddle of the Sands*, a volume of Kipling, and at mother's insistence, a copy of the Psalms, which might well remain in its wrapper. My heart was thumping. Today was the day and all that. Sudden change, as I was to learn, was the spice of life. But even as father drove the Studebaker from the car ferry to Lime Street Station and despite the opportunity which had come my way, I couldn't help thinking about Margaret. Even if she was a prick-teaser and a snob and we'd squabbled last time we met, we'd been puffing and panting in the park for at least two years. Happy days! I would try to phone her from London, if only to get one over on Hugh.

And now here we were, whistles blowing and steam billowing all over the place as a big engine drew in.

"Good luck, son," said father, summoning a porter and giving me a hug and a peck on the cheek.

My new life with my new mentor was about to begin.

CHAPTER 5

AS THE STATION clock struck noon, Jacky was shaking my hand—not in the manner of a man who, drunk the night before, wished you would suddenly vanish in a cloud of railway steam, but as a valued acquaintance. Lime Street Station was as smoky and crowded as ever, but we were soon heading out of its ravine-like approaches and on our way. I wondered what Chips and Ian were doing—penance, or had they too met some luck?

"Coffee?" asked Jacky as locomotive, tender, luxury carriage, attendant's car, and guard's van began to gather speed. Fisher's father, I later learnt, went to Ceylon as a planter to make a fortune out of London speculators' short-lived love of coffee. But the market collapsed, and the family became so poor that, along with other children, Jacky had to be sent back to England—he to the Royal Navy, where guts, hard work, and a pleasing personality brought success. He now had a handsome salary, but compared to Beatty, he was a financial minnow. Still, he didn't care about money, which, in some people's eyes, made him doubly dangerous. Also, having been born in the tropics, his broad features and bulging eyes suggested something Oriental in his make-up, not recommended at a time when foreigners were, like the English Jews, subject to relentless prejudice from the gentry. To some, he was Chinese Jacky—an upstart, not one of us.

He sipped his coffee and grumbled at his paperwork. His present job, working for Churchill, was to oversee the changeover from coal to oil.

Why? We hadn't got any home-grown oil, whereas we sat on millions of tons of the sooty black stuff. His answer: our peerless Navy would protect our oil tankers, and if we showed any sign of running out, we'd requisition it from the nearest neutral vessel and give them a chit for later encashment. Coaling was a curse on the Navy, who had to manhandle thousands of sacks down into the bunkers. Coal smoke was also a dead giveaway to even a small squadron at 25 miles on a clear day. Oil made warships practically invisible. So as Jacky saw it, "Get it from anyone at every opportunity and don't take no for an answer."

He rehearsed his reasons as we clicked over the rails. "Let there be no argument. We must have it, and we shall have it, and there's an end to it. Do you know that oil-burning ships keep a silver-plated shovel inscribed with 'Lest we forget' in a prominent position so they'll never forget the misery of coaling? And how many injuries are suffered by seamen who lose their footing and slide down into the bunkers?"

I quickly found that Fisher loved his mercurial and youthful boss, Winston, who was to insist on restoring him to First Sea Lord in October 1914. This followed Jacky's great *Dreadnought* tenure, 1904-1910, when he had piled into the Navy establishment, fists flying and making so many enemies—some wanted him hung from a lamp post—that he was eased out by Prime Minister Asquith on his sixty-ninth birthday with a peerage as compensation. Churchill wanted his energy, gratitude, and compliance. He got the first two but, knowing Jacky, not automatically the third. For now though, with war less than two years off, they were as thick as thieves.

Over a pre-lunch sherry, sitting on dimpled armchairs as the countryside flew by, he suddenly burst out: "You're sure to meet Winston in London unless he's off inspecting ships. In which case, God help them."

"I thought they'd be jolly proud to have the First Lord on board," I ventured.

"No, they wouldn't. They would rather have Lucifer himself on board." Jacky's face beamed with delight. "He looks at every rivet. He will also, to the profound annoyance of the captain, insist on currying favour with the Lower Deck. He's driving everyone mad. One of my informants sent me this note"—he giggled and produced two pages of typescript—"in which Churchill ordered an entire battleship's complement on deck then asked the officers if they knew their men by name."

"Sounds a little like abusing his authority, sir," I said, risking a rebuke for criticising such a stratospheric figure as Winston. But I don't suppose Jacky liked toadies any more than I liked toadying.

Jacky hardly noticed, wheezing with laughter, tears of mirth brimming in his eyes. "He sets out so vigorously to offend." He found the line again, stabbing it with his finger. "Here we are. He asked one officer for the name of a seaman.

"'Seaman Jones' was the reply.

"'How can you be certain?' barked Winston.

"'Because that is his name, Your Lordship.'

"Winston then turned to the sailor and asked him his name.

"'Jones, Sir,' replied the innocent tar. 'Ah, yes,' Winston said, suspicion mounting, 'but is your name really Jones, or are you only saying that to back up your officer?' Which was quite enough to produce purpling rage among the commander and officers."

"Can't say I blame them, sir."

"Yes, but that's Winston's trouble in a nutshell. He's all for ensuring that the men's treatment is fair. But in this in case, all he did was humiliate the officer and suggest that a British seaman would be so cowed as to forget his own name, the silly ass. None of the other Sea Lords can stand up to him. I can. Mind you, some of them can hardly remember their own names, even given a head start. But old 'Ard 'Art Wilson's come and gone and so has Francis Bridgeman, and now we've got Prince Louis of Battenberg, who's brilliant but not exactly ideal because he's a hereditary sausage eater, and I don't see him lasting when push comes to shove. What do you think?"

"Winston needs you back, sir—and the sooner the better," said I, earning more good scout points. I was grateful for Jacky's candour, although I was later to find that he used—and abused—confidences bestowed. But he couldn't really hold back; mostly you could see where the turrets were swivelling, and his peppering of correspondence with 'most secret, destroy at once and burn this note at all costs' virtually guaranteed publication in those newspapers, which he shamelessly used to carry his point of view, including clobbering his opponents.

"Oh, don't worry, dear boy, I'll be back," he said, tucking into his luncheon steak and kidney and downing a glass of claret. "There are too many cloth ears around. In a very short time, the call will go out again for men who can make things happen and fast! All the rest will have to fill out forms and toe the line." At that, he closed his eyes but not before opening one and inquiring: "Fancy a hornpipe, Mister Tucker?" Then he laughed quietly and nodded off.

Actually, I could have done with another rough night out with my friends Chips and Ian in Liverpool. And over the clickety-clack of the train over the tracks, sleep and vivid dreams closed in. I was in the hospital "quite poorly," and Dr Greta doing her rounds was going to "make me better."

Not for long.

I was awakened by two frightful explosions which almost turned my bowels to water. Back in reality, I saw his Lordship standing at the open window, ejecting the cartridges from a double-barrelled shotgun. Was Jacky defending the train? Was I still dreaming?

"Ah, there you are, Tucker," he said, "lost to the world," his voice almost lost to the wind as he leaned out of the window to see if any damage had been done. "Excuse the racket, but it passes the time wonderfully on these interminable railway journeys. I give the nod to the mess steward, he shouts an order to the fireman who pulls a clay up front there, and I try to shoot the thing. Excellent practice in deflection shooting if you have to down one of those aeroplane things. Like a go? Of course you would!"

I'd done quite a bit of rough shooting with father on holidays in Killarney—I once got two rabbits with three shots from a .22—so I accepted without hesitation. The mess steward loaded the piece with a slightly haughty look on his face, and I stood by the window, barrels pointing towards the sky.

"Pull!" cried the steward as Jacky peered over my shoulder. And damn me if I didn't hit two clays on the trot, bursting them over the ripening Northamptonshire corn.

"Good grief, the man's an ace," exclaimed Jacky. He took another piece from the steward, ordered pull, and scattered buckshot over the deserted fields. He cursed as he once more missed by a mile but goaded me into further attempts, but by this time the barrels were overheating, and the constant gunshots from the "Fisher Special" provoked one lonely stationmaster to telegraph ahead with lurid reports of a Jesse James train raid, passengers at peril, etc., all of which were studiously ignored. Jacky had toyed with the idea of mounting a Maxim gun on his special, the better to blaze away at anything which caught his fancy, but the gun on order mysteriously failed to arrive. Just as well for the neighbouring farmhands. I failed to register further miraculous hits, but two were enough for Jacky, who—lacking experience of a major sea fight—was impressed.

"Gunnery officer—that's your opportunity, Tucker. Once we've got simultaneous firing on all our ships—with that strange computer Dreyer's invented—you'll be able to sit there at the foretop with some optical gadgets, looking at the enemy ten miles away, squeezing the trigger and blowing them to Kingdom Come with eight tons of broadside." He paused, summoning up the appropriate quotation. "And there shall go a fire before him and burn up all his enemies." Bit of a Bible-basher was Jacky. He once listened to four sermons in one day; three were quite routine.

"They'll be just like sitting ducks, Sir."

"Yee-es. But they will be firing back at you, Tucker, don't forget that. We may believe that the Germans will be dozily sailing around in antiquated gunboats—anyone who believes that is an imbecile. You'll see their shells coming towards you like bluebottles, getting bigger and bigger and bigger until they either burst on your ship or fly over your head and explode in the sea. God help the cod and the haddock and all the rest. Don't fancy their chances. No, there will be danger, even on a British ship, which of course is a manifestly superior vessel."

Well, I hadn't thought much about the danger. But the fact is, you never quite know in the Navy whether you are going wake up to the routine ministrations of your servant or gripped with fear by thunder as your cabin is visited at high speed by a 12-inch German shell. Still not at all sure of myself, I had visions of being ignominiously discovered after a battle still quaking with fear under the sheets.

The shotguns had been stowed, the window closed as the mess steward served tea. Fisher's face suddenly grew serious; his eyes hardened. I was stopped in my tracks.

"Tell you what, Tucker."

"Sir?"

He leaned forward, eyes widening and drilling into mine.

"You've done me a favour, and by delivering you to Dartmouth Naval College with my personal recommendation—I know it's hell on earth but has to be done—you could say I've paid the bill. But I think there's a little more you could do."

"Just say the word, sir." Looking back, it would of course have been madness to try to defy the wishes of Jacky Fisher. I had yet to see him turn his broadside on those who tried to upset his plans, but consigning their careers to particles of dust would probably have been just a start.

Jacky's was like the Old Testament God, heavy to wield but terrible in execution, just like the old Saxon broadsword. But whatever he had in mind had to be an improvement on cutting chops. Dear old father—would he ever get used to the loss of a son to the business? If he had any sense, he'd employ one or two of my old cronies from the Commercial School, thick as two short planks but not quite thick enough to slice their thumbs off. I tried to rein in a feeling that I had already become important, but the bogus swelling of the head and the ego was impossible to resist. Why should humility punish a lucky break? At that very moment, somewhere in the world, scores of perfectly harmless people were being filleted by bayonets, turned out of cellars, picking up their last pay packets, and contemplating suicide. And the only way I could conceivably help anyone was by keeping the good luck coming. In that sense, Jacky's power—and the bonus of a sense of fun—were impossible to resist.

He yawned, no doubt missing his Maxim gun. The train smoke occasionally drifted across his practice range, and we could hear the White Ensign, an eccentric addition to the guard's van, snapping in the wind through the partially opened window. "You'll be going," he said, "to that estimable holiday resort called Dartmouth to find out what buttons to press, which levers to pull, and all that technical stuff, which is considerably more fun than sailing in my view.

"But"—and he leaned forward menacingly—"no shinning up rigging and all that Nelsonian claptrap. I expressly forbid it."

"Yes, Sir," I replied, somewhat startled. And how right he was as another broadside rumbled towards me.

"If any fuddy-duddy lost in the past tells you to go pissing about on a yardarm, tell him to piss off and refer him to me. Is that clear?"

"Perfectly, sir."

"And knots—no messing about with cleaves and hitches. I'd rather you were caught messing about at the local brothel. Understand?"

"Completely, sir."

"I will not have the Navy destroyed by backward glances to HMS *Pinafore*. Do the army still parade around with swords and muskets?"

"Certainly not, sir. A few bursts from a Maxim, and they'd all be down like ninepins."

"Yet you'd be surprised, Tucker, how many of the General Staff still have visions of huge cavalry charges with swords and lances. And much good will it do them! Well, here's what I'd like you to do, Tucker: keep me informed about what's going on. Nothing too detailed. Just a line now and then, telling me how practical and up-to-date your instruction is." His neck grew crimson as he considered the reactionaries in both Army and Navy.

"Any attempt to deny the technical methods needed to keep us ahead in the race with the sausages I regard as high treason. I won't have it, d'ye hear Mr Tucker? So keep your wits about you and keep in touch! And that's an order!" His eyes flashed alarmingly and then melted back into their usual spangle of tolerance and amusement. "That all right with you? It's better be!"

"Assuredly, Sir," said I. "I'll do my best to be an accurate correspondent."

"Not just accurate—opinionated. I can get facts from all over the place—manuals of them. Enough facts to bore you to pieces for six months without a pause. I read them every night and annotate them *fiercely*. No, what I want is impressions, sensations, straws in the wind. Your own feelings about morale—and don't spare feelings about rank. I don't care if some stiff-necked admiral has fifteen years' service. If he talks poppycock and seems capable of landing his ship or an entire squadron up a creek, then I want him sacked, sunk, capsized now, this instant! *Comprenez?*"

And thus I became one of Jacky's spies. I could hardly have refused, could I? If so many of the admirals were dimwits, maybe I could become one myself. Frankly, spying for Jacky appealed to me in a funny sort of way; the ability to have a direct line to the top without accountability, however harlot-like, rustled up all sorts of delicious images of being able to get back at enemies—God help Senior if he every fell within my grasp—while bestowing preferment on friends like Chips and Ian, even if they were better at pub-crawling than attacking an enemy ship. If a worm like Schmidt, my sadistic maths master at school, were to enter the service, I'd have him out of the wardroom and into the stokers' hold in three shakes of a hammock.

"I think I understand you perfectly, Sir," I said, looking him in the eye as snappy as could be.

"Capital!" said Jacky, ringing the bell for the steward. "Tea, Mr Tucker?"

No one could have impressed me more in the half a day or so I had spent with him. The sheer exuberance was exciting as was at least the pretence of being frank with a potential recruit.

He was the schoolteacher I had always wanted, who taught ambition, common sense, and a sanguine philosophy. It can only be done by those who sincerely like the young and have the humanity to take them as they find them with all their faults.

CHAPTER 6

THE FISHER SPECIAL fairly ate the miles to London. I inquired of the steward at one point about our speed, and he whispered reverentially: "About 75 mph, Sir." At Euston, the steps were wheeled out, and we then boarded Jacky's limousine. Where was I going? Was I about to be dumped in some second-rate young officers' hotel with gaslight, leafing endlessly through dog-eared copies of *The Field* and not knowing from one day to the next where the Admiralty bureaucrats were going to send me?

"The Admiralty," Fisher barked at the driver. He leaned back in the studded leather seats of the motor, and I was suddenly aware of the frostiness in the air.

"What a bloody awful suit," he said. "You look like a cross between an off-duty Liverpool copper and a clerk."

"It's my girlfriend's favourite, sir," I protested. This was getting too personal. "She chose it herself at one of Liverpool's best outfitters."

"Well, get rid of her. I wouldn't give you much a chance if I took you to the Admiralty with that outfit. About ten Marines would be on top of you before you reached halfway up the stairs. This is London, Mr Tucker, not a provincial toytown like Birkenhead. You have to look the part, bear yourself well, and be bloody dangerous when needed." He rapped on the window separating us from the driver with his cane.

"Gieves," he ordered. "And make it snappy. Better get you measured up for a uniform, Mr Tucker—you won't get far in those togs." The upshot of all this was that I entered Gieves with a chit from Jacky ordering an off-the-peg reefer, flannels, etc.; my offending brown suit sent to the Sally Annie (or the furnace more likely) and a full uniform to be ready the following day. All on Jacky's account of course.

Jacky didn't like sitting doing nothing, so there was a dong as he entered the front of the famous tailors and began peering at accessories. Then with a chuckle, out he went again. And when I emerged, natty in blazer, white shirt, and cadet tie, he pressed a box of silver cufflinks into my hand and said, "Twice the man!" as we sped off to Whitehall.

On the way, he even became contrite. "Sorry, I was a little brusque, laddie." He laid his gloved hand on mine. "And I'm sure your girlfriend's a corker. But just occasionally, the strain shows through."

I thanked him of course, then swallowed a little with my own strain as we drew up at the Admiralty. Here is where the First Lord, the Sea Lords, legions of Admirals, and shore-based captains did their best to bring the Navy to heel—nearly always succeeding—to the misfortune of those in peril on the sea and those at sea who knew that you couldn't win battles by referring to manuals.

But the great marble staircase, vaulted ceilings, great canvases of heroic deeds, and busts of fighting admirals all conspired against the pretence that those at sea knew the big picture, for the big picture—however grossly distorted—was here expressed in oil paint and stone. The Admiralty ruled the waves, and those who tried to waive the rules must be carefully measured for a straitjacket at Gieves before being torpedoed, driven hundreds of fathoms deep like the *Titanic*, wedged into a crevasse, and slowly eaten by crustaceans. I must have looked a little awestruck and communicated this mood to Jacky.

"Very impressive," he said, looking around him with practised indifference. "But to be on a great ship at sea is much more so. I can't think of anything worse than spending my entire naval career anchored in Whitehall in a place seemingly dedicated to the men and ships of the past. The pomp here is mighty impressive, but I am about a thousand times more interested in the here and now. As is Winston, as you'll find in a minute."

The youthful First Lord of the Admiralty, Fisher's boss, was barking down the phone when we opened the door to his office, and I was struck by the sheer energy of the man. One of his secretaries was trying to gather up a bundle of correspondence. Winston waved him away impatiently, then threw an India rubber at him, which hit him on the ear. His desk was almost as large and solid as a billiard table, and on it sat various gadgets—vulcanite intercoms, levers, microphones, telephones, and coloured lights—providing instant contact with his underlings. Beside him was a huge .45 Navy Webley revolver—probably with one up the spout—as though he expected the enemy to burst in at any moment.

As Lord Fisher led me into the room, I saw him wince once or twice at this display of technical marvels since he was frequently at the receiving end—which was difficult for the older man because while he worked a fairly heroic day, starting at six and finishing around five, Winston started much later and, after his post-lunch doze, was still in full cry at midnight.

To his credit, Jacky refused to alter his routine and endured the demands for his opinion well past his bedtime. Even so, it was apparent to me that here was a mutual admiration society.

"Ahem!" said Jacky to try and gain attention. This had not effect, so he bashed on loudly: "This young man saved my life yesterday. Some horses were trying to crush me to death."

"Not before time," said the First Lord, still scribbling away.

"Blast!" he added, slashing at the draft with his pen and taking a sip from a large brandy and soda; it could have been cold tea, but the decanter and soda siphon were close to hand. He then rolled the offending script into a ball, accurately fired it at the wastebasket, and finally looked me up and down. It was hard to know when Winston gave you the once over whether he was wafting you with Caribbean sea breezes or burying you in the Arctic ice. But then a smile illuminated his pugnacious features.

"And I suppose he wants a medal and a line in the Telegraph," he said, relighting a large Havana. "And what is our hero's name? Jacky sometimes forgets life's little niceties." He chuckled, then laughed out loud, puffing out a dense cloud of smoke. "And sometimes he isn't nice at all!" We shook hands over the desk and smoke.

"Reginald Tucker," I said through the murk.

"Well met, Tucker—sterling work. Without Admiral John Fisher, we'd have a fleet of well-polished pleasure boats with brass popguns rather than a fleet of great brutes that can knock anyone else flying with the first punch." Beside me, I could sense Jacky swelling with pride. "And apart from capsizing the entire Victorian Navy and lowering the flag on most of its ludicrous ceremonial, he's now practically engineered controlling interest in the Anglo-Persian Oil Company for about two million quid. Now, that is a man well-worth saving."

"Glad to be of service, Sir," I blustered.

"Can't write speeches, can you? If so, you can help me with my present labour, which is a fairy story about naval estimates for the Commons, dozy lot. Can't seem to get the thing right. I would very much like to suspend the Commons, seize the Exchequer, and do what I like with the money— guns, guns, ships, and more guns. But you have to be terribly careful not to hurt people's feelings. I mean, I'd like to dictate a letter from King George to second cousin Willy, saying we know perfectly well he wants to immerse the whole of Europe in a bloodbath and suggesting he change his doctor before the fantasy gets worse. But it's no good. You'll have to help me with this one, Bunty," he said, referring to Jacky by his pet name.

"I'm afraid I've never tried speech-writing, sir. But I'd like to," I said.

"Well, like it or not, you will. Being able to make a decent speech is axiomatic to success in most walks of life, more's the pity," said the man who could, in a 90-minute oration, convince most audiences that black was white and that one and one made five. He tapped his cigar ash into a sawn-off brass shell case as big as a frying pan. "But never look at a note—they'll kill you."

"I have advised Reginald to enlist and aim for service with the battlecruisers," said Jacky.

"Good show. We need every bright man we can get to sail against the German Navy, which seems hell-bent on sinking the lot of us." He picked up his revolver and waved it about in a dangerous fashion. "And the only solution is to keep several steps ahead and shoot first. That right, Bunty?"

"Damned right," said Jacky, clenching and unclenching his fists as though personally preparing to throttle von Tirpitz, head of the German Navy.

"Shoot first and ask questions afterwards. Just like in Dodge City. Think you can do that, Tucker?"

"I think it's an excellent philosophy, sir."

"Philosophy? More like a necessity, if you ask me. Unless you want Kaiser Willy and his beastly army goose-stepping down the Mall with his tuneless bands playing, you hobble the lot of them before they take one step. And then send a band and a few dragoons clip-clopping up the Unter den Linden. And that means . . ."

"Sending the High Seas Fleet to the bottom, sir."

"Excellent, my sentiments exactly. Mind you, the German Navy is no pushover. Even if most of them are conscripts and can't tell port from starboard, we've still got to keep a damned good lookout."

The secretary edged into the room again, placed a small pile of telegrams and letters on the corner of the great desk, and tiptoed away. Winston threw another rubber after him.

I thought this a little childish but of course didn't say anything. If I was the chap, I'd spike his brandy with senna pods.

"More damned paper, no wonder I'm here day and night. And half of this lot could be written in a couple of lines. They wander along, paragraph following tedious paragraph, like a camel train without a map, reaching no oasis of refreshing conclusion and instead suggesting that to their eyes 'possibly the matter should be examined further,' etc., etc. And the Parliamentarians are the worst—far too much time on their hands. They should all be running the chain ferry at Sandbanks."

"Can't you just ignore them, sir?" I suggested.

"Hum, a bigger wastebasket would help, which reminds me, I have about twenty letters to dictate to old Bald Pate, my correspondence secretary. But the man who can tell you about the battlecruisers, Jacky's Splendid Cats, is my Naval Secretary, Rear Admiral Beatty." And manoeuvring out from behind his desk and dislodging his pistol at the same time, Churchill took me into the next office and introduced me to Rear Admiral Beatty. The First Lord then shook my hand.

"Well, good luck to you, Tucker. You seem to have managed commendably so far. And I personally won't forget that you saved Admiral Fisher. Lord knows what we'd do without him. Keep it up!"

If meeting Winston was like encountering a somehow benign but restless tornado, then at least I'd been prepared. Beatty was a different matter. He was taller than me—a shade off six feet—and shared my thick black hair. In other respects though, comparisons would have been inaccurate. He had the bold good looks of a fictional hero—Rupert of Hentzau perhaps?—with eyes which looked as though they could penetrate six inches of armour plate. But though his appearance was young, distinguished, and handsome, there was something in the heavy lines of the face which qualified the sense of youth. Perhaps, as I was to find, it was because naval warfare in the twentieth century was an infinitely more demanding business than lining up muzzle to muzzle and sword to sword and slogging it and also because of his marriage to the former Ethel Tree, after her first short-lived marriage, was finally annulled.

Ethel—soon to become Lady Beatty—was heiress to the fabulously wealthy Marshall Field's department store empire of Chicago. Meeting in the hunting field, Ethel and Beatty had fallen head over heels in love and taken little notice of tut-tuts from strict observers of protocol in court circles because of her divorce. Quite apart their magnetic attraction, her fortune, and therefore influence, was understandably attractive to the young captain. Whether she overdid it at times was a matter for debate. On one occasion when he earned a rebuke from the Admiralty for running his ship too fast and burning out the engines, Ethel famously said: "Criticise my David? Tell them I will buy them another ship!"

Nevertheless, here was the Sea Hero I had been looking for. Notwithstanding his upbringing in Anglo-Irish hard-riding, hard-drinking country circles, Beatty was lured to the sea like a dangerous fish to water. He had a captivating smile, and it lingered for a moment, even before the sickly gaze of an unknown cadet.

"Dartmouth, eh," he said. "Well, keep your wits about you. When I went training there, I was billeted aboard a dreadful old wooden hulk so rotten you could drive a scout knife right up to the hilt in its timbers. I was lucky to get out of there alive. And most of the time was spent learning sailing drill, knots, and God knows what—skills like that would last you about two minutes in a battle today. What about you? Do you like the sea?" He smiled, opened a gold cigarette case, and lit one.

"Good old Birkenhead," he mused, "workhouse of the Wirral. Most of the people I know there live in whacking great houses and play golf most of the time. Not a bad spot for making money." *And teeing up at the Royal Liverpool while your manager or foreman did all the work*, I nearly added.

I felt I had to return to Jacky's point about redundant activities like sailing drill. "He actually said I should tell them to go and take a running jump, sir."

"Well, you can try it if you like, but if you do, I'll bet my bottom dollar they'd find some way of clapping you in the brig for a while. What *are* you interested in?"

"The latest techniques in gunnery, sir."

"Good God, a latter-day Prometheus. And then?"

"And then I'd like to join the battlecruisers, sir."

"How interesting." There was now a definite gleam in his eye. He inhaled his cigarette. "Why?"

"Because they're the fastest ships afloat—unless you count the destroyers—and it sounds as though they would be right in the middle of the action. Speed and the big gun. Sounds exciting, Sir." I was almost bouncing up and down with enthusiasm—Fisher, Churchill, and now the dashing Beatty, all within 24 hours.

"And it is!" Beatty's expression broadened into a bow wave of a smile as he saw in his mind's eye the cavalry of the sea riding down its helpless opponents like Hannibal's elephants at Cannae. He couldn't wait for his next command.

"Admiral Fisher said the battlecruiser would be like an armadillo lapping up ants," I babbled.

"Did he? By jove!" The Admiral flashed a smile before his face contorted alarmingly into a grimace. It only lasted less than it takes to fire off a small pan from a Lewis gun, but I was to see it again—an involuntary twitch which may have been hereditary or been caused by too much exposure to the mercurial Winston or Fisher's roaring and shaking of fists.

His face relaxed. "Well, if it means anything to you, young Tucker, the battlecruisers are in the bag for you—as long as someone doesn't post you to a battleship, great lumbering things that they are. If you're up to it—*really* up to it—I don't see what'll stop you, certainly not me. Jacky has built us a wonderful weapon, but can we use it?"

My heart leapt. And at the same time I was beginning to see the tensions within the service. The senior men in the silent service—probably the noisiest service on the planet, in fact—were far from seeing eye to eye. They were divided into camps, and victory over each other's schemes mattered nearly as much as capsizing the Germans. The pompous Lord Charles Beresford believed that the Navy was virtually in German control and thought Fisher was a dangerous saboteur who'd deliberately scrapped the majority of our cruisers. But a cruiser couldn't face a full-rate battleship or battlecruiser, so what good was it? And of course as I had already learned from Jacky, Churchill spelt scurvy for his belligerent attitude to our seagoing knights—entering a ship's wardroom uninvited and ringing a bell to summon the commander, for instance. On his part, Winston—though very much a friend—regarded Fisher as a dangerous lunatic to be caught and tamed as far as possible.

And there were countless other feuds although few raised a voice against Fisher's choice to lead the mighty force which was to become the Grand Fleet—the mild-mannered Admiral Sir John Jellicoe, respected throughout the service for his decency. The only trouble which came out later is that all these conflicting opinions gave few clues to captains how to act when battle was joined. The nearest theory, when push came to shove, was to follow Lord Nelson's tactics and lay your fleet next to the enemy—eight miles away in today's era—and blaze away until he either blew up or slid under. Those who made a religion of strategy and tactics still held to Victorian ways: form line ahead and fire relentlessly away until it was settled.

And no one seemed able to sort out the muddle. Gunnery was still regarded as a rather noisy and dirty speciality, and any restlessness was becalmed in a sea of secrecy. Even the mouths of North Sea fishes were sealed, as the journalist Filson Young, whom I was to meet later aboard *Lion*, rather aptly put it before he was netted and hurled back to dry land. Jellicoe treated reporters as busybodies and wouldn't have them near, which is why his Navy was less better known than Nelson's. To Horatio, publicity was addictive, even when it penetrated his private life; to Jellicoe, it was anathema.

"When are you off to Dartmouth?' asked Beatty, leaning against a filing cabinet, lighting another gasper, and leaving plumes of petroleum spirit and tobacco hanging in the air.

"I thought I'd catch a train tomorrow, sir. Lord Fisher gave me a chit."

"Ah, one of Jacky's famous chits. Where would we be without those? Collect enough of them, and you'll be in the front of any queue within seconds. But let's see, why not hang around—getting myself out of Winston's clutches might take me half an hour—and then come up to Hanover Lodge for the night? I'm sure Ethel would love to meet you. And there will be some battlecruiser men around, many of them are going to be on my team. Dartmouth is quite bad enough without getting a decent send-off."

"Thank you, sir. I'd love to."

"And don't be afraid to chip in. Trouble is, and I know Jacky agrees, that we're not exactly churning out the chaps we need. The public schools produce an impressive team spirit, but they think they can win the day by just charging the enemy—like shooting fish in a barrel, as Ethel is fond of saying. In the Navy, things have become a bit technical, more like playing chess. I know the dreaded Hun spends more time on technique than we do. So if you don't want a watery grave, keep your eye on the ball. Anyway, Ethel loves meeting aspiring young officers. It's a social occasion, and some of them are as very rich, including me—or rather Ethel—and you're not. Still, we can't all be from the top drawer, and my lot certainly weren't. Big country house, smelling of riding boots and drink. So just in case you're wondering, I don't care that your father's in trade—Jacky mentioned it when he phoned last night. I don't think it's anything to be ashamed of, especially if you blow up lots of enemy cruisers, in which case medals and promotions will come tumbling down the Shining Ladder in no time at all.

"All it takes is a lot of effort. Slight northern accent—you might well work on that, but don't get too posh. It's a dead giveaway. Togs are okay. Yes, Tucker, you'll do—and you might as well come and get some decent food inside you before you have to start gnawing away at that Dartmouth pigswill. Shouldn't think that's changed much since Omdurman. Now off you go. I'll see you in the anteroom as soon as I can get away from Winston." His eyes flashed in a friendly fashion.

I looked around for Jacky but couldn't see him anywhere. Then the Marine on duty in the anteroom handed me a sealed envelope in the great man's handwriting addressed to the authorities at Dartmouth. With it was another personal note. "I was having a chuckle at your expense. As a reward for saving me, I am consigning you to the dubious delights of Dartmouth. Still, better than Dartmoor, what? Remember what Winston and I told you: when in doubt, remember you can't go far wrong if you shoot first. Do well and keep me posted! Amen, Fisher."

I lounged on a large green chesterfield, lost in thought. So only a faint Northern accent stood in the way of my rapid rise in the Naval ranks and in Society because there was definitely going to be a big bust-up before too long. Getting noticed was relatively easy for Beatty because he was banging away heroically in the Opium Wars and in Sudan, where he was noticed by Winston for bombarding the Dervishes. Battle apart, though, details counted when you're moving up fast, ten years ahead of the rest. Ahead of the pack. Why else did his monkey jacket have six buttons instead of the regulation eight and his gold-braided cap have a peak, which jutted out two inches further than anyone else's? Maybe the fact that Ethel's dad could buy a large estate from the petty cash prompted his desire to stand out from the crowd.

In this sense, he resembled Jacky, who may not have cared a fig about money but whose sensational dancing livened up the endless small talk of many an otherwise dull London party. But for sheer style, Beatty won by a head—not least because of his screen-star good looks and the youthful fitness which shone out of him, compared to some of his contemporaries who were already becoming grey-haired, rheumy-eyed, and stooped. Stamina was important in the Navy. To reach a crowded, tricky port at dawn, many captains would stay up all night, taking only very brief naps in their sea cabins on the bridge.

But a lot of effort? Hum . . . Perhaps quite a lot of effort—and a lot of luck.

CHAPTER 7

A S BEATTY AND I emerged into Whitehall, he explained rather crossly that Ethel had just fired Henry, their chauffeur, for getting tipsy with the "pantry girls" and taking them for a nocturnal ride around Regent's Park in the Rolls.

"Bloody shame, really," he said, striding out into the middle of the road and flagging down a cabbie. "Henry had some of the wickedest jokes I have ever heard. He was a bit overfamiliar with Ethel, and I had an idea she was waiting for her chance to strike. We were motoring around Italy last summer when she asked him whether we had time to go to Pisa and see the famous Leaning Tower."

Beatty's face creased into amusement with the recollection. "'I've got the inclination, your Ladyship,' he said, 'if you've got the time.' Then he winked or leered or something, and that was it—the Son of Satan. Bloody good lad, Henry—just couldn't keep his mouth shut. Once drove me all the way from London to Portsmouth to catch my ship after I'd missed the last train—never miss your ship, Reginald.

"Anyway, despite the appalling journey, I nearly wet myself with laughter on several occasions. Did the same Portsmouth dash with a miserable cabbie who hardly said a peep all the way. And the fare! It nearly blew up his meter. Henry will be back, you'll see, after I have clandestinely arranged for Ethel to be ruinously late for several important social occasions—though if you ever repeat any of this, you will of course be pegged out somewhere off Malta and used for target practice by the whole Mediterranean Fleet."

"Quite, sir. Wouldn't dream of it," I said.

"But actually there are no secrets in the Navy, they can't survive the proximity. The officers can't leave the ship or murder each other, so the only sensible thing to do is develop comradeship, nothing more of course, although I dare say what occasionally goes on below decks would make your hair curl. Ten or so years ago, there was one cruiser whose reputation was so bad it was called HMS *Buggeration*. On another, the captain and crew of HMS *Haveanother* were so permanently pissed that they rammed one of the few rocks in the Indian Ocean."

By now we were in the taxi; Beatty promised the driver a quid, and we started threading our way through the tangle of motor cars, omnibuses, carriages, and whips in Trafalgar Square. Beatty tipped his cap to Nelson's column in salute. "Great strategist—could sum up a situation in seconds. Made his plans and then discussed them with his captains before implementation. How his conscience allowed him to cuckold poor little Hamilton for so long, I'll never know, but I suppose he paid for it in the end."

Once up in Regent's Park and approaching Hanover Lodge, we saw a lady rider on a black stallion racing the traffic—and easily beating it.

Beatty grinned and leaned out of the window.

"Tata!" he bellowed. How Ethel heard him, I don't know, but anyone who got to know the Beattys well knew there was some remarkable chemistry about that marriage despite its occasional difficulties. She looked over, cocking an ear in our direction.

"One more for dinner!" bellowed the admiral, looking admiringly as she galloped towards the big house. They had met while in the saddle, and it was soon all over for Mr Tree, her then husband. There was some tut-tutting in influential circles, and they were cut off from court since divorce was still frowned on in those days. Ethel's millions, her feisty personality, and her undoubtedly head-turning beauty, however, exerted a strong pull, as did David's reputation as one of the Navy's brightest stars. And they were soon back in court circles again.

"You know, the speed of a battlecruiser, Tucker, is the same as a galloping thoroughbred," Beatty observed, retrieving his handsome head from the window. The taxi slowed down as it crunched up the gravel drive; the sun was starting to set over the rooftops of the lodge, glinting on well-tended greenhouses with the great trees of the park swaying gently in the evening breeze.

And then the double front doors were flung open, and Ethel appeared still in riding gear, her long dark hair swinging around her shoulders, her riding crop smacking her gleaming boots.

"Hi, David," she said, joining us as we alighted from the taxi. "And who is this youngster? He looks a bit like you did, David, when we met— all those years ago." She took my arm and squeezed. "What's the matter— rattlesnake got your tongue? Or are you the strong, silent type?"

Beatty was handing over a crisp one-pound note to the cabbie, who knuckled his forehead in thanks. Ethel peered over.

"A pound?" she exclaimed. "He's lucky to get ten shillings."

Beatty bristled. "I promised him a pound." And the heiress and the Rear Admiral sparred over this matter of national importance for several minutes before the taxi driver chipped in to say he'd be quite happy to get ten bob if he could then get going. Beatty grumpily took back the pound and, fishing out ten bob, gave it to the driver, who crunched around in the drive and began to head off.

Beatty suddenly stamped hard on the marble steps to the front entrance. "Damn it," he said and thrust a ten-shilling note into my hand. "It's his because I said it would be. And that's important. Run after him, Reg, like a good chap and bung him the rest."

It was a direct order. And not a bad runner, I sped down the drive, catching the cabbie by yelling at him just as he turned out of the main gate. I bunged him the extra, and he gave me a wink, and then I returned to the famous couple.

Ethel was chiding Beatty. "You only stay rich by being economical with the details, David," she drawled, nodding to me and saying: "Well run, son."

"Well, all I know is that if you promised ten bucks to one of your American cousins in Dodge City and then tried to pay 'em five, you'd be up in Boot Hill within three shakes of a coyote's tail."

"Coyotes don't have tails," said Ethel, laughing.

And then Beatty laughed, hugged her, and kissed her on the cheek. "Bet you anything they do, Tata. I think you just like arguing for the sake of it."

"Sure, but I'd rather win, honey."

"Well, you can't always win. Look at Napoleonic France. That was the whole concept of duelling. Pistols at dawn—one wins, the other loses."

"Or in Dodge City, a .45 slug in the back up some dark alley."

I had a feeling that I was intruding on a private game. Then a maid curtsied as we entered a long cool hall which seemed to be entirely decorated with pictures of horses and warships pitching up and down in a kind of artistic steeplechase.

It was time to make a mark.

"I don't know whether I'm strong enough to rein in that stallion of yours, your Ladyship, but as for your question a moment ago about whether I was the silent type, I think *garrulous* would be more accurate."

"Good God," said Beatty. "I still haven't introduced you. Ethel, this is Reginald Tucker, en route to Dartmouth and, he hopes, a distinguished career with the battlecruisers. I took pity on him as he doesn't seem to know anyone in London. He's from Birkenhead."

"Good, hard-working town, just like Chicago," said Ethel. "And drop the *ladyship*. I'm no Lady—not yet." She patted me on the shoulder. "In the Windy City, where I hail from, most of the ladies pack .38s and swear like stevedores. That right, David?"

"I'm afraid it is," he said, leading me into a large bright drawing room dominated by Lazlo's portrait of the fabulous couple. Ethel's arms were round my shoulders, and she pointed at her own likeness. "Don't altogether like it," she said. "Puts five years on me—and that a lady doesn't need—and my eyes look hurt, as though I've just heard some bad news." I looked at her eyes, which were clear and bubbling with amusement.

"And I think I look too skinny as though I've been in a siege. I think women, as well as men, should have some meat on their bones," she said. "You look as though you need fattening up, Reginald. Put on a few pounds, or they'll all start calling you Bony at Dartmouth, which will never do. Get out to the local inn and get your teeth into beefsteak and lots of red wine as often as you can. We're having steak and kidney pudding this evening, express orders from O. de B., which will put you on the right track. A little more flesh on the bones."

"Champagne?" she asked.

"Well, thank you, ma'am"—calling her Ethel seemed a little impertinent at this stage—"and who's O. de B.?"

"One of David's captains-to-be. And as I guess you are the lowest form of naval life at the moment, he shall be called Captain Osmond de Beauvoir Brock." She sipped her champagne and smiled encouragingly. "You'll be okay, junior, as long as you agree with him—nothing worse than an opinionated novice, know what I mean?"

I was sure I would have no problems deferring to Captain Brock, but another matter was commanding my attention. I was hoping that the occasional drift of my eyes down to Ethel's décolletage was not causing her embarrassment. I tried to summon up an image of Margaret standing beside her, but it would not materialise. Margaret, as I ascended in my lucky balloon, had become a distant country cousin, her pleasant features blurring into forgetfulness. She stood as though waving from Liverpool Pier as I cast off, but I could no longer distinguish her from the rest of the cheering crowd. Social climbing even for a beginner had a price, and I had begun to pay it; old friends, even loved ones, cast aside.

"And he won't be the only one of the very senior captains or Rear Admirals here," continued Ethel. "Horace Hood is going to show up if he can, Vice Admiral Doveton Sturdee, who's very brilliant but who gives the unfortunate impression that he's the only one who's ever been to sea, and one of my favourites, Roger Keyes. Then there's David's favourite, Captain Chatfield. Keep your wits about you," added Ethel, "and you could get quite lucky, young Reginald, especially since you saved the life of that crashing old misfit, Fisher."

"Is he coming?" It was very ungrateful of me, but I thought I'd seen enough of Jacky for the time being.

"No, he's one of David's favourites—but too much of a Bible-basher for me. Last week, he cornered one of the Sea Lords in his office and shouted at him for an hour without stopping, thumping the table and shaking his fist until the poor old boy went chalk-white and collapsed. Had to take a week off. No, he may be a genius, but he's an old bully. Anyway, I'd rather talk about you. You'll have to come hunting with us when they give you leave from that crammer you're off to. Got a good seat on a horse?"

"Oh, yes, horses," I said, my experience limited to trotting along New Brighton Beach aboard our pony Matilda, looking at girls' legs as they paddled in the sea. But the alcohol was starting to work its usual mystery.

"Great fun," I lied, taking a good slurp of my second glass of champagne. "Used to go barging around a bit with the mid Wirral hunt. The odd five-barred gate, that sort of thing. Bit out of practice though."

"Capital, I'll get David to arrange it. I always think riding is a great test of character and courage. And—though it doesn't apply to you, young man—it is a terrific antidote to boredom and malaise. When you're going hell for leather for a darned great fence, there's no time for dwelling on anything else. No time for doubts, fears, worries, and all that claptrap."

"Ah," she smiled at a new arrival, introducing me to the Hon. Sir Reginald Aylmer Ranfurly Plunkett-Ernle-Erle-Drax, better known as Reginald Plunkett.

"Dartmouth?" He smiled. "I was so relieved when I left that bally place, I got drunk for a week. Hope you fare better."

The other fellows were now arriving, and I took the opportunity of helping myself to a large gin and French, a drink with a kick; it was Dutch courage of course, but I didn't want to be tongue-tied. I suppose after a few minutes they would all know I came from trade, and I was determined to put on a great show about acres of sausage factories and being a scratch golfer at the Royal Liverpool and a family friend of old man Laird. After we sat down, I pecked away at some smoked salmon but then made a complete pig of myself with the steak and kidney pudding and Baked Alaska. Ethel looked on approvingly as though she had rescued a starving youth from a workhouse, and I repaid her interest by ogling her more times than I should.

"Jolly good nosh, sir," I said to my neighbour, Roger Keyes, who had obviously twigged my interest in Ethel. He looked as though he could put on some weight himself.

"Yes, David keeps an excellent table," he replied, "and a very decorative one," nodding at Ethel, then reddening a little in the cheeks. Meanwhile, Beatty was having a moan about bloody journalists and especially Filson Young, who had been causing him endless embarrassment - translate that into secret pleasure - by writing long features in the *Daily Mail* and *Daily Sketch* predicting that he had inherited the mantle of Lord Nelson.

"One eye and arm gone and then the target of a damned sharpshooter, I hope I get better luck than that!" he roared.

And everyone laughed like drains and had another glass of claret.

There was then a commotion in the hall, and Winston, the greatest self-publicist of all, arrived unannounced just as dessert was being cleared away. He sat down, still with his hat on, devoured several brandies, then began to suggest playfully that the gunnery theories of the assembled captains, including Beatty, were all up a gum tree.

He proceeded to try and elaborate this with the help of a box of matches. There was an atmosphere of expectancy and resignation around the table.

"Concentration of fire is the solution," he said. "Don't fight ship against ship. Select the first three ships in the van and smother them with salvoes."

He laid out a small armada of matches on the table, rudely dislodging Brock's unfinished dessert. He pushed out his formidable chin. "Then after they've sunk, start with the rest."

The First Lord struck three matches and then blew them out as if to prove his theory. Then he lit three more flaming lucifers and propped them precariously around the table.

"On they come," he chuckled. "And meanwhile our own ships remain untouched." He waved his arms about as if to prove his point.

"Gosh," said Beatty. "Surely unless hypnosis is part of this theory, they'll be shooting back, won't they?"

"Yes, but very wildly," retorted Winston. "Had the idea yesterday. Wanted to see what you chaps thought." He then knocked over his brandy, which raced towards the lighted matches and set fire to the tablecloth.

Plunkett was forced to admit that there might to some merit in the First Lord's arguments, as he plied the soda siphon in the direction of the flames.

"But, Winston," he said cheekily, "we have just had an admirable lesson in keeping the magazine well away from any ammo." He then directed a jet of water at the brim of Winston's smouldering Homburg, some of it splashing his face. Ethel began a giggling fit.

"Hum," said the First Lord, dabbing his face with his handkerchief. "But there are some things which the average Naval mind cannot grasp. I fight for the Royal Navy all the time." He fanned his arms around again and knocked over the candelabra, adding more fuel to the fire. "The Admiralty demands six new dreadnoughts. The economists and reformers offer four, and we finally compromise on eight. And a bloody good thing too!"

He stood up and puffed his Havana at the assembled company, nicely complementing the fumes from the smouldering tablecloth. "It's good to be here at the heart of the Navy. We have excellent administrators, experts of every description, fine sea officers, great navigators, and brave and devoted hearts. But as we near conflict, we need more captains of war—fighting captains, just like you, chaps! And now, I must dash off to see Fisher before I try and frighten a few more millions out of those dolts in the Commons."

"Think I could finish my dinner now?" asked O. de B. politely, reaching for his plate after the First Lord had motored off.

"I'm afraid," said Plunkett, "you can hardly ask Winston to grasp Naval facts. His only experience of the sea as far as I can recall is filling the Admiralty yacht with cigar smoke and talking lots of twaddle, especially when he's had a few."

"He's always had a few!" exclaimed Beatty. "He'd be completely unbearable if he hadn't. If Winston ever took the pledge, the next place you'd hear from me would be Winnipeg."

"He's just so sure of himself," said Ethel, still giggling as she surveyed the wreckage caused by the great man's brief visit. "I can't help liking his drive. But there's a fat chance of him sending round a new tablecloth, let alone a bunch of flowers. What his friends think doesn't seem to bother him. He thinks he flies higher than the rest of us." She paused, then laughed out loud. "And blow me down, maybe he does!"

"Judging by tonight's fiery performance, he must be worth at least three divisions," said Horace Hood.

"Make that five," said Beatty, opening a big sash window to let some of the smoke escape into the evening air.

I dimly asked Plunkett what he thought Winston had been banging on about. He said something about masking a fleet's main broadside during a deployment to starboard. In those days, the idea of independent action—so beloved of Beatty until he succeeded Jellicoe—was anathema. The dreadnoughts had to line up like formation swimmers and move around with never a bow wave out of step. Anyone trying to cut corners would probably biff his neighbour and so on until so many own goals had been scored that all the captains would reach for their revolvers and blow their brains all over the bridge—those that had any, that is. Or Winston or Jacky would do it for them.

At this point, I was starting to wonder about tomorrow's train to Dartmouth. Beatty must have had similar thoughts because he tapped his wristwatch. My trunk had already been hauled upstairs, and all that remained was to say thanks and goodnight to the brass and, lastly, to Ethel. "It's been quite a day," I said.

"And quite a night!" she said. "Hope you learned something. These sailors are all the same. Once they start playing war games with the cutlery, the meal turns into a farce. Still, as long as they enjoy it. Shall I send you up a cocoa?"

I thanked her again, made my way upstairs, and was just starting to drift off when there was a knock on the door. It was Ethel holding a steaming mug.

"You look quite fetching in bed, Reginald, a possible recruit to David's team. But I don't think David would appreciate more than a momentary goodnight. So drink your cocoa and have a good sleep, Reginald. And write me from Dartmouth. If it's too beastly for words, I'll try to pull a few strings. But I'm sure this isn't the only time we'll meet."

"I hope not."

"How sweet. Well, sleep well, young sailor man."

"I will," I croaked as she left, closing the door quietly. She was compelling. But could I really be David's protégé and Ethel's admirer at the same time? In the end, I could only admire from a distance and would have to accept that. I had better be careful—and to demonstrate why, there was soon another knock on the door, and Beatty looked in.

"Bit of a lark tonight, what?" he said. "There'll be a taxi arriving for you at 7 o'clock in the morning. Bit early for me. Got your chit? Good man. Well, there's no point in pretending that Dartmouth is Antibes, but it'll pass quite quickly. Good luck."

It sounded as though I would need some luck as I prepared to face the rite of passage at the famous naval college. But a feeling of unease didn't stop me from sleeping like a baby and no doubt dreaming about Ethel on her racing stallion and Greta wearing a Prussian guardsman's helmet taking the salute.

CHAPTER 8

DARTMOUTH'S IMPOSING NEW building may have been an improvement on the old hulks Beatty had mentioned, which were still sulking on the banks of the Dart below the college, but attitudes had changed little.

Fisher's letter was taken little notice of, although it seemed to me I did spend a little more time on gunnery and signals than some of the others. The world of Hanover Lodge, let alone Birkenhead, was a million miles away. Never having been to boarding school, I was appalled at having to sleep, in alphabetical order, with other cadets, some snoring and threshing about in the grip of nightmares, and some abusing themselves into a lather.

But the worst thing—and they still cling in my mind—were the Cadet Captains, who rang bells and bellowed orders as if we were performing dogs at a circus.

Ding, ding, ding! "At the double."

Ding, ding, ding! "Small arms drill."

Ding, ding, ding! "Clean your teeth."

Ding, ding, ding! "Say your prayers."

Ding, ding, ding! "Lights out. Silence!"

Ding, ding, ding! "Rise and shine. You've had your time!"

But I did learn a useful amount of technical stuff. How do you fire a shell weighing a ton so that it lands on an enemy twelve miles away? First, you use an optic which coincides with the split image of the enemy until you have the exact range. Then using a mechanical computer, you dial in the estimated speed of the enemy, the speed of your own ship, wind force and direction, the air temperature which affects the cordite needed, the drift or spin of the shell, and the rate of change to keep hitting the target. Finally, in its infancy, director firing which is located in the foremast and allows all guns to be fired simultaneously instead of turret officers using periscopes and their own judgement.

But it was still a chancy business; besieging armies probably had more luck with their trebuchets than we did, trying to hit castles in the sea that were only a smudge on the horizon.

I kept my promise and wrote to Fisher, riling against the harsh discipline and conservatism which I encountered. An instructor was, as a result, removed to improve the manufacture of evidently defective torpedoes in the Midlands; one tin fish is reputed to have rounded on the dreadnought that fired it, then chased the ship and nearly sank it.

As my training wore on, Rear Admiral Beatty hoisted his flag on *Lion*, then left Chatfield, Flag Captain; Frank Spickernell, his secretary; and Ralph Seymour, his Flag Lieutenant, to carry on the dirty work of fitting out while he dashed off to meet Ethel in Monte Carlo, where she was enjoying herself at the casino. He spent some happy days in Paris, then returned to *Lion* in time for some fleet exercises.

Meanwhile, I had passed top in gunnery and was among the first ten in signals. So there seemed absolutely no need for me to stay the rest of the term, being driven mad by the Cadet Captains. And so I cheekily wrote to Ethel, begging for her intervention. She replied by the next post, having telegraphed some cock and bull story to the college, and told me to get a chit for Southampton right away to meet on board her snappy steam yacht, *Sheelagh*.

I did learn a few knots—but not enough to bother Jacky—and the poor cadets were still square-bashing as I sauntered down the steps the next morning and boarded a taxi to the station. A youngster was just arriving for his tour of punishment. He dropped his bag and gave me a ramrod-straight salute—probably my best moment at Dartmouth.

"All right, carry on, lad." I stepped past him, and when I looked back, he was still standing there agog. I looked at the college for the last time. In a few days, poor lad, he'd be wondering what hit him.

CHAPTER 9

GLEAMING IN THE sunshine, *Sheelagh* was anchored in the middle of Southampton water. A launch was waiting for me at the dockside, and in a few minutes, I was reclining under a canopy in the stern, sipping champagne in the company of Ethel and Lady Gwendoline Churchill, Winston's attractive young sister-in-law.

I summoned up the blood as much as I could, but I must have looked a little ill at ease as Ethel eyed me up and down approvingly. "Well, Lieutenant Tucker, you sure have filled out a bit—quite a card in that uniform too. I won't ask you whether you enjoyed Dartmouth, but when I asked David, he made a few inquiries. And when he found out you'd got top marks in gunnery, he couldn't wait for you to join *Lion*. Quite a little shooter, eh, Gwendoline?"

"Quite," said Gwendoline admiringly.

"So we're waiting now for David and his party and we are then off to Russia, to wring the hand of Tsar Nicholas II—nice-looking fella but as dull as ditchwater apparently."

I must have looked curious because Gwendoline chipped in: "Kaiser Willy, our German nemesis who as you know is appointed directly from heaven, used to carry on a sentimental correspondence with Nicholas, the Willy-Nicky mutual admiration society."

"Both candidates for the booby hatch," said Ethel. "And Whitehall was a little afraid they might just decide to hold hands during the big show instead of whacking the daylights out of each other."

"Anyway," she added, "while we're waiting, let me show you around." She got up and ushered me along the deck. "*Sheelagh*'s only a pipsqueak compared to *Lion*, but we make up for it in luxury. Take a look here at our stateroom." This was a huge and expensively furnished bedroom with deep-pile carpets and a bed with a gold satin cover glowing in the sunshine. Ethel drew me inside.

"The privileges of wealth," she whispered as I gaped at the decor. From such distractions, I was saved by the man himself; the First Battlecruiser Squadron had just swept into the harbour, firing salutes and sounding sirens as if in battle. Then there was a tap at the door.

"Thought you'd better know, David's just cast off in his launch," said Gwendoline from outside, "and is on his way at the rate of knots."

"He's always coming at the rate of knots," said Ethel. "Sorry about the abrupt end to the tour. You all shipshape, junior? You'd better be, David is quite a different man at sea."

"Hope so." I opened the door with some trepidation. Beatty's launch was heading towards the stern.

And then a professional shock. There they were—*Lion*, *Queen Mary*, *Princess Royal*, and *New Zealand* gliding in to anchor—four ocean giants more than two hundred yards long and as handsome, sleek, and purposeful as any warships built before or since. The late afternoon sun glinted off the eight massive gun barrels. The signal flags snapped in the wind; their steel bows met the choppy seas inside the harbour, sending spindrift high into the glinting sunlight and cartwheeling up and over the open bridges. I had never seen anything like it and was a battlecruiser man from that moment on, in love with those long, lean ships, the greatest warships ever built if you went by looks alone, which was all I was qualified to do in those days.

We rejoined Lady Churchill. "Well, we should give the Russians something to think about," she said, "taking their minds off their medieval religion and the knout for a while. Cruel bastards." Whether the notorious knout was any worse than being crushed to death by the machinery of a modern battleship was debatable. But there was no time for that as Beatty was stepping aboard. I approached him and snapped a salute.

"Lieutenant Tucker reporting for duty, Sir," I said. "Very good to see you again, Sir."

"Right-o, Tucker. At ease. Bit out of order to write to Ethel, but I can't fault ambition, and of course I can't deny her anything. Are you going to be a good officer and punch your weight?"

"Yes, Sir!"

"I fondly hope so. Now look lively and bash off in the launch, and I may see you later if I've got time from all this play-acting I have to get into training for."

"Meeting our Russian friends, sir?"

"Exactly. And it's all got to be in French, damn it. Now off you go and get acquainted with *Lion*. It may not rival *Sheelagh* in opulence, but there's a lot to see, a hell of a lot to learn. I expect you to be a good officer, Tucker, as well as an asset to the wardroom. Understand?"

"Yes, sir!"

"And you will receive no preference for saving Lord Fisher, writing to my wife, or being on intimate terms with King George himself, for that matter. Understand?" The famous grimace flitted across his stern features.

"Absolutely, sir. I wouldn't have it any other way."

"Just do you duty—nothing else matters."

Ethel shook my hand before I stepped aboard the launch, a grand confection of brass and polished woodwork and Marines with fixed bayonets.

"You'll do just fine," she said warmly, giving my hand a squeeze. "See you in St Petersburg. We might even have one of those funny Russian dances. Take care, Reginald." And by golly, if she didn't peck me on the cheek, which made my head spin, especially as David was looking on impatiently, his face again creasing into its familiar grimace.

It was time to go. I saluted, stepped aboard, then the launch surged across the harbour, carrying me into the labyrinthine world of the battlecruiser *Lion*.

My ambition was achieved at last.

CHAPTER 10

AFTER BEATTY'S GRUFF welcome, a cheery face greeted me at the top of the companionway to the dark-grey giant. It was Frank Spickernell, the Admiral's secretary and head of Signals and Intelligence.

"Welcome aboard," he said, smiling. He had eyes as piercing as a seagull looking for scraps, but they were never unfriendly. "Gather you took what the wireless people might call a short circuit to get here. Well, nothing wrong with that, providing you're up for it. The Admiral asked me to show you the ropes—not that we've got many of them, but no one can resist a request from David. Besides which, you might otherwise get hopelessly lost."

We started walking around the two turrets at the bow with their enormous guns. "The guns are 13.5 inch—beat anything the Germans can muster," said Spick before vanishing down a steep flight of steps with the skill of an acrobat. I followed rather more gingerly, emerging into an endless white corridor bathed in the glare of electric lights. "This ship is the size of a fair-sized village with one intent—to put the shits up enemy vessels, beat them as they start running, and then sink them in a hurry," he said. "And you can easily lose your way. The main areas to avoid are the lower decks—where most of the seamen kip, eat their meals, and have their rum—because if they don't know you and sense for a moment you don't know where you're going, they'll chase you like a pack of hounds.

Shall we start the Cooke's tour now, or would you like to wet your whistle in the wardroom?"

I opted for the tour.

"Tell you what," said Spickernell, "it's a wonderful night for wireless—you can hear all sorts of things going on. How's your Morse?"

"Could be better, sir."

"Well, most of it is scrambled anyway; thank God we've highly trained operators who can tell where a signal's coming from because every operator has his own keystrokes, a kind of signature."

On the main deck in the dazzling light and amidst the department-store busyness of the main thoroughfare of the ship, scores of men were slinging their hammocks and preparing to turn in. We had to duck to avoid disturbing them.

Down another steel staircase, across the ship, along the mess deck, and up another and steeper ladder, we came at last to a white-enamelled door, on which were inscribed the words "Wireless Office." It was crowded with knobs and switches in brass, copper, and vulcanite and furnished with two small desks and, in the midst of it all, a cage containing a thick cable that climbed right up to the foremast—the vital aerial that joined us to almost anywhere in the planet.

The chief of the small band of seamen and petty officers was watching the clock. He nodded respectfully at Spick as we entered his private world.

"It's Norddeich, sir, the Berlin station, you can set your watch by him. He's just knocking out his pipe, I reckon, to deliver his usual propaganda. If the young gentleman would take these earphones, he'll hear him now."

I put on the heavy earphones and listened. A black vulcanite disc, which tuned the hundreds of various wavelengths on the air, was set to a certain number on the dial. I heard a ghostly buzz, a chorus of insect-like noises, then a loud, strident signal.

"There he is!" said the chief.

All very well if you could understand it. From what I was told, the dit-dit-dahs spoke of the growing strength of Germany and the necessity to arm itself against the growing strength and dreadfulness of its enemies, including forging a High Seas Fleet which would be a match for the Royal Navy—a fanciful notion since our size was half as a big again.

"Sounds like tosh to me," I said.

"And we have to listen to that arrogant propaganda every night," said the chief. He then turned the dial so I could hear bits of sound from the Eiffel Tower, the Commander-in-Chief of the Atlantic, then the Russian Commander-in-Chief of the Baltic. All were gobbledygook to me. And then came a plaintive message from one cargo vessel to another, somewhere between Ireland and Iceland. The chief translated with a grin: "Two thousand lbs of marrowfat peas intended for me, addressed to you in error. And I have the same number of potatoes. Can we swap at some suitable point and achieve a more varied diet?"

And that was that. The night was turning sour after a peerless summer's day, and Spickernell, on duty, had to leave me to my own devices. I followed him towards the stern with its clumps of hammocks, ducking and weaving, but he was too fast for me. I had to find my own way back.

I could hear the water gulping and slurping up the great ship's side, agitated by a fair chop as the wind gained strength. Towards the bows, the corridor was coated in white enamel and dazzling in the electric light. Between the wardroom and the Admiral's quarters, it resembled the corridor of a modern hotel. The numbered cabin doorways on each side were screened against drafts by red curtains, which wafted back and forth in the corridor as the *Lion* rolled sleepily in its moorings. A seaman was suddenly beside me, tugging at my sleeve.

"Haddock, sir, your servant. This is your cabin, sir. I've unpacked your trunk and laid out your clothes for dinner." He cleared his throat. "There is the small matter of your .38 revolver, sir. Unless you think you might be firing at anyone tonight, I'd suggest stowing it in the small arms locker. Is that all right?"

Good grief, a servant of my own. To me, it was surprising that servants fitted into the modern dreadnought navy. But if you ask me, anyone who is offered a servant to deal with life's mundanities—like having a sharp razor and a clean shirt twice a day—then turns him down not only robs the chap of a perfectly decent job but is a prize idiot.

"Hello, Haddock," I said, trying to look more authoritative than I felt. "I hope we'll be good friends. Yes, stow the pistol if you want to."

"Thank you, sir. Dinner is in half an hour. And I thought it might be fun if you popped along to the wardroom and got acquainted with your colleagues and have a stiff one."

"Excellent idea," said I, warming to Haddock and his ministrations, and in about ten minutes, the raw recruit was standing at the wardroom door.

Spickernell was already there. "Found your way," he said with a twinkle in his eye. "Here's one of your contemporaries, Lieutenant David Highet." Highet stood up and shook my hand. He was tall and dark-haired with a permanent curl to his upper lip and attempted to crush my fingers, but I gave as good as I got.

"In trade, I hear," he said pleasantly enough. He was trying to put me in my place at our first meeting, the pompous ass.

"And your old chap is a bank cashier," broke in Spick, coming to my aid. "Doesn't exactly own the bloody bank."

"Wish he did," said Highet glumly. He would dearly have loved a private income, but the threadbare carpets at home, as Spick told me later, were trampled under the feet of hungry brothers and sisters galore. For that reason, if no other, he had to be watched in the wardroom, where he had a tendency to cadge drinks so, with savings on his mess bill temporarily achieved, he could bung ten bob home.

"Don't think there's much in it," said I with a wink. "Our sausages are the talk of the north-west. Our factories"—laying it on a bit thick—"can barely keep up with demand." He had no possible way of checking the sausage consumption of Cheshire, Lancashire, and North Wales, but I managed to conjure up visions of vast production floors full of girls with white aprons, churning out sausages, ready for delivery by a fleet of waiting Tucker's vans. *One-nil*, I thought, but Highet would bear watching, even when he became a firm friend.

"Commerce it sounds like, hardly trade," said Spick, although I suspected he thought I had gone a bit over the top.

I was delighted to hear that Beatty and his Flag Captain Chatfield were being invited to the wardroom for dinner—a rare event—to celebrate the Russian trip. It promised to be a bit of a rag. I met Flag Lieutenant Ralph Seymour and several other officers and must have sluiced down four pink gins by the time we were called to the table. A marine band began to play in the wardroom flat. Compared to Dartmouth, this was paradise.

The conversation began quietly enough, becoming more rousing as the claret began to flow, then became plain boisterous. At this stage, Beatty's special guest arrived, the gentleman journalist Filson Young. "So sorry, been wiring some copy to the *Daily Telegraph* in London," he explained, drawing up a chair and tucking into a large pink and pâté de foie in order to catch up.

"Not telling porkies about us already, Filson?" said Beatty who had just sped back from *Sheelagh*. "I think we ought to censor your copy."

Young laughed—I liked the look of him—and glanced with amazement round the long table. "Grief, I am so hemmed in with restrictions that if I ever write anything interesting or remotely factual about the British Navy, the Admiralty will seize the very lead from the compositor's hands and hurl it back into the furnace. Am I allowed to say that boats float on the sea powered by screws? No, a few scraps from the table is all I'm allowed."

"Quite right," said Highet with characteristic pomposity, running his hands through his dark hair.

"Oh, why do you say that?"

"'Cause all journalists are stinkers and write about what they don't know," Highet said. "They just make it up. I'd start by snapping all your pencils."

"You would prefer, I expect," said Filson, "to be entertained in the salons of London, where Mrs Asquith and Lady Astor dictate their useless gossip to the war staff and tame editors and somehow have some divine way of knowing about great military and naval plans before they've even been conceived. If a good-looking woman invites Sir John French to dinner, he'll rehearse a whole battle for her, giving away his whole strategy and tactics. And he's not the only one."

Reginald Plunkett, whom I'd met at Hanover Lodge, threw his oar in. "I think it's interesting having you aboard, Filson, but I'm damned if I know what you can tell anyone about the Navy, not having the faintest idea about it. Still, it might make the public understand us more, which I suppose is all you're after when all is said and done."

"And who, pray, gives a damn what the public thinks?" asked Chatfield.

"Well, I suppose, if you put it like that," Filson said, laughing. And I really thought I ought to come to his aid.

"Well, I've only just joined the ship," I said as all eyes swivelled towards me. "But I must say, it was articles by people like Mr Young which informed me about the Navy. Otherwise, I'd be completely, well, all at sea."

"And what makes you think you aren't?" haw-hawed Highet.

The gins followed by the claret made me dash on regardless, and I heard myself saying: "Well, I think in about two months' time we'll be exchanging fire with the Germans, and what I think is that we'll make sauerkraut out of them because this is the best Navy in the world. Print that, Mr Young."

Beatty rose to his feet, glass in hand, and said: "Bloody good show!" And everyone got up and joined the Admiral in the then popular toast: "Confusion to the Kaiser."

"And what have we got?" asked Beatty, still on his feet and waving us on as if conducting an orchestra.

"Speed!" went to the wardroom chorus.

"And what else?"

"Hitting power!"

"And what do we do when we see an enemy?"

"Shoot!"

"Too damned right," said the Admiral. "And what other vital ingredient?" No one spoke, and all eyes were on him. Chatfield, *Lion*'s captain, aglow with good spirits, sat beside his chief, waiting.

"Champagne—Fizz!" bellowed Beatty. And a procession of mess waiters entered, bearing Magnums. "Now get your drinking boots on, gentlemen, because we are off to see the Tsar, and if I see any officer in the First Battlecruiser Squadron unable to better his Russian counterpart bottle to bottle, I'll put him on soda water till Christmas. That understood?"

"Yes, Sir!" we all answered, then fell about laughing.

"I don't care how well lit up you get at night as long as you're burning bright by morning."

"I think the Russians have a couple of tots of vodka to get themselves going in the morning," said Spick. "Bit like the Frogs with their coffee and cognac."

"No wonder their ships go around in circles all day," said Young, who now looked as though he was in the bosom of his family. "They don't practise good tactics like we do." This was a little too familiar for a mere scribbler among seasoned pirates, and Chatfield stuck his oar in again.

"What tactics?" he inquired with a look of feigned astonishment. "Tactics haven't really altered since the Armada. You see the enemy, make sure it's not a passing ferry boat or a neutral cargo ship, then shoot the beggar." He then bowled an accurate bread roll, hitting Filson on the ear. Others joined in, shouting "Shoot!" and leaving Filson to duck and weave, then finally mumble that he thought it was all more complicated than that, and bury his nose in his glass.

"Anyway, for the moment, gentlemen," Beatty said, "we have to pay homage to the Tsar of all the Russias, where when the sun is sinking at one end of the playing field, it's hoisting itself up at the other—that is, unless the Japanese are twisting their tail. So even if they have the most chronic navy in the world, let's drink a toast to Tsar Nicholas, Alexandra, and the lovely Grand Duchesses."

"Tsar Nicholas!" said Seymour, no doubt wondering what strange signal hoists would be required when he arrived at St Petersburg. Signals by flag were a delicate form of communication between languages, and he had never quite got over signalling a Turkish cruiser during a Mediterranean exercise to "turn two points to port and proceed up your own bottom."

Still, Fisher thought it was a great joke; Ralph went on to commit so many more scrapes that I wondered whether he had cast a spell over Beatty or simply hoisted any mixture of the many coloured silks up the rigging while artfully concealing that he was congenitally colour-blind.

He was rumoured to have once directed a sizeable squadron to steam at full speed to Birmingham, the bands no doubt playing "We Plough the Fields and Scatter" as they went. Still, while it was one thing to gloat over the incompetence of others, it had to be remembered that a more competent enemy was always waiting to pounce.

"When do we actually set off?" I said foolishly, finally hitting my own coral reef.

"Good God, Tucker, we've been underway for at least an hour," said Beatty. "You couldn't see Old Blighty now with a telescope a mile long. And I can't see that happening unless Filson makes it up."

"We're almost in the b-bloody Baltic now, Tucker," said Highet, his stammer appearing as he clenched talons for the kill. "Haw-haw, haven't you been to sea, Tucker? A rowing boat at Blackpool Pleasure Beach perhaps?"

Fortunately, Filson came to my aid as the laughter echoed around the steel walls. "An easy mistake surely. *Lion* is so smooth, you barely know it's underway. And I am convinced that Tucker is an excellent seaman. He just got carried away by the excellence of the company."

"Exactly," I said, screwing up all courage to gaze at all the company in turn, with a particularly sickly smile in the direction of Highet. "I am clearly among giants and am enormously proud to be here." That should do it. And it did, until the next time.

"Do you think it's time to pass the word to the crew where we're going, Sir?" Spickernell asked the Admiral.

"Can't do any harm," Beatty said. "And give 'em an extra tot without causing a riot if at all possible."

"Do you know where I like to be, Sir?" piped up Low. He'd had a few.

"In my own first-class hotel."

"Good grief," said the Admiral, looking around the table in mock wonder.

"We'd have a huge garden, be near a golf course and major road, and have a trout stream handy."

"Yes, I'll join in, and we'll have no men about the place, just maids with old-fashioned names," said Spick, enjoying the fantasy hugely. "Jolly names—tuck you up in bed names."

"Penelope," offered Plunkett.

"And P-Prudence," said Highet.

"And Phoebe," I said, just for the hell of it.

Quite contented by this vision, Low took a good tug at his champagne. "Changing the subject, do you know what they call the children of the Tzar? I've just thought of it."

"No," we all said in wonderment.

"Tzardines! You can get them in a can at the grocers, as many as you like. A whole dynasty in a can!"

Evidently no royalist, Low did quite well with this one and there was much spluttering around the wardroom table. Plunkett nearly wet himself, and Beatty twitched with laughter.

"On you go then, Frank," he said, back to the business of the moment, which was telling the ship's company where we were headed so they could knock off some of their grog—125 per cent proof Navy rum mixed with water—and join in the fun.

And so the word was spread. People were fetched out of bed, and a minor riot ensued. Those officers not in their cabins were locked out of them. Those already in them were locked in. There was a point-to-point over various chairs and sofas, resulting in several breakages, and the keyboard of the piano was covered in trifle. I managed to dig Highet in the ribs during one of these "races," which gave me great satisfaction. "Rule, Britannia!" was meanwhile being lustily sung from the mess decks.

Spickernell, in one of the great traditions of the service, led a raid to the Midshipman's gunroom, producing two specimens for the game of "running torpedoes," the torpedoes being the unfortunate snotties, who are hurled face downwards along the length of the table by all available forces. The "torpedoes" have to enjoy this game; if not, it is repeated until they do. By about 11 o'clock, the whole of *Lion* was alight, and the Marine Band was playing "A Life on the Ocean Wave," complete with raspberries from the trombones. And as they played, *Lion* was pulling us at more than 20 knots towards our erstwhile allies in the land of vodka and the knout.

In time, everyone sloped off, the Admiral towards his stately quarters and the rest to their cabins, leaving me and Filson Young and a mess waiter hovering in attendance.

"This is all a bit like being at sea, isn't it?" He laughed, looking around with affection at the wreckage of the wardroom. "Care to join me for a nightcap in my quarters?"

His quarters, as the Admiral's special guest, were magnificent, fit for a King. Hunting prints lined the walls; there was a broad picture window, not a porthole, looking at the moonlit sea ruffled by a strengthening wind. He signalled his servant, who brought a decanter of brandy and two snifters. Pouring away, he told me how he had managed, through various stratagems, to wangle an RNVR—the wavy navy—commission to the *Lion* on "special service" through toadying to Fisher.

He laughed. "I employed the old and very simple trick of a man who comes to you and says he has the promise of work in Montreal if you will give him ten pounds for his passage and then writes to Quebec that there is someone who will pay for his passage if he gives him a job. Not bad, eh?"

I nodded approval. Obviously a man after my own heart. I told him about Jacky and the runaway horses. "Incidentally, did Fisher ask you to keep in touch—keep him informed of developments and all that?" I asked.

He nodded, smiling. So we were both Fisher's spies. "What I can't understand," I said, "is that Admiral Beatty hardly seems to know him."

"That's pure affectation—he loves the old geezer. But one who doesn't is Clementine, Churchill's wife. She won't have him in the house." He laughed again. "You are either in one school or the other: the Winston school, which is considered brilliant but dangerous, the Percy Scott school, who insists on technical brilliance well beyond the reach of most in the

Admiralty, and the Jellicoe school, who believe in very tight central control and no questions asked."

He got to his feet and piped: "'Please, Sir, can I go to the bathroom?' And the commander radios a signal to the Admiralty in London, who replies that in order for an officer to leave the bridge for a natural call, certain conditions calling for immediate acceptance must prevail. If the ship is at action stations, another officer must be found to take the position of the one who wishes to relieve himself. The officer must take no more than two minutes to fulfil his function and, if longer, must be deemed lost in action and so on. Now you either piss in your trousers or disregard such instructions as staff rubbish. Or let them pee over the side of the bridge so long as ordinary seamen aren't looking, which would set a bad example. Not that that would matter much, most of the lower deck thinks officers are tossers anyway and pee over the side without blinking an eyelid."

Filson took a swig of brandy and looked out of the picture window at the wine-dark sea, through which we were moving at a swift 22 knots. As a journalist, he had his hands tied. He went to the sideboard and produced a camera. "I'm not supposed to use this, but that's one regulation I will gladly flout. Good God, Billy Russell had more freedom in the Crimea than someone writing about the Navy in the twentieth century."

"Rear Admiral Beatty seems to like you having aboard, Sir," I lied.

"Perhaps, but Beatty actually plays the publicity hand rather well. He and Ethel pretend to dislike it, but in many ways, they make sure they get in the papers and the journals in the right way. And after he's appeared in *The Pictorial* calling him the New Nelson, he complains about dreadful scribblers but is really as pleased as Punch."

"So that's why you're here."

"Yes, but if it comes to the crunch, I will pack my typewriter away and do what's necessary to defeat the enemy."

"And then write about it," I teased.

"Why not? Someone's got to keep a record. And all this secrecy is a bloody imposition on the public, the taxpayers, history, and the Navy itself." His face was growing red and knew I had hit a deep vein of resentment.

"You can't run a war like a club with only some self-important oafs and rich old tarts in London knowing what's going on. Winston understands that, but he can't be bothered to do anything about it. He knows he's either riding for glory or a nasty fall. Helping journalists is a sideshow. And the same goes for Jacky Fisher. And now, matey, I'm going to turn in."

"Thanks for your hospitality—and your insights," I found myself saying.

"Tucker?"

"Yes, Sir?"

"You seem a good fellow. Let me know if there's anything you think's worth a line, will you?"

"Right-o."

"And, Tucker. Don't make too many mistakes, like asking whether we're underway yet. I know you're new, but that sort of thing is supposed to be in the bloodstream, as it were. If you're not sure whether we're underway or not, go up on deck and have a shufti."

"Fact is, sir, I've never been to sea before."

"Grief—well, keep that under your hat. This is smooth sailing tonight, but being in one of these things in a gale is bracing to say the least. Prepare yourself."

"Goodnight, sir," I said, saluting and leaving Filson to ponder his eccentric and, in many ways, accurate view of the Navy, including the fact that many lieutenants, including me, had about as much experience of the medium on which they travelled as a wooden duck.

It must have been either the booze or the excitement which made me wake up in my cabin four hours later—that, or the roll of the ship, which had now entered the heavy seas of the Baltic. I was ecstatic at being on *Lion*, and it was that, more than anything, which led me to put on my greatcoat and white silk scarf and take a proprietorial tour around the nerve centre of the ship—the bridge—and delve into its secrets.

Passing the Admiral's quarters, I climbed a spiral staircase, suddenly going from light and peace into darkness and the beginnings of a storm.

Through a steel doorway lit by one dim light, I was engulfed by blackness and the roaring of the gale as the great ship surged ahead.

Then I was in the lee of the superstructure, feeling gingerly for the first of three ladders which led up past the four-inch gun deck, past the recording office, and the Admiral's and Captain's sea cabins to the searchlight platform. The marine standing outside Beatty's put a finger to his lips, indicating that he was snatching one of his brief rests at sea. Another clap of wind, and I was at the foot of the ladder leading to the signals bridge. Shadowy figures loomed; Seymour, the Flag Lieutenant, paced up and down beside the bo'sun, trying to keep warm. The ship's speed and a strong wind made the temperature keen despite the fact that it was early summer.

Next, I went into the Admiral's chart room lit by switches operated by the opening and the closing of the door so not a chink of light could escape and give a clue to *Lion*'s position. Oddly, I found closing the door difficult and tugged at it while a lieutenant, trying to look up a signal, cursed the sudden blackness. Apologising and thinking it was a mechanical failure, I gave the door everything I had and then gave up the unequal struggle with what was a stronger force. The door opened and closed easily this time to reveal in the light David Beatty who was not in the best of tempers. A light rain had started to fall, which didn't help matters.

"Oh, it's you, Tucker," he sighed. "What are you doing—sleepwalking?"

"Sorry, Sir, but I couldn't sleep, so I decided to have a look around."

"Good God, it sounds as if you're on the *Mauretania*. You'll be promenading round the decks next in your dressing gown. But the fact is, you need your sleep, Tucker, because in a few hours' time you're due at the signals office. So off you go." He suddenly grinned. "Bloody good rag, what? Old Brock on *Princess Royal* claims to have the best rags, but in my view, no one does it better than *Lion*. I thought Low's hotel idea was inspired. Can't wait to go. Now come on, you're not a gormless schoolboy any more. Go and put your head down. I want us in top form for the Russkies. Nothing less will do."

"Right away, Sir," I said, thoroughly chastened and ducking out fast. In my confusion, I ascended to the compass platform which was open to the elements where the Officer of the Watch and the Navigating Commander ensure the ship is on perfect stations. But this was not the way to the signals office nor my bunk, for that matter. Below in the dark conning tower shaped like some huge medieval helmet were the spotting scopes, steering wheel, telegraphs, voice pipes, and navy phones that made up *Lion*'s war room. Though much tempted, I decided not to venture into this department because Beatty might arrive at any moment and a second encounter would involve punishment—perhaps a one-way trip such as a seaplane raid on Zeppelin sheds.

Seaplanes weren't highly regarded as offensive weapons at the time; they were lowered into the water with all the respect and care given to old Queen Victoria alighting from a train, and how to get them on board again in the unlikely event they did complete their mission was anyone's guess. The damage they might do to an enemy dreadnought—grenades chucked or lobbed by hand—was even more pathetic. Jacky of course was the only one who could see their potential, developing them in his imagination into fearsome battleships of the sky firing aerial torpedoes at each other and laying waste to whole cities. I didn't see how you could get 30,000 tons of battlewagon to fly. One had to admit the flimsy but impressively large Zeppelins had warlike potential, yet they too were too much at the mercy of the elements. No, in 1914, a battlecruiser was the place to be, protected by plenty (but not actually enough) armour plate.

Chips and Ian, dozy buggers, had volunteered for the Royal Flying Corps, reckoning that it stood the best chance of any service in providing not only the excitement of flying but also of ample booze and obliging French girls captivated by their flying jackets and goggles. Girls weren't available on board a ship of course, but Ethel was not far behind us in *Sheelagh*, settling herself in her queenly bed and perhaps reading a bit of the racing form before she went to sleep. She was quite out of my league of course but nonetheless beautiful, and I sensed in her a typically American appreciation of any young officer with aspirations and drive. How different from attitudes at home, which invariably regarded ambition as a disease.

We did of course have our share of Nancy Boys, but they didn't seem to bother anyone very much, and no one in the wardroom was that way inclined, so far as I could see. Dressing up in ladies' clothing was of course a favourite pastime during the various dire shipboard entertainments, from pantos to variety and one-man bands. Coquettish and ridiculous attempts were made to mimic the opposite sex. In this way were the men "entertained" during the coming war, but I think they'd have been just as happy with an extra tot of rum and a game of cards. Certainly, boxing matches between all ranks were far more popular.

On the way down from the bridge, Beatty's mention of a "promenade" round the deck amused me. There was now a good sea running, with waves splashing over the bow and running down the slope of the deck, but risking damp and salty shoes, I started out. The sky was now light, though scarred by lumps of thundercloud. The sea crowded in around the ship, seeking out every crevice, looking for a crack in a plate. I imagined an enemy battlecruiser lying low on the horizon, the turrets' steel ball bearings rolling round as they sighted their guns, then the shells and silk cartridges being fed into the breeches, and the sudden spurt of fire as the shells came roaring towards us at well over a thousand miles an hour.

And then nothing. The water would close over and entomb the vanquished ship. No memorials possible on the rising and falling sea to show where it had met its end; no bodies to bury, just the transcript of a final morse message, "M'Aidez," and a final transmission from the Admiralty: "Under no circumstances are ratings to be allowed to exchange socks for cigarettes and rum rations. This practice must cease . . ." Too late, you bullying, bungling bureaucrats; they're all bloody dead.

I was drifting. I would never make it to the stern, let alone round the ship. I headed down the nearest ladder, found my cabin, and fell into a dreamless sleep.

CHAPTER 11

WHAT WITH ALL the liquor and the roll of the ship, I could have been feeling better the next morning as I struggled with a cut-throat razor at the unholy hour of 7.30 a.m. I still had to find my sea legs.

Spickernell popped his cheerful face round the cabin door. He gave me quite a start, and shaving was a difficult enough job at the best of times.

"The Captain thought you might like to pop up aloft into the foretop as we're having a spot of gunnery practice at eight o'clock."

"Right-o," I said, nicking myself painfully under the chin. This was obviously Beatty's revenge for my nosiness during the night. Blood ran down my neck. "Don't slice your head off," Spick laughed. "That might happen soon enough. And remember, keep a bloody good hold of that steel ladder."

I yelled to Haddock for a bacon sandwich and some coffee. Then ten minutes later, I was standing, terrified, at the foot of one of the two 60-foot-long steel ladders placed astride the foremast. *Lion* was making 25 knots, and the resulting headwind was strong. As I started climbing, I thought the slipstream must have possessed a malignant force of its own. The moist steel grips were smooth, and I wondered whether my grip was strong enough to win a fight with the gale. I looked down once during the climb; just beside me, the nearest funnel was blowing hot coal fumes right across the grey giant. Men taking exercise around the deck—including a seamen's gym class—looked tiny against the battlecruiser's length.

At the end of the climb, as the ship swayed, I was dismayed to find there was a yawning gap which had to be spanned, striding across to a small foothold below the cross trees. Open air beckoned, and reaching over it, I then found a handhold which allowed me to get my knee on to the edge of the trapdoor into the foretop. At last I was there: a miserable steel box bolted to the mast with a surround so low you could only kneel on the rivets of the floor. But the view! Compensating for the discomfort, it was endless: a beautiful morning with pink clouds among the blue and the sun glinting off the wave tops, a far better view than that from the bridge. The elevation made a tremendous difference.

From about five miles to starboard, *Princess Royal* was limbering up to make a pass with the target, a great wood and canvas botch-up on a very long cable. She must have been making some steam because she towed the target across the range on an interception course with *Lion*—a distance of about 8 miles. Meanwhile, the sea had got up again, and *Lion* was plunging up and down too much for my liking and it was then that I felt the shaking through the mast as our eight 13.5-inch guns rumbled around to face the adversary.

A navy phone beside me started ringing.

"Spot fall of shot," said a disembodied voice.

"Yes." Oh well, nothing like joining in the fun. I tried to stand up in the box, but it was like being hit by a knock-down gale, and I continued to crouch. I then heard a deafening roar above the shriek of the wind. X turret had fired, its smoke drifting across the range. Cordite blew in my face. I got out my field glasses and looked at the target. The flight of the shells, which I could easily see, lasted about fifteen seconds. They landed short, throwing up waterspouts 100 feet high, which fell slowly back into the sea. Then the guns roared again—this time, a full broadside.

No point in wittering on about it. "Short," I said down the phone. After a thirty-second pause, the guns boomed out again, the cordite rising in the air and smudging my face. Funny, I've always liked the smell of cordite—rather like the hot tar applied to roads.

"Over," I said. "Down a fraction." My eardrums were cracking from the gale and the shattering noise of the guns.

Down below, I could see Beatty and Chatfield on the signal bridge following progress with their own glasses. Conditions were good, visibility fine, but no hits. Then all turrets started to fire at random, making spotting almost impossible. Which turret was getting closer, and which was still 500 yards off? Over the phone receiver, which I still clutched, I heard somebody say: "The Admiral's offered an extra tot of rum for the first hit." This seemed to do the trick because the next broadside blew the target sky-high, and as there was nothing else to fire at, the huge smoking guns trundled back to their usual positions fore and aft, like bloodhounds panting after a chase.

Anxiously, I began to descend the ladder, but it proved easier than going up, and I soon was among the assembly on the signals bridge from where Beatty liked to conduct his battle practice and his battles. He should, in theory, have been in the protection of the armoured conning tower, peering through the slits like Sir Galahad going into the lists. But he and Chatfield liked fresh air and took their chances.

"Well?" said Beatty, adjusting his cap.

"Bracing, Sir," I said bravely. My face was rimmed with cordite, and one of my ears was bleeding from the detonation of the guns. I had a sudden sense that I was going to collapse at the great man's feet; I gripped the rail until my knuckles whitened and the spell had passed. But I had to say something about the shooting—possibly unpopular but at least something I was supposed to know about.

"Not a bad outcome," boomed Beatty. "You don't often see a target so comprehensively smashed as that one."

I cleared my throat as Chatfield, the Navy's gunnery ace, joined us. Seymour was also in view and just about in earshot.

Here goes. "They took a while to find the range, Sir, if you don't mind me saying so. If it had been a real enemy, they might have got our range first. Might have been a bit hot for us, sir."

"Oh." The dashing admiral looked a trifle crestfallen since he, among a very few in the 1914-18 Navy, treated junior officer's opinions with some respect. "Maybe in a real action, we'll have to speed up."

I had an audience, receptive except for Seymour, who looked as though I deserved a week in the brig on bread and water.

"Director firing is the answer. All the guns coordinated, aimed, and firing from a central point, bringing the full power of the weapons to bear." And that was straight from one of my more enlightened Dartmouth lectures.

"So you'd blow it to bits the first time?" asked an amazed Chatfield.

"Not necessarily, Sir. But we'd have a fifty per cent chance of scoring hits than usual gun laying. Or certainly forty, Sir. A control position would be where I was, sixty feet above the turret periscopes with vastly better visibility. Coordination of fire would be a piece of cake. And in a busy action with many targets, aiming could quickly be returned to individual turrets if that was thought necessary."

All this had to be shouted because of the prevailing headwind, but I thought I'd scored a point. A young officer capable of discussing gunnery with his superiors and getting them to listen? Almost worth a commendation. It was the new Navy talking, Fisher's navy, where technical points were supposed to be listened to because they were new. There was among a few of us a thirst for knowledge, which stemmed from an absence of tactical ideas about how battles would be fought with the power and range of the big guns and the galloping speed of the ships. Nelson was a source of inspiration but provided no practical clues. It was a different kind of warfare; seamen carried spanners, not cutlasses, and the guns had grown to elephantine proportions.

"Very interesting," Chatfield said solemnly, and Beatty nodded. Later, I was pleased to hear from Spick that Beatty had written to the Admiralty and demanded that director firing be installed at the next refit.

My first contribution to the ship, I thought to myself proudly, but of course you never get any thanks in the Navy, just a complete bollocking if anything goes wrong. Still, the name would be registered, fed into conversation, and you might well find yourself in contention for an early promotion—possibly out of your depth but a small command of your own, a torpedo boat, a destroyer, or worse, an armed trawler looking for U-Boats or stray mines.

To show their smart-alec new lieutenant the ropes, I was assigned to join X turret during the next practice firing later that day. The Admiralty preferred captains to be miserly with the ammo because of the expense, but Beatty couldn't care a fig about that nor about the targets which, as they cost the extortionate sum of a twenty pounds each, were the subject of endless memos from the Admiralty's cost-cutters.

Not to have exercised the Big Cats in their proper role of blowing enemy ships to Kingdom Come would have been rather futile. Besides which, Beatty was clearly addicted to cordite smoke, dense clouds of which surrounded the great tongues of flame which leapt from the muzzles of the guns hurling the shell towards the horizon at thousands of miles an hour.

I clambered into the turret, feeling queasy as *Lion* corkscrewed, and was greeted by a midshipman called Muirhead, whose main job was to leap up and down with enthusiasm and squeak with delight when the big guns fired. I had expected protective clothing and earmuffs. But there was no such sissy stuff in 1914.

About 35 ratings manned the turret, but much of what was done was automatic. From the shell room, the deepest hold in the ship, the 1,000 lb projectiles were carried by hopper to the base of the ammunition hoist. They then picked up cordite charges in their silk bags. Shells and charges moved up to a curved track to the breech of each gun and were pushed hard into the firing chamber by hydraulic rammers. Then, once the heavy breechblocks were screwed shut and the guns had moved into the proper angle for firing, the order came: "Shoot."

It wasn't the ear-splitting roar I had expected being so close, more like an impact which travelled through the body like a seismic shock. With the deadly projectiles travelling into the outer reaches of the atmosphere, the great guns recoiled about 18 inches and were then ready for service again after the barrels had been sprayed with compressed air and water to stop any flaming fragments catching the next cordite charge and blowing up the gun house. It was a smooth operation—I counted two shots a minute (not the three that Beatty claimed)—but didn't like being in the turret. An electrically lit fortress of armour plate with only a periscope to see out, I found it claustrophobic.

"Good, eh?" said young Muirhead as the guns boomed again.

"Very impressive," I said, looking down the hoist to the depths of the magazine, a giddy twenty feet below. There were precautions to prevent an explosion in the gun barrels, but what if an enemy hit caused a cordite flash down to the magazine? The whole ship would go up like a big firework, everyone aboard burnt to a crisp.

"What about that then?" I said, explaining my doubts to Muirhead without trying to scare him unduly.

But he brightened. "It is recognised as a problem, Sir, but the trouble is, if you put antiflash shutters all over the place, it would slow everything down dreadfully. Actually, Admiral Beatty likes to pile up cordite charges at the bottom of the hoist to speed things up. He's determined to get us up to a regular three shots a minute, sir."

"Good grief." I knew Beatty was a bit reckless, but surely this was carrying his lack of technical knowledge too far—the hunter, always going for the highest fences and risking a fall.

"But I think on the safety angle, the Admiralty are looking at it, Sir," piped up Muirhead, a nice youngster in reefer and flannels, his face almost entirely covered in freckles.

Oh, no, they're not, my lad, I thought as I thanked him and clambered out of the gun house into the late afternoon sunshine. In my mind's eye, I saw a salvo arrowing down and an exploding magazine splitting a bit ship in half and blowing it to atoms, the smoke rising to a thousand feet. And a thousand men dead, Muirhead and his freckles vaporised, rather like my nightmarish thoughts during my early morning reverie.

Then and only then would the Admiralty do something—in the following order: 1) find a scapegoat; 2) send scapegoat away to a lonely colonial station where, with any luck, he'd drink himself to death; 3) appoint a committee of experts and ask them to report; 4) neatly file report away; 5) forget completely about report, 6) lose report.

Worth mentioning to Filson Young or Jacky Fisher? I should have really but then decided against. I'd only get into trouble. Predictions of doom or vulnerability were highly unpopular in the Navy. And I wanted to get ahead. Stay bright, Tucker. And remember, it is easier for a horse to get into heaven than for the Admiralty to take the blame.

CHAPTER 12

I T WAS JUNE 1914 when the squadron steamed majestically up the Baltic as the pell-mell diplomacy and the irresistible threat of a European ding-dong added more heat to the already-scorching weather. Sunburn aside, whether, as some suggest, this moment marked the high tide of civilisation, I don't really know. I frankly doubt it. Still, there was a good deal of military preening, which would do nicely instead. As we rode into our anchorage at Kronstadt, past the Tsar's yacht, *Standart*, on June 23rd, we fired three ear-splitting salutes, the gun smoke drifting over the Winter Palace and deafening the flag-waving thousands who came to welcome the four grey giants from Britain. Then came ten days and nights of partying that drained the city of champagne and—importantly—helped ensure the Russians were allies when it came to the crunch and when the strutting turned to shooting.

When I look back on it, I challenge anyone to even begin to suggest that this was not the biggest and best eve-of-war party ever given.

It began with Beatty and the officers motoring into St Petersburg proper with bands playing and people scuffling to get a look at the "New Nelson," as the St Petersburg press had already dubbed him. The *Novoe Vremya* welcomed "the floating steel islands of England and their manly occupants." Then under coloured awnings and cheers from the crew, we were entertained for dinner on the Russian flagship and were agog at the colossal capacity for food and liquor of our hosts. After being greeted by the Mayor, Count Tolstoy, who was thanked by Sir George Buchanan, we soon found ourselves standing at a table crammed with tempting cold dishes of all kinds: goose, salmon, trout, and caviar in large bowls with outsize teaspoons. The drinks were mainly sherry and vodka.

I looked around for Ethel and was surprised to see her at the other side of a gigantic table in animated conversation with Highet. I had never rated Highet as a lady's man. But he did look quite the part in full fig, and they were getting on famously—he whispering in her ear and she smiling behind her fan. I felt a pang of professional jealousy and a distinct sense of being let down with a thump. Quite why, I have no idea. Then as Ethel was guided away to the aristocratic party, Highet joined me, intent on cramming as much food and drink down his throat as possible.

"One could say," he confided greedily, "that we're all sorted out." He scoffed his plateful and went back for more, including about a pound of caviar. We bowed to a number of well-rouged ladies and attempted conversation in fractured French with some Russian navy types, who—since their crushing defeat by the Japanese in '05—didn't rate very highly and generally lowered the tone all round. I laid off the nosh a bit and hogged a few vodkas, which started the little people dancing in the brain. Then Highet, having stuffed himself to the gunwales, poured himself another large sherry and drew one of the Russian officers aside.

"Jolly good supper!" he said, beaming and patting his swollen stomach.

The Russian looked at him with amazement, then laughed and looked with incredulity at his colleagues who were sharing the joke. "Supper? Lieutenant, this is not supper, this is the Zakuska. In a moment, we start dinner. Then we really eat!" And sure enough, we were moments later being fanfared down into the main dining room, where we sat down to a truly enormous dinner.

Highet, full to bursting, was fairly choking at the prospect of dinner as grace was said by a funny old ship's pope facing the icon. I had noticed a certain amount of corpulence among even the young Russian officers, and this is obviously why. They did themselves very well. We sat down to soup, junket, cheese, pates, crayfish, chicken, and ices. The drinks were champagne, vodka, claret, hock, and sherry. Every five minutes, everyone had to clink their glasses and empty them. Ethel was now enjoying Seymour's company; they pinged their glasses together with merriment. But it was just Ethel being friendly with another young officer. Given his pompous performance during my first wardroom dinner on board *Lion*, she would no doubt find Seymour as much of an ass as I did myself.

Then after dinner, which Highet shuffled round his plate like someone with a bilious attack, an enormous bowl of punch was handed round. As each fellow got it, the others shouted "Pedada, Pedada!" clapping their hands until it was emptied, then refilled, and passed to the next victim. I managed quite well, then it was Highet's turn, after which—the final straw—he was invited to clog dance.

Some of our party, by now slightly off balance, had been doing the Russian dance on double knee. He started quite well, poor chap, but by the time the cup had been passed to him again, he went very red in the face and clawed his way out of the stateroom to be sick. I went to find him; he was retching his heart out in the ornate gentleman's room. We had lost a little face, and I told him so.

"Come on, Highet," I said. "Back to the party."

"Just don't tell Beatty," he gulped.

Then it was back to the banquet, where a passing smell of mussels and the whiff of Cointreau and ice cream got Highet's eyes revolving again.

Ambassador Buchanan was in the midst of a toast to the Royal Navy, which was very grand, overly long, and self-congratulatory. Being officers of the Flagship, we were expected to be attentive, but I could tell Highet was fighting an intestinal struggle of titanic proportions.

"And what of the British sailors of today and tomorrow?" Buchanan was asking. "They will still possess the same high qualities of seamanship, of dogged courage, and of devotion to duty as the great captains of the past who lived and died in their country's service."

As if transported by this vision of patriotism and pride, Highet went a deep shade of purple and buried his face under the tablecloth, where he vomited his heart out, some of it splashing over my shoes and socks. He came up for air, red-faced, and looking about as appealing as a pig at a slaughterhouse.

"This won't do, David," I said mildly. "Come on now, toast the Navy—least you can do." winking at the matron opposite, whose dress may well have been sullied by the attack. His eyes rolled, pissed as well as stuffed.

"Your friend not so very hot?" the lady asked in passable English. "Our food a little rich for his taste? Perhaps on board your ship, you have simplified fare?"

"Very simple meat and potatoes compared to this, your ladyship," I replied nibbling a large prawn and cracking open an enormous lobster with relish.

"I don't think I should like that, lieutenant, oh no." She was obviously as stoned as a gull, and I decided not to mention how British seamen used to stone gulls in order to make their infamous stew, Oooosh.

"Anyway, what your friend needs is a good dose of vodka—very good for settling the stomach. We use it for almost anything" [certainly true]. "And tell him he won't reach high rank if he's sick over everybody. This is the first time I have worn this dress. I shall have to throw it away or give it to the poor."

Taking her advice, I gave Highet a large iced vodka, which worked like a charm. He even wanted to stay, but I had a quiet word about ladies' dresses, huge expense of replacement of same, and being in debt to the purser for months on end, and eventually we walked unsteadily back to *Lion* to sleep it off.

The first of our marathon entertainments lasted until about 5 a.m. Luckily, watches had been relaxed since we were ostensibly in friendly waters.

"Get home all right?" I said brightly to Seymour the next morning. He was looking a little pale. "I had to look after Highet, sick as a dog all over a Duchess."

"Too much of that bloody fish jam, I expect," said Seymour—fish jam was our pet name for caviar.

"I'm sure Lady Beatty enjoyed talking to you at the banquet."

"I expect she did. You have to be a bit senior to engage in conversation with the Admiral's wife."

"Bet she absolutely adored it." At this, Seymour blushed.

"Watch it, Tucker. Any cracks like that, and I'll . . . I'll."

"What?" I said in an exaggerated whisper.

"Help you less than I have already and not show up your weaknesses. Like not knowing whether we're at sea or not."

"About as helpful as a ball and chain, Seymour," I countered. "Is Ethel coming to the reception at noon?"

"Of course, you oaf," he replied. "My God, the bloody Tsar is going to be there with the Grand Duchesses. And Alexandra, the Tsarina. Fail to show up for her, and you're on the next train to Siberia with lukewarm potato soup for company."

So only a few hours later, there we were in full dress uniform—epaulettes, swords, pistols, the full imperial regalia—waiting to welcome the Tsar and his royal party aboard *Lion*. With us were Ethel and Lady Churchill; despite desperate efforts by Seymour to corner Ethel by the bar, he was caught by Gwendoline, who wouldn't let him go. This could have been to annoy Ethel; they were both, after all, headstrong young women, used to getting their own way, and Seymour was a good-looking sod, apart from when he got flustered and blushed like a choirboy.

So I sidled up to Ethel, sipping a pink gin to oil the mental cogs and wheels.

"Good trip?" she asked, looking ravishing in a long cream number. She was sipping champagne.

"I've got a lot to learn," I said solemnly. "Especially, well, about the thinking of the Navy . . ."

"Don't even try, junior," she said with a twinkle in her eye. "There isn't any."

"Well, heartfelt thanks for getting me aboard. This is an occasion I won't forget."

"And I don't think our Russian friends will either. What a gathering!" And she patted me on the arm just as I was taking a sip of gin, which splashed over my nose, making me sneeze just as Beatty gave a glare in my direction. Ethel tittered away as he approached.

"Go easy on the drink, Tucker. You'll develop a seaman's liver in good time." He turned to Ethel. "Look after him, darling. I shouldn't be saying this, but young Reginald is one of our brightest recruits, and we don't want him too distracted, do we?" There was the faintest Long John Silver grimace, then he turned towards the canopied entrance and the gangway. Our big battlecruiser reception had built up a head of steam and was about to begin.

Had the Admiral actually said "one of our brightest recruits"? The sheer pleasure and pride I felt at that moment mingled with the grandeur of the gathering. This was surely a dream come true.

Our Marine Band began crashing out its version of the Russian Anthem, and next minute, other marines fired a salute as the Russian royal party filed up the gangway and stepped on to the main deck.

In view of the Admiral's praise, I almost imagined they were playing for me. And here came Tsar Nicholas, looking fit and the spitting image of cousin George V; Alexandra, the rather severe-looking Tsarina; the frail young figure of son, Alexis, crippled as he was by haemophilia and dressed in a sailor's uniform. Then the four daughters: the younger Marie and Anastasia; Olga, the eldest, with her sad but beautiful features; then Tatiana who was seventeen and whose grey eyes, slender figure, and dancing smile made my heart skip a beat. She could hardly compare with the mature beauty of Lady Ethel, but her dazzling white dress and black sash brought out her healthy complexion and a sense of other-worldliness, simplicity, and care for others—certainly different to many of the ladies of St Petersburg, who'd give you a bottle of champagne and a lot more in their private parlour as soon as look at you. And then cut you dead a day later.

"Well, we'd better get mixing," said Ethel with some resignation, characteristically—and quite properly—making for the Tsar. And as she left, Tatiana was beside me. Always the most forthright of the Tsar's daughters, she said: "Good God, Captain, what are you drinking?" looking rather wide-eyed at my pink gin. Her eyes flickered up to mine, and I had a feeling of weightlessness. I don't know whether she was experiencing the same feeling but knew that even if we talked about crop yields in Ukraine, it wouldn't matter. Mutual attraction was the answer, and the only shadow cast over a delightful meeting was that she could never be mine, nor me hers. The social gap was too wide.

"It's called a pink 'un," I said, blushing slightly. "And actually I'm not a captain, more of a lieutenant. Real captains are very old, more often than not over forty."

Her eyes danced with amusement. "And what, pray, does a pink 'un consist of? Looks a bit like cough medicine to me."

"London dry gin and some aromatic bitters with a splash of water. Actually, we drink it because it's quite cheap. And yes, it does taste a little like cough mixture."

"Ugh, I don't think I should like that. And gin is so cloying." She spoke exactly like an upper-class English Girl, the sort of girl featured in comics of the period—*Fiona of the Remove*, pillow fights and scrapes with rough girls from the village.

"I think that's why we put the bitters in—to remove the cloyingness." And I giggled a bit at the construction, and so did she.

"Cloy-ing-ness. How delightful. And are you going to learn a bit about Mother Russia while you are here? Or just stand upright like the perfect British officer sipping gin and bitters and thinking of home?" she teased.

"Your servant, your Royal Highness. If I had a good guide, I should like nothing better than to see as much as I can."

"Can you ride?"

I cleared my throat non-committally.

"Well, when you come out to see us for a day at Tsarskoe Selo, we can go for a ride. And now I should mingle. There's father looking a little lost—he's not at all keen on these functions, which is why we live like country bumpkins. One English magazine said he was a model of the perfect English country gentleman and that he was an unlikely character to be the leader of the Holy Russian Empire."

"Yet there he is, looking the perfect monarch," I said politely. Alexandra certainly looked more like a monarch with a smile which flitted across her features like wan sunshine through gaps in the cloud. She was certainly beautiful but was never popular among the Russian people and kept private a lot of the time although exerting a large influence on her mild-mannered husband. She knew that trouble, internal or whipped up by foreigners, was coming to Russia, and things would never be the same again. If the Baltic was threshing with British battleships like fish in a barrel, it would make no difference. It might be surprising if any came at all; the visit was posturing, nothing else.

She wished she was back at the palace, relaxing in her mauve boudoir. Who was coming next in his enormous warship? President Poincare of France? And so it went on. Still, the girls—the grand duchesses—seemed to be enjoying the attentions of the young officers, and Beatty was every bit the dashing, youthful inheritor of the tradition of Hawke and Nelson with his square jaw and cap perched at a jaunty angle. If only Russia had a Navy she could be proud of. If only Nicholas could be a little more forceful like the dashing British admiral. His wife was obviously enjoying herself talking animatedly to a lieutenant who must have been ten years her junior.

Tatiana was back at my elbow. "Come and meet Papa," she said, guiding me towards Nicholas as the other guests parted to make way. It was a command. Tatiana was only seventeen, but after all, she was in line to the throne. So over I went.

My first impression of the Tsar was his uncanny resemblance to King George. Handsome, grave, and wishing no doubt that he was back at Tsarskoe Selo with a good book. I didn't know whether to kneel, bow from the waist, kiss his hand, or what, so I nodded my head like an obsequious Prussian and took his hand, which was unusually rough. The Lord of All the Russias was obviously pretty handy with a hammer and chisel or a wood axe.

Tatiana looked pleased. She adored her father; everyone did. They just wished he wasn't so, well, placid.

"Lieutenant Tucker of the *Lion*, your Highness," I said. "I am more pleased to meet you than you could ever imagine. Our visit is so short. We can only touch the fringe of Russia, but your people have made an excellent impression, and I am sure that friendships forged here will last. And you can depend on the men of the British Navy—the greatest fleet in the world—to uphold your cause should any trouble arise."

"Jolly good," said Nicholas, looking a bit dim and distant.

"And Lieutenant Tucker would like to come riding at Tsarskoe Selo, Papa," said Tatiana.

"He shall, he shall," replied the Tsar. And he looked at me and shook my hand again. "What a handsome ship you have, Lieutenant. It must be an honour to sail in her."

"Yes, and with your permission, I thought Grand Duchess Tatiana might enjoy a short tour of the ship, would you, Mademoiselle?"

Tatiana nodded enthusiastically. "Yes, but it can't be too long. I have other engagements today."

We first inspected the wardroom, where I wasn't surprised to find Low trying unsuccessfully to pick out a ragtime tune on the piano. However, I was surprised to see Highet and a female guest sharing a bottle of champagne and giggling together on the sofa. Highet was stabbing his scabbard on the carpet. "Manoeuvres!" he explained.

"So I see," I replied.

And I was surprised to hear Tatiana say "What tosh!" before we moved to the forward gun house, where the lads shuffled around a bit awkwardly, and Tatiana peered down the ammunition hoist. I couldn't risk her life aloft of course, but I decided to breeze along and impress her with a few dit-dahs and squeals of interference from the wireless office.

Down endless ladders we went until we accidentally emerged on to the mess deck, where an uproar of men were trying to sleep, read, eat, and sing songs—and even seek the privacy of their own thoughts as they penned letters home. I was quite lost. In the great floating village that was HMS

Lion, I had brought a royal guest to a place where even experienced officers feared to tread—or at least were expected not to intrude.

"Wrong place," I said briskly to the duchess. By now the wolf whistles had started along with the "Cor blimeys" and "Ullo, darlin'" and "Fancy a stroll in the woods?" And I was mortally embarrassed. If he heard about this, the Tsar would probably ask for my head, and Beatty would give it to him on a gold plate.

Then a saviour. "Can I help, Sir?" said a little ship boy with a twisted smile.

"Wireless office," I snapped.

"Up the first steps, past the barber's shop, and Bob's your uncle, Sir. I'm afraid *Lion* is a bit of a warren hereabouts." And he escorted us up to the right steps, then stood behind them looking up Tatiana's skirts as she tripped upstairs, the dirty little devil. Still, I gave him five shillings—a good day's pay for his trouble.

The lads in the wireless office were somewhat taken aback by Tatiana but couldn't have been more courteous, teaching her how to send "God Save Tsar Nicholas" into the ether. She wanted to send a second message— along the lines of "Watch it, Wilhelm"—to Berlin, but what with the delay in getting lost, it was time to return to the party; I decided to spare her the engine room, however much its fascinations, because the steam and soot would have marred her spotless white dress.

So back we went.

"Need an escort?" Tatiana smiled mischievously.

"You should see me in battle," I retorted grandly.

"You haven't been in one yet, have you?" But her teasing fitted the general mood—one which I shared—that the whole world was involved in a party that would never end.

Back in Beatty's cavernous stateroom, the Tsar was at my elbow. "Oh, there you are. Tatiana, all right? Now where has your Admiral gone?" *Probably*, I thought, *trying to unfreeze the severe Alexandra somewhere in the stern.* Beatty was aware of his dashing charm and liked nothing better than a challenge. The Tsar drifted off in a dream, like a ship with neither helm nor helmsman. He appeared under the influence of some drug as the precipitator of his extreme calm, probably prescribed by the archscoundrel and seducer of St Petersburg Society, Gregory Rasputin. Or perhaps he was just bored, gloomily contemplating the arrival of Poincare a few days later looking for a dozen Russian divisions to take the heat off the anticipated German drive towards Paris.

Tatiana's eyes sparkled in contrast to her father's dullness. "Are your royals allowed out to enjoy themselves?" she asked. I thought of the late King Edward, who had—like Strauss in music—brought pleasure-seeking to new heights. Rumour had it that in one of his favourite brothels in Paris a special chair had been designed so the young ladies could maintain maximum thrust against a belly as big as a balloon. "Well, they certainly like country pursuits," I said plausibly. *And town pursuits too*, I thought—though Edward was no fool, indeed had been highly regarded for his judgement; pity he hadn't been allowed a longer innings.

Then Beatty appeared, the Tsarina on his arm. And unfortunately—for it was involuntary—the grim facial twitch came into play just as he bade her goodbye for the time being. And it locked, gargoyle-like, for a good ten seconds as the Admiral said goodbye to the royal couple.

"Back to the country," said Tatiana sulkily. "Father dressed like a peasant splitting logs and those horrid secret police noting down where we girls are at every moment." And away she went, her hand being kissed by Beatty—his face back to normal—at the gangway, with the Marine Band blowing their heads off at some classical Russian piece which was well beyond their abilities.

But anything we did to cement relations with our Russian hosts was good news as far as Beatty was concerned. The British Ambassador (whom I was to meet later in rather different circumstances) was often around to lend a helping hand. But the spotlight always fell on the Admiral. And even after a jorum of champagne, he never put a foot wrong. Rather like the stars of the movies, he managed to convey an impression of effortless charm. Behind the scenes, however, he worked like a bugger at getting things right—even if many of the night's parties didn't end until five a.m.

His succession of encouraging speeches had to be made in French. This put a burden on Spick to vet his efforts. Late at night, he'd be called to Beatty's quarters, provided with a stiff whisky and water, and asked to pronounce on his latest effort—the might of the British Fleet, the integrity of the Baltic, the huge Russian army, and the fate of the Germans, who could run but could not hide. He would stride up and down intoning this soothing stuff in his diabolical French until Spick was satisfied or had fallen asleep. Still, the efforts paid off: Beatty made a huge impression—not just because of his attempt at French, but because of his good looks, jutting jaw, and aggressive demeanour. *Here was a man*, thought members of the Duma, *we can count on.*

In these endeavours, I was asked to help even though I was usually half cut—or soused, as the men used to say—but that simply put me among the vast majority of St Petersburg citizens as the mists of war closed in. Spickernell, who never missed a trick when it came to paperwork, peered into my personnel file and found the legend: "proficient in French." *Only when the guillotine's about to drop*, I thought. "Rein, jamais," I protested as he led me into the Admiral's rooms.

Beatty was in a fairly evil mood as a short but savage shower had exposed the many leaks in the deck above him, and he had hoisted his golf brolly for protection. "They give you quarters about ten times bigger than Nelson ever enjoyed but then make them leak like a sieve," he complained, glaring above him at the drips.

I could see Spick was finding it extremely difficult not to laugh, then he suddenly exploded into a great snort of mirth. This brought on the famous grimace, and I was forced to bury my laughter in my handkerchief. Finally, the drips stopped, and the Admiral paced about, looking strained after five days and nights of orgiastic festivities.

"Now," he finally said, "I want to say that wherever the Russian Navy meets a superior force of Huns, the British will spring to assist them," he said, rubbing his forehead. "The damned thing is of course that the last place even a sloop from the British Navy will be found is in the Baltic, fighting to save the Russian Navy. They'll go down with all hands before we fire a damned popgun. Well, Tucker? You're a bit of an intellectual by accounts."

Was I? Bless my cotton socks. But it was an easy one—particularly for a lowly lieutenant with no responsibilities for diplomatic affairs.

"Well, sir, I'd just say that in order to protect all its allies, our navy will keep a careful watch over the North Sea, which has been erroneously called the German Ocean, but will, if circumstances permit, detach a squadron or two to assist our friends whenever necessary in other sectors. Outdated cruisers, I really mean, Sir."

"Good oh," said Beatty. "Write that down, Frank."

"A bit cold-blooded, but yes, fair enough," said Spick, quite impressed, scratching away with a pen on his clipboard. "Have you got it in French?"

"I don't think I could do it as well as you, sir," I said, my head in a bit of a spin. I'd only slept three hours the night before and felt like death.

"Oh, very well."

And we went on like this for what seemed like hours. I added several further testimonials to King George's determination to do everything possible to help our Russian cousins, short of giving them a commitment worth a damn. Spick had fallen asleep again in a leather armchair, and only Beatty, whose stamina was quite extraordinary, was left striding about his quarters, rehearsing his lines. Finally, he let me go.

How hard those in high rank had to work. In a bit of a daze, I walked around the deck, bumping into some other officers who, in the great naval tradition of walking the deck, pretend you're not there and move on like ghosts. From below decks a bluejacket could be heard singing:

> *Night, and the stars are gleaming,*
> *Tender and true;*
> *Dearest, my heart is dreaming, Dreaming of You*

What sentimental rubbish—but a curiously potent reminder of home and hearth. Birkenhead, with all its shabby confidence, seemed a million miles away. I looked at the bewitched city of St Petersburg and the gleaming Winter Palace. It was another world. Even some of the rich, decorated aristocrats we were meeting every day seemed to belong in the past. And the soldiers and the poorer of the citizenry—the vast majority— had wide staring eyes, the pupils frequently offset, indicating a vacancy, an acceptance that their lives would be brutish, short, marred by hunger and bad treatment. Anything which gave them food and shelter for another day had to be saluted.

I went below, got into my cabin, and slept like a log but not for long enough. I woke early thinking of Tatiana, realising I was quite bewitched, and rang the bell for Haddock and a steaming mug of coffee. Tea is all right when you are in equilibrium, but when the blood is full of booze and longing, coffee works best—black and with a good spoonful of sugar.

As with other days on our ten-day visit, stamina and liver permitting, this was one great holiday camp. But it was quite a strain. The men were treated with the same lavish hospitality, but most of them could not stomach caviar, which they called fish jam. Vodka, however, was much to their liking. There were banquets and theatres in St Petersburg, and the usual time of returning on board was 5 a.m., making it difficult to fit in the Russian hours with ship routine. Various small crafts, including a small imperial yacht, were placed at the disposal of our squadron and were continually ferrying officers and men to and from St Petersburg along the Neva.

Shortly after I awoke, I learned that we had to turn up in full-dress kit—frock coats, swords, and holstered pistols—for a lunch party en famille, with Tsar Nicholas, Alexandra, and the girls, at Tsarskoe Selo's Alexander Palace, a modest yellowish 100-room confection adjacent to the fantastic blue-and-white 200-room Catherine Palace—but decidedly more homely. Both, I thought, made Buckingham Palace look exceedingly drab. But Catherine—how many peasants had died in its construction?—had certainly done her best to create heaven on earth.

"Back in the land of Peter the Great," whispered Chatfield as we were shown into a gilded coach and footmen in golden livery and cocked hats. "I feel rather like Cinderella going to the ball."

As one of a small number of lieutenants chosen, I felt duly honoured but wasn't used to ceremonial at the time and kept tripping headlong over the stupid sword at my hip. Beatty noticed this, and I overheard his comment to the Lord of the all the Russians. "He may not be able to take a head off at full gallop, but some of these youngsters can sink an enemy cruiser at ten miles."

And so I damned well could. But the Tsar just nodded dreamily, and we were then shown to a number of round tables hosted by Russian royals; and I was pleased enough to find myself sitting next to the spirited Tatiana. Sitting down wasn't easy, mind you. I nearly skewered myself with my scabbard and was being effectively throttled by my wing collar. And the weight of the huge .45 Navy pistol—Haddock said my .38 wouldn't do—gave me a lean to the right rather like a ship being canted for the removal of barnacles.

"Hello, your Highness," I said weakly. "What a pleasure to see you again."

"Why, lieutenant, you look flustered. Is anything wrong?"

I fumbled around with the scabbard, encountered a table leg, then rested it against the boot of some old general whose chest full of medals gave him a useful lean towards his soup.

"It's my sword that's giving me problems, your Highness. I am not accustomed to wearing them. I find them a complete nuisance and, what's more, a relic of past conflicts."

"Well, don't tell that to a Cossack. I take it you are not an admirer of tradition, Lieutenant?"

"Not a lot. There's no point. The idea of beating your opponent man-to-man is gone. He can get you from ten miles away—a whole company and most of your friends too."

"How beastly!" It sounded like Cheltenham Ladies College—or at least how I imagined it to be. Yet there was a sheen to the skin, a sparkle to the eyes, an excitement which was not English. It was the extraordinary presence of a girl born to rule, brought up in a curiously upper-class English setting, whose empire was falling apart by the minute but who could still order the Cossacks to arrest anyone who displeased her. Not that she would of course. A one-way ticket to Siberia would do nicely.

But something was happening, something irresistible; I was starting to fall for this engaging girl. Others at the table seemed to melt away as we talked. I wanted to know about the scandalous monk, Rasputin, who clung on to life—otherwise fiercely endangered—because of Alexandra's belief that his healing powers helped relieve the pain of little Alexis's maddening haemophilia. He had even taken a seat in the Duma to the consternation of its President, Rodzianko.

"Mama will not hear a word said against him," said Tatiana matter-of-factly, "despite his well-known drunkenness and lechery. You can see him this afternoon if you like—he'll be at his apartment, laying on hands and drinking large amounts of sherry. I think he's quite harmless." She gnawed away contentedly at the roast pork, potatoes, and mustard which, with cabbage soup to start, was Daddy's favourite, accompanied by a glass or two of port.

"He's quite nice really, even though half of St Petersburg is out to get him. When we were a bit younger, he used to come into our bedchamber and tuck us up. Father sometimes shooed him away."

I bet he did. The dirty old peasant was probably a child molester as well. How different from the life of our own royals.

I was having difficulty eating the pork crackling. Attacking it with gusto, I overdid it, and a piece flew off my plate and landed on Beatty's.

"Thank you, Tucker," he said dryly with a shadow of a grimace. "But I have quite enough on my plate at the moment." Beside Ethel on the same table, Highet spluttered with laughter, the rat.

"Very sorry, sir."

Then Alexandra giggled, and I went as red as a plum. And Tatiana joined in the fun.

"I say," she whispered, "isn't your Admiral a bit fierce?" Beatty grimaced back and then gave a small encouraging wave. I think he was finding all this diplomacy heavy going, especially with Russia's quiet and impassive Tsar.

"He can be." I grinned. "Especially if you start throwing food at him."

"Yes, do excuse the food. Years ago, we had two jolly good French chefs, but they put too much sherry in a trifle and back they went to Paris. Since then, it's been cabbage soup and black bread all the way. Look at me—I'm a stick!" Then laughing, she started to choke on a piece of pork. I patted her gently on her slender back.

"Harder!" she ordered. So I gave her a good biff, which did the trick but caused a few eyebrows to raise around the various tables.

"We're not in the wardroom now, Tucker," chided Beatty.

"Went down the wrong way, sir."

"He was gentleman enough to do my bidding, Admiral," said Tatiana, hauling him up at the next fence, "and I am much better as a result," receiving a Beatty smile in reply.

"But is your young officer there all right?" she then asked Beatty, looking at Highet, who was starting to get into trouble himself. I noticed he was showing the same signs of gastric turbulence which he had exhibited at the banquet. He might well have eaten too much pork—the crackling was certainly difficult to eat—or the port wine might have been too much for him, given his weak head for alcohol. Whatever the cause, his face was going red, and his eyes were starting to glisten with the awful knowledge of what was going to happen next.

"Do excuse me, your highnesses," he croaked, getting up from his chair. "I'm afraid I seem to have taken a turn."

"Come on, Highet," the Admiral said sharply. "Don't let the side down."

But it was too late. All eyes were on Highet as he crossed the room, his hand over his mouth. At least he made it as far as a side table when he retched up into the soup tureen.

Now this kind of thing might well have been overlooked in *Lion*'s wardroom but not in the company of Tsar Nicholas II.

"We have some stomach powder which might help our young friend," said the Tsar consolingly as Highet was taken aside by a footman. "I am sorry the lunch didn't agree with him."

"My profound apologies," said Beatty with the best smile he could muster. But I could tell from the grimace which quickly accompanied the smile that Highet was in for trouble when he returned to the ship.

CHAPTER 13

WHAT A STRANGE life. The iron fences of Tsarskoe Selo were patrolled day and night by bearded Cossacks in scarlet capes and black fur caps carrying lances, carbines, and sabres which could sever a limb with one blow. Inside, the palace grounds covered eight hundred acres of lawns, follies, ancient trees, and even a Chinese pagoda. In addition were five thousand troopers of the Imperial Guard and, oddly, scores of plain-clothes police who prowled around, watching everyone like hungry crows.

I was now firmly under Tatiana's spell and, like all young men, although entranced, tried very hard not to show my emotions. She was a little on the young side for me, but even so, I looked forward to being shown around. This means I could spend more time with her, and we escaped soon after Beatty's now-mind-numbing speech about the fate of Russia's enemies.

"We shall tread them down to the ocean floor, never to rise again," he thundered. "Rest assured, we shall never let our Russian cousins down." Then—God help him—he retired for a more intimate chat with the Tsar and his Admirals, leaving us free to look around the grounds.

After an endless walk down a vista of pavilions, statues, and accompanied by two footmen waving jars of incense, we were met by two Cossacks holding a pair of beautifully groomed horses.

"Good girl," I said to my mare, which nuzzled me welcomingly in the ear before I swung into the saddle. A walk turned into a trot but nothing faster than that. Tatiana cut a fine figure on her horse, and in my mind's eye, I saw myself getting quite accustomed to going on frequent rides with her—and maybe one day trotting off the beaten track, settling down to a picnic, and getting to know her better.

A squadron of Cossacks followed us, which I found quite encouraging since I was not entirely happy on horseback and nervous of falling off and skewering myself with my sabre. We visited a rather dull folly, where I was surprised to find a secret policeman taking notes. What he was writing down, I cannot imagine. Presumably, he would have to go back to his office and painstakingly type it all up into a report which would be carefully filed away.

"Now," said Tatiana, mounting her horse again. "Let's go and see the starets. I really think you ought to meet him, not the best example of our race but a real Russian, big and smelly and as mad as a hatter. Someone to write home about."

So disregarding the troop of Cossacks following at a discreet distance, we cantered off to the great seer's apartments, no longer in the palace because of the scandals of his behaviour in St Petersburg but close enough so that he could be summoned by the Tsarina in case Alexis's condition flared up again. A mere stumble could do it, poor lad, and then the agony, the endless visits by quacks, and the sudden arrival of the strange bearded figure whose laying of hands brought mysterious relief.

Superficially, Rasputin had cleaned up his appearance by 1914. He no longer lived and slept in peasant outfits, never washing and smelling of goat's cheese. His man showed us into his chambers, where we found him wearing a pale-blue silk blouse, black velvet trousers, and soft leather boots.

But his eating habits hadn't improved. The Grand Duchess and I found him plunging his hands into a large bowl of fish soup or stew and wiping his hands on the tablecloth. A fair amount of the concoction had dribbled down into his beard; the general impression was one which combined a Viking feast with feeding the sea lions at the zoo.

"Come, my dears, and have some vodka," he said, fixing us with his mesmeric stare, "or sherry." I took a glass of the former. Something possessed me, and I couldn't resist pointing at his messy bowl.

"Sorry," I said, "but why don't you use a spoon?"

"For why?" His eyes darkened and looked into mine.

"Well, if you used a spoon, your hands wouldn't get all greasy."

"But the spoon would, so I'd have to take the trouble to wash that. I see from your uniform that you are English, who have so many eating implements you could starve before you worked out which to use first. In my home, I do what I like. And I like contact with my food, it's more sensual. We Russians are very alive to the senses, as I'm sure Tatiana would agree."

"Most Russians are alive to the difficulty of staying alive and trying to pay their taxes—that's all I know," Tatiana said, mirroring her father's paternalism.

"I can tell that you are worried, Tatiana," said the starets, sucking the fish concoction greedily off his fingers. "And who is this rude young man?"

He had heard of the endless feasts and banquets since the Battlecruiser Squadron arrived, and I could tell he didn't approve, not that he would have been invited anyway.

"Come, my dears," he said. "You are too pampered. Follow me to Pokrovskoe, to the great freedom of Siberia. We will catch fish, work in the fields, and then you will really learn to understand God." His hands dived into the bowl again.

Not likely, I thought. Mind you, it must have been the vodka—100 proof, I guessed—but the piercing eyes of the man above the enormous beard were difficult to deny. He moved towards Tatiana and stroked her long straight hair with his fishy hands, much as he had done when he had access to the royal bedchambers.

"A terrible cloud is over Russia," he said gently. "A sea of tears immeasurable, blood in torrents. There are no words, for the horror is indescribable. If we are not careful, the madmen will triumph and destroy themselves and all the people."

"I hope you don't think Britain is going to put up with that," I said hotly.

"No." And he smiled, refilling my glass. "Have fun on the oceans, English. But that is just a sideshow. I am talking about Russians fighting Germans and then taking arms against themselves. And the best place to be in those circumstances is lying in a hayfield against a woman's breast with a bottle of wine, a thousand miles from the front."

Him and me both. I liked him for his peasant wisdom and his selfishness and could protest no more the lie that all would be well as long as the tripod masts of a British battlecruiser were on the horizon. His flowing beard, almost insane religious sense, lack of hygiene, deviousness, and sexual appetites were a long way from my experience. But you had to admit, he had the courage to be himself.

Yet there was something haunting about the scene, which I wanted to be rid of. The great eyes were making me feel uncomfortable. The predictions of doom were not entirely logical, and I suddenly felt a need for the simplicity of *Lion*, the japes of comrades, the blast of sea air through the hair, and the boom of the guns deciding matters between opponents based on logic, morale, science, and a degree of luck.

Compared to these certainties, he seemed ill-fated, unreal.

He approached me and laid his fishy fingers on my cap. "You have a lot to learn, English," he said solemnly. Then there was a squeak—a female squeak—from his bedchamber. And the great eyes were saying it's time to go. Whoever it was, she couldn't wait any longer.

"You have a patient waiting?" Tatiana asked with the faintest twinkle in her grey eyes.

"She needs me," said the starets. "Do excuse me."

Even my mother would have said it couldn't have lasted—certainly not for long enough to change Russia and hurtle the Romanovs into oblivion. Watch out for bearded seers with boozy breath, mesmerising eyes, and a meandering way to God is what I think, even if they do relieve haemophilia.

But for now, there was nothing for it but for us to canter back to the palace, where I was surprised to find that Ethel, obviously bored to tears by the proceedings, had complained of a headache and been driven back to *Sheelagh* in a motor car accompanied by the sickly Highet.

On our ride back in the gold coach, Beatty was in fine spirits and asked me how I'd enjoyed the afternoon.

"Very fine, Sir," I said. "Grand Duchess Tatiana took me to see a folly."

"The whole dang place is a folly!" said the Admiral as we passed the ostentatious mansions of the palace acolytes. "And what's that smell of fish? Probably one of the coachmen. If they ever have a bath, I would be surprised. And now we're going to give these peasants a party they won't forget in a hurry before we steam away back to civilisation."

"What a good idea, Sir," I said with enthusiasm.

The fifteen miles or so back to our berth didn't take long, what with Beatty's scornful running commentary, and I stayed with him till we reached *Sheelagh* in deference to his concern for Ethel's health. We tiptoed aboard in case we disturbed her rest. She was indeed taking a nap in her stateroom.

"The poor dear found the Great Belt quite difficult," Beatty whispered to me. "She's much more in tune with the Med.

"And now let's get back to *Lion*. I want to have a word with a certain colleague of yours." It was Highet. And if he was going to get it in the neck, I wanted to be there. Pure curiosity of course.

He wasn't in the sickbay of course, where he might sensibly have taken refuge with his stomach upset. We found him sitting in the wardroom as pissed as a parrot. He gave a sloppy salute as we entered.

"Highet, stand up in the presence of your Admiral," Beatty snapped.

He stood warily at salute. I was tempted to give him a wink for good luck but decided against it and stared stonily ahead of me.

"Your sickness seems to have improved," Beatty said, his face contorted well beyond its usual 10-second time limit.

"Please accept my humblest apologies, sir," said Highet, who seemed to have difficulty breathing. "Too much to drink, I fear."

But Beatty was very angry—unusual for him. "You let us down in front of our hosts here. I need men who can go to action stations in the middle of a state dinner rather than vomiting in front of a royal party we were trying to impress. You can blame gin, port, bubbly for a lot of things, but not for letting it get the better of you," he said in his best clipped manner. "Highet, you are to be placed under armed Marine guard and confined to your quarters until I decide what to do with your hide."

"Thank you for your support, Tucker," said my Admiral as two Marine sentries as big as houses and with bayonets fixed marched the stupefied Highet away. His goose was truly cooked. Admirals had considerable powers to inflict misery. A posting to a leaky armed trawler in the Falklands? A message-carrying sloop in the boiling Mediterranean Fleet at Malta? Testing defective mines in the Hebrides? Perhaps retraining as a seaplane pilot—lucky to launch off the sea with a bomb load as lethal as a bag of liquorice allsorts, let alone land safely again? What would it be?

This became clear the following afternoon. It was a tradition of *Lion*, as with other warships, that fitness combined with entertainment was an essential part of any seaman's routine. For the officers, this usually involved deck hockey in which a wooden puck was propelled around the deck until invariably it was lost overboard. Most took part in this since not to do so would indicate a wardroom laziness, which would be noticed and reported on. Beatty himself was noted for his long ten-mile tramps across the countryside. There were races with skiffs and longboats and gymnastics—and boxing of course.

None of these activities had any class distinction about them. Lieutenants were pitted against petty officers and against stokers—that race apart which regularly shovelled tons of coal into the ship's furnaces.

So I came out the following morning and was not surprised to see that a boxing ring had been rigged up on the afterdeck. Duties, apart from getting over the previous night's hangover—not to be underestimated— were light, so I strolled down in the company of Low and Seymour to see the fight.

Highet, well-built though he was, looking pale and faintly ridiculous in shorts, was in one corner of the ring. In the other was a lean but very well-muscled stoker called Williams. The referee was Woodley, Beatty's steward.

Chatfield strolled up and joined what I could only suppose was clearly Beatty's revenge—perfectly well judged and, well, without prejudice. But pride and prejudice it was going to be. Practically, the whole ship's company was there, waiting in silence for the action to begin.

The gong went, and the fighters started to circle. Highet took a couple of wild swipes into thin air and then received two swift blows to the solar plexus and retreated to the ropes. Williams followed him with a blow to the side of the head and toppled him into the corner. Beatty joined our group and made some blithe remarks about the importance of physical fitness. That he was getting any satisfaction from the spectacle, I wasn't sure; he wasn't a man with any cruelty in his soul. Jacky Fisher would have had Highet loaded into a torpedo tube and fired, but nothing I saw about Beatty suggested any remedy for wrongdoing but the value of a short sharp shock, then back to normal.

The bell rang again, and Highet—determined to put up a good fight though outgunned—managed to connect a passable uppercut, which made Williams sway. This was rewarded with a "good on yer, sir" from a few throats. But then Williams—you had to have muscles of steel to be a stoker—gave Highet a one-two round the kidneys, which made him gasp and sink to his knees. Standing again, he was hit twice in the mouth and the eye and went down again. This was getting very one-sided, and I yelled out "Stop the fight!" which made Chatfield blink.

Then Highet just managed to connect with Williams's ear, and he too went down. Highet bravely waited for him to get up and then connected well with his jaw. At this point, I saw Beatty grin; the debt was being paid without a complete rout, although he must have known the outcome. Williams was down for a count of two seconds but then, no doubt thinking of the jokes he would have to endure from his mates if he was beaten by a mere lieutenant, screamed with rage and battered Highet against the ropes so thoroughly that he went through them, hit the deck, and lay still. A knockout. "Ten!" yelled Woodley. Justice had been done, or rather rough justice, within the ship's rules had been accomplished. Highet had been punished, but in a fair fight.

Beatty adjusted his hat to an even cockier angle than usual. "The fight goes to Stoker Williams!" announced Woodley. And there were cheers all round. "And a hand for our gallant loser, Lieutenant Highet!" he added. And damn it all if there wasn't a thunderous round of applause for Highet, now unsteadily on his feet, who was then led below.

I hoped Beatty was satisfied—and it looked as though he was. "Fallen at quite a hard fence—always difficult," he murmured to Chatfield as we strode back aft towards the nerve centre of the ship. Ethel, whom I could see watching through glasses from along the quay, retired to her quarters and doubtless ordered champagne.

"Good fighter though, that Highet," said Chatfield.

"Yes, it's good to see the wardroom lads having a go," Beatty replied, which could have meant a number of things. But that was the end of it. And I rather think it did him credit. I didn't say so; I wasn't expected to.

CHAPTER 14

I THOUGHT ABOUT it for a while, but while there had been something deeply satisfying about seeing Highet hit the deck, I nevertheless decided to show some sympathy. After all, it could have been me.

I knocked on his cabin door, then finding it unlocked, strode in.

"What's up?" he said. "Here's Beatty's messenger with another piece of news. Would I mind reporting for duty and being towed out to sea for some small-calibre target practice? Might sting a bit. That okay, old boy?" He actually sounded quite bitter though several admirals would have had put him in the brig for the remainder of the trip. "Are the lads outside all right? Would they like a cup of tea?"

"The Marines have gone, Highet," I said. "You're a free man. I was just up on the compass platform, and Beatty asked after you quite pleasantly."

"His bark is worse than his bite. Hope we don't find that when we go into battle, which I reckon will be in a few weeks."

"No, he just wants a happy ship, short of everyone waylaying his wife. Something tells me he'll be much harder on the Germans than drunken lieutenants who throw up during diplomatic visits." I could have added a few more comments since he had clearly let the side down, but he was still nursing his wounds.

"That bloody fellow Williams nearly tore my head off when I knocked him down for the second time. I'd quite like to get him up some dark alley on Portsmouth with his back to me and a large cosh in my hand." I noticed his smashing black eye.

"You'll need an eyepatch for that."

"Why, pray?"

"Take a look at yourself, Highet. Be sensible."

I called out to Haddock in my nearby cabin who, after seeing Highet's distress, returned in a few minutes, grinning from ear to ear and carrying a patch straight from the *Pirates of Penzance*.

"We keep a couple in the medicine cupboard in case chaps lose their eyes with shell splinters," he said matter-of-factly.

"Highet, the hero. You'll be our Nelson tonight," I said, stretching the elastic over his head and popping the eyepiece over the offending bruise.

"Ouch!" said Highet. "Anyway, what do I need a bloody Long John Silver patch for? What's up?"

"The biggest party St Petersburg has ever seen, sir," said Haddock, who was privy to some of the preparations. "And if you'll allow me to raid the theatrical department, we could fix you up with a wooden leg and a stuffed parrot in no time, sir." He tittered, and so did I.

"Thank you, Haddock, and I am glad you find my plight amusing. But good God, haven't we impressed them enough with our fearsome ships and our ability to drink the town dry?"

"Tonight is the big one," I said, suddenly feeling quite sorry for him. "Come to the wardroom, and I'll buy you a pink." Something would have to begin to fortify him against the almost certain prediction that his eyepatch would certainly make him a figure of comment. It might attract some fabulously rich and beautiful Russian ladies who would enjoy some story of derring-do from one of their young English hosts.

True to his word, Beatty staged a ball unheard of in scale even in St Petersburg. *New Zealand* was moored alongside *Lion*, one ship providing the ballroom and the other the cloakrooms and supper rooms. Covered gangways connected the two ships; the upper decks encased by red-and-white-striped awnings. The ships' carpenters, whose job in battle would be to fix holes in the armour plate, made two hundred circular tables out of rum barrels, seating six apiece. Woodley procured twenty 20-lb salmon from somewhere or other and managed to obtain a hundred dozen bottles of champagne—quite a feat since the city had nearly run out. And after all these exhausting preparations, a sun-kissed evening began with the arrival of the first of 2,000 guests to the blaring of the Marine Band.

The day, as it happens, was June 28th, 1914, when a young pro-Serbian fanatic shot Archduke Franz Ferdinand, heir to the creaky Austro-Hungarian Empire, and his wife, Sophie, during their visit to the Bosnian capital of Sarajevo. As a result, Austria made impossible demands to Serbia, provoking Russia in turn and encouraging Germany, which pranced up and down indignantly on its high horse. But for now, the rumbling from the Balkans was barely digested, the scale of the party only adding to Beatty's reputation as the true Nelson of the modern Royal Navy—enjoying a dance while keeping his huge guns primed for the big fight which he and the British Navy had been looking forward to for years.

Tatiana arrived looking beautiful and as fresh as a daisy. "Saddle-sore, lieutenant?" She giggled. She waved her fan. "Still quite hot, isn't it?"

"I am fine," I said. "It was quite an easy ride really."

Her fetching grey eyes were twinkling with amusement. "Well, in that case, I hope next time we go faster—and a lot further." I was beginning to get that slightly giddy feeling again. "Good, I shall look forward to that. Now, are you going to be my escort this evening?"

"Nothing would give me more pleasure," I said. "But first I have one or two other duties to attend to. I will be as quick as I can." This was true enough since Spick had asked me and others to keep an eye on certain vulnerable luminaries—that is, the high-ranking, filthy-rich Russian piss artists, whose safety was particularly treasured.

Actually, I was given quite a good old boy: Grand Duke Vladimir, whose livid red face shone almost as brightly as the rows of medals pinned to his chest. He was as fat as a pig and rolled aboard as though we were in a force-eight gale and, after the bowing and scraping of introductions, fixed me with a rheumy monocled eye.

"Bet you have a bit of fun in these boats, lad," he observed.

"We prefer to call them ships or, more exactly, battlecruisers, sir," I said pleasantly. "Boats are, well, for boating."

"Oh, really? Well, I don't care if you put them on the railway line and drive them up to Moscow," growled the old lad. "Where can I get a drink round here?"

"Champagne, Sir," I offered, beckoning to a mess steward.

"Pish, tosh. Vodka, my boy—the great drink of Russia! Do you know how the French put the bubbles into champagne?"

"No idea, Sir," handing over a large iced vodka.

"They fart into the barrels."

"Really, Sir. And they eat frogs and snails."

"You bet they do!" He looked around and spotted one of Woodley's giant salmon resting on a bed of ice.

"Fish!" he thundered. "Fish . . . scaly things with gills. What's the matter with pork, the Tsar's favourite—big fat porkers with apples in their mouths? Can't put an apple in a fish's mouth, can you? Fat and crackling—that's what we like, what? Fire the bloody fish from your guns."

"I'm sure there'll be plenty of pork as well, Sir." The old boy was quite good value really.

"Lost my wife in the crowd," he said with apparent contentment. "Now, young man, what about showing me around?"

So I happily showed him the guns on *Lion*, went below to the wardroom, which was thronged with people, and when we went out on the main deck again, he said he wanted to see the other "boat," *New Zealand*, because among other entertainments, Beatty had rigged up a cinema showing Great British achievements. These consisted of a number of inventions calculated to impress Johnny Foreigner: an electric kettle, a speeding car, a speeding aeroplane, a speeding train, the White Cliffs of Dover, and a cameo of Tsar Nicholas and King George, looking as alike as two peas in a pod, grinning at each, and generally looking rather too pleased with themselves. I didn't think old Duke Vladimir would like it because there was no violence. I had told Spick the show—which I had seen before—was far too tame for the Russians and should contain at least one Wild West shoot-out, but he insisted that the programme could only be changed on pain of death because the content had been selected by the new Ministry of Propaganda. This sounded a bit like the Naval War Staff which Jackie scorned and fought against calling it "an ideal department for the arrangement of newspaper cuttings."

"You British own *New Zealand*, don't you?" said Vladimir as we prepared to go aboard.

"That's right, Sir."

"Funny place to own. Nothing there, is there?"

"Sheep, Sir."

"How very tedious. Can't hunt sheep, can you?" And he started to move towards the nearest gangway just as the night breeze stirred the two great ships; I could see guests holding on to their hats and on to the rails. I followed as best I could among the chattering crowds but got a bit delayed. Clutching his vodka, Grand Duke Vladimir picked his way along the swaying gangway like a large infant taking his first few steps. And when a small downward roll from *New Zealand* coincided with an upward roll from *Lion*, he lost his balance, crashed through a gangway rail, and flew, bellowing, down 25 feet into the small gap of turbulent water separating the battlecruisers.

There wasn't a tar in sight, just a sea of overweight Russian socialites.

"Get a lifebuoy!" I shouted, but no one seemed to understand. "La vestment pour la mer!" I tried in my appalling French. But that didn't do the trick either. So of course I had to jump.

By God, you hit the water hard from the deck of a big ship. I'd torn off my frock coat and thrown away my cap, and when I surfaced, there was the Grand Duke thrashing about like a whale in his death throes. I paddled towards him and got a hold, but he lashed out and hit me between the eyes.

"Hang on!" I said, "I'm only trying to help." And I got a mouthful of seawater for my trouble. Then there was a bugle call from up on the deck, and down the side of *Lion* came a sort of knitting pattern of hemp and cork. I got hold of the old lad's collar, starting to feel the numbing cold of the Baltic even in summer, and tried to drag him towards the tangle so we could both clamber up. But I knew he couldn't manage the climb. And meanwhile, the hulls of the two big ships were starting to surge towards each other. If they closed up, we'd be smudged against the steelwork like jam. Still, at least I got him to hold on to the rope ends and corks and get his head out of the water. Then I caught hold of the ropes myself, coaxed him up a little further, and trussed him up like a turkey. A few medals dropped off, but what the hell. Then I looked up the sheer cliff of the ship's side, saw some tars, and yelled "Pull!" at the top of my voice. They soon got the idea; we started to rise as fast as a lift in a department store, and we were hauled over the rail in a great tangle of rope—to shrieks and, finally, thunderous applause.

Spick was standing there, smoking a cigarette, looking as cool and unflustered as ever. He landed me a hot cocoa laced with whisky. "That old chap is closely related to the Tsar. He will be very grateful."

I could see Tatiana looking rapturously in my direction. Ethel Beatty, smoking a cigarette out of a long holder, was nodding approval and waving. Then Haddock led me below to get changed.

The rest of the night was sheer bliss since of all the things most calculated to improve one's outlook on life, nothing—absolutely nothing— quite beats being a hero. I danced with Tatiana, who obviously regarded me as the matinee star of a film possibly called *Tucker Pulls It Off.*

"Now I have to recognise that the British Navy is made of sterner stuff than I thought." She laughed as I held her by her slim waist and guided her around the brightly lit dance floor on deck. "Daddy is rather fond of old Duke Vladimir. And you didn't even hesitate—not a thought for yourself."

The grey eyes were now showing admiration, affection, and something else. "I think, if you don't mind, lieutenant," she said suddenly as they lit up with all the confidence of a royal command, "I rather think you deserve a kiss."

And so whilst still dancing, we moved away from the main party of dancers towards the side of the ship, ducking under one of the flower-decked party awnings and finding ourselves next to one of the large grey ventilators in complete privacy.

And then, as I continued to hold her around the waist, she cupped my face with the long fingers of both her hands and gave me a long lingering kiss on the lips. It still seems like yesterday, a moment of unalloyed joy which probably shines the brightest of all my memories.

I tried to pull her towards me and repeat the process. But she put her fingers to her pretty mouth. "Let's leave it like that for the moment, lieutenant, and hope there may be other opportunities in the future. But we don't want to get into trouble, do we? We had better get back to the party before we are missed."

We returned to the party, and the rest of the night seemed to pass as in a dream. Tatiana went to join her family. Ethel Beatty was among those who gave me a pat on the back and even whispered congratulations; there was nothing she enjoyed better than something that broke the stuffiness of a state occasion. Thanks to congratulatory drinks—a mandatory ocean of the stuff from Grand Duke Vladimir's family—I got rather drunk, and recognising the warning signs as the whole scene began to revolve slightly, the voices turning into a babble, I made my excuses, found my way below, and fell on to my bunk.

God, the Navy is a cruel master. It hardly seemed five minutes after my head hit the pillow that Haddock was cruelly shaking me awake, proffering a steaming mug of tea.

"Bloody hell, Haddock," I said. "Can't the Navy allow a hero at least one morning's lie in?"

"I am afraid not, sir. The Admiral would like to see you in his quarters. He awaits your pleasure, Sir. I'd say you've got about five minutes."

"All right, Haddock"—I had to bully somebody—"but can you bring some strong coffee instead? I would far prefer coffee, particularly after a gallon of booze and only an hour's sleep."

"Of course, sir. Just as you wish." Haddock would never understand coffee.

Beatty's vast quarters on *Lion* had dried out—unlike most of the officers who were still tipsy, me included—and I reflected on the brave attempt to make them resemble the sitting room of a large country house.

Fox-hunting prints decorated the walls, along with horse brasses and other reminders of the admiral's savage and dangerous peacetime hobby. A copy of Lazlo's famous portrait of Ethel also adorned the panelled walls. But what was this all about? Was I not a hero? Had I inadvertently strangled the old Russian and put paid to all our expensive diplomacy? Was I going to be thrown to the wolves?

Beatty indicated that I should perch on a sofa and nodded towards a large ebony box sitting on the table between us.

"Good morning, sir," I said, trying to sound brisk and not still half-cut.

"Morning, Tucker. You know I had slight qualms about you, particularly after you wriggled your way out of Dartmouth. But then you fished old fatty Vladimir out of the water—blow me down, it was well done—and now you've become our biggest asset. The Russian papers"— he flapped a newspaper around—"are giving you so many column inches they're going to run out of ink."

"I haven't given any interviews, sir," I said.

"Well, to hell with that." He coughed, leaned forward, and opened the cabinet. "Prize money, Tucker. The old lad had it delivered first thing this morning. I've had a word with Spick, and we think you ought to keep it. No one forced you to commit that act of heroism. You weren't in a battle when you'd be expected to cleave to your gun even if you'd had your arm shot off. You could have looked the other way. No, Tucker, it was altruism pure and simple. So what I'm saying is that this little lot is yours."

This little lot turned out to be a treasure chest of roubles worth about ten thousand pounds, a considerable fortune in those days when you could order a custom-built Studebaker for about £250. Wouldn't take very long to dispose of at the tables in Monte Carlo, but it looked very good to me.

"Can I really accept this, sir?" I said, absolutely flabbergasted.

"You can, and you will," said Beatty gravely; like most rich men he was always a bit solemn about cash. "With your permission, I'll get Frank to put it in a safe place in the paymaster's office, and knowing Spick, he'll get you a good exchange rate and send a credit through to the Admiralty for you with as little tax shaved off as possible. Nothing wrong with having a bit of money behind you, eh? You could buy your father another sausage factory, what?"

Earning as I was the princely sum of 11 shillings and sixpence a day, I could only say: "Very welcome, sir." Whether one sausage would be extruded as part of my windfall was open to question.

"Well, just don't waste the damned stuff, it's hard enough to come by." And he looked me straight in the eye, and I knew what he meant: Ethel's millions didn't come without a human price. "And to cap it all, I am inviting you to lunch on *Sheelagh* with dear Ethel and Lady Churchill. Bit early, but care for a spot of champagne?"

"Thank you, sir."

We even clinked glasses to "good fortune and success." My head swam with the addition of alcohol to that already coursing through my bloodstream, and the thought of ten thousand quid in the bank—good grief, you could buy rows of shops with that—made me feel quite giddy.

"Tucker," said Beatty as I bowed out. "I think you might have the stuff we need because, Tucker . . ."

"Yes, sir?"

"Things are going to be pretty bloody before long. And it's going to make Hannibal and the Romans look like a bit of a picnic."

"Every party's got to end sometimes, sir," I said bravely. And then I retired to my cabin to try and work it all out, mightily helped by a strong pot of coffee and a bacon sandwich thoughtfully provided by Haddock. It looked as though war clouds were blotting out any chance of having another outing with Tatiana. *C'est la guerre.*

Haddock had run a hot bath, and pressed my uniform, polished my shoes, and in all respects, got me ready for lunch on board Ethel Beatty's steam yacht, *Sheelagh.* I stepped aboard with Chatfield, Spick, and of course Beatty himself, determined to stay sober and add to the general air of merriment.

The vessel, moored close to *Lion,* was a world away from the battlecruiser—a lady next to a knight in armour, with its sleek white-painted hull and swept-away bow and ochre funnel and triaxial stay covered with triangular flags. Everything that could be polished was gleaming in the sun, speaking of luxury and leisure. And there to greet us were the two society beauties I had met soon after my rigorous spell at Dartmouth. Only now, I had climbed a few steps up the shining ladder and become the guest of honour.

"Great heavens, if it isn't our young hero," said Gwendoline.

"Welcome aboard and congratulations again," said Ethel. She clicked her fingers to a mess steward. "Champagne?"

"Thank you," I said, determined to stay well within my limits.

"We were just discussing the visit, and I rather think your rescue of that old Duke was worth at least five more banquets and a parade of the entire ship companies through St Petersburg," Gwendoline said. "For that alone, I think you ought to get a medal, don't you, David?"

"The thought had crossed my mind," said Beatty.

"But what I would like to know is your honest opinion as a young officer of our Russian hosts. And you can be quite frank." She laughed and looked around melodramatically. "There are no secret servicemen here."

Here was my chance to make a good impression on Winston Churchill's rather beautiful sister-in-law, whom I was sure moved in the highest circles. So I laid it on a bit thick or, looking back on it, said what I really thought.

"Well, I think they have given us an outstanding welcome, but in some respects, I think they are living in the past. There seems to be a massive gap between the other ranks and the officer class. Compared to all the technical and industrial advances we have made, they still seem to be in the Napoleonic era. I met Gregory Rasputin, the mad monk, and he doesn't seem to think Russia has much of a future at all."

"When did you see him, Tucker?" asked Beatty, looking a little alarmed.

"When Grand Duchess Tatiana took me for a ride around the palace grounds after our lunch, Sir. She wanted me to meet him. He is quite well regarded in a funny sort of way. He looks completely unkempt and may well be a real rogue. But his powers of healing means he's allowed at the heart of the family when Alexis is distressed, particularly after even the smallest fall when he starts to bleed internally. And all he does is lay his hands, and the little boy gets better. Empress Alexandra never wants him far away because he's the only one who can help little Alexis when he gets one of his turns."

"Quite a gift," said Beatty.

"And he thinks the whole country is in for very hard times."

"I wonder what he meant," inquired Lady Churchill, leaning back on her chair and sipping her champagne.

I gathered confidence. "Because the Empress trusts him as the only person to help the boy, in the same way, she thinks he has other supernatural powers and uses him to tell the family fortunes. And when we saw him, he suddenly said he foresaw a terrible storm cloud hanging over Russia. First, there is going to be a terrible war against the Germans, then the Russians are going to turn and start butchering themselves in a long civil war. And it is going to be a very bloody business."

"And what about our visit in the here and now?" asked Beatty.

"I am afraid he thinks our visit is almost totally irrelevant, Sir. We even could sail the whole of the Grand Fleet into the Baltic, and it wouldn't make much difference. Mind you, that's only the way he sees things."

"So he is what the Irish call a seer," said Beatty, waving his empty glass at the mess steward. I didn't know then that Beatty had consulted fortune tellers himself and clearly had some faith in their abilities. "Well, blow me down."

"And the worst thing is that I can readily see it coming myself," said Gwendoline, exhibiting her very sharp intelligence. "The people here are ruled by Tsar Nicholas II, a dim retiring young man who buries himself away in a palace and pretends he's living the life of an upper-class English gentleman in the Home Counties. And his German wife, Alexandra, goes out of her way to make herself as unpopular as possible. That certainly wouldn't work in England, would it? What they need is a strong ruler who won't take no for an answer, like Catherine the Great."

"What's her story then? Do go on," said Ethel, her interest perking up.

"Well, I can go for hours about Catherine. She is very much a heroine of mine, and it really starts with her mother, who was determined to better her lot in life. And if she could not do that directly—a divorce would have left her languishing in a convent—she would have to do it through her daughter.

"The girl shared her mother's frustration. Gifted with good looks, a talent for learning, and remarkable energy, she hated the restrictions of life, which squashed her aspirations, far from the balls, the gossip of court, and the chance to meet new friends.

"Then her life suddenly changed dramatically as she was eating her New Year's Day dinner with her parents in 1744, when a letter arrived. It came from her distant relative Elizabeth, who ruled the vast Russian empire hundreds of miles away and had decided to marry the 15-year-old girl to her teenage heir, Peter."

"Sounds exciting," said Ethel, quite captivated as we all were by the story.

"This was the opportunity she and her mother had been waiting for. With little preparation, they set out from Stettin on the journey east, their carriages jolting across the frozen landscape, the freezing Baltic winds whistling around them. After a month, at last they saw the great walls of Moscow. It was evening, and torches blazed in the palace courtyard as the girl was greeted by Empress Elizabeth, who immediately liked what she called her freshness, intelligence, and discreet manner."

Lady Churchill laughed, threw her head back, and took a gulp of champagne. "But then came terrible disappointment. Meeting with Peter, her husband-to-be, must have drained much of the life out of her. If she was a racehorse, he was a donkey. At fifteen, he was very short and thin with a pale face, wide mouth, and receding chin. He was ignorant of the world and interested only in his toy soldiers and wine. He showed no interest in her physically and also hated everything Russian—quite the opposite of Catherine, who learnt fluent Russian as fast as she could and also embraced the Russian Orthodox Church.

"For nine years, Peter declined to consummate their marriage, spreading toy soldiers across the sheets and playing war games well into the small hours. Meanwhile, Elizabeth stubbornly refused to accept the failure of the marriage, and Catherine patiently bided her time."

"Good grief, it must have been horrible for her," said Ethel.

We paused as the mess stewards ushered us into the yacht's dining room for lunch. It was another fine summer day, and we started with cold Vichyssoise soup with chives.

"But here comes the best bit," continued Gwendoline. "In 1762, after Elizabeth died and Peter succeeded to the throne, he immediately went completely bonkers. At Elizabeth's funeral, he cracked jokes and stuck out his tongue at the priests. He wanted to scrap icons, build a Protestant church in his palace, redesign his soldiers' uniforms on German lines— and even change sides in the seven years' war in which Russia was against Prussia.

"This was too much for Catherine. And in June, while her husband was at his summer retreat, she pounced. Riding a white horse as colonel of an elite guard regiment, she seized power with the support of an army of fourteen thousand men. Almost meekly, Peter agreed to abdicate, allowing himself, as Frederick the Great remarked, 'to be dethroned like a child being sent to bed.'"

"So she finally showed her claws," said Beatty.

"You bet your life she did. And she was absolutely pitiless. Stripped of his uniform, Peter was given an old dressing gown and a pair of slippers. In prison, he sent his wife a series of letters, begging her to have pity on him and let him go back to Germany. But even his imprisonment in Russia might have proved a nuisance. The letters went unanswered. And eight days after the coup, Peter was strangled by a group of officers loyal to Catherine."

"Blimey," said Spick, clearly a little shocked. "She had him murdered?"

"Well, Catherine pretended he had died of colic, but nobody really believed her. When she asked her friend the French philosopher Diderot what they were saying in Paris about the death of her husband, he promptly changed the subject.

"But her pragmatism stood Catherine in good stead. For 34 years, she ruled Russia with a strong grip. She never remarried, although her affairs were notorious. She enjoyed talking about reform but did little to improve the lot of Russia's serfs and, in foreign affairs, proved as ruthless as any emperor before her, swallowing what remained of Poland as well as territory conquered from the Ottomans. By her death in 1796, she was probably the best-known monarch in Europe and certainly the most famous and accomplished female ruler since Elizabeth I."

Gwendoline leaned back on her chair and smiled. "And that is the kind of rule Russia needs now, not the namby-pamby Tsar Nicholas II and Alexandra currently leading the country. I think Lieutenant Tucker's mad monk might be right—there are some hard times coming to our hosts. And they have certainly had some hard times in their history."

"And what's the situation as you see it now?" asked Beatty.

"Well, following the Revolution of 1905, the Tsar made one last effort to keep his regime from being toppled and offered reforms similar to most rulers when pressured by a revolutionary movement. The military remained loyal throughout the Revolution of 1905, shooting hundreds of revolutionaries as ordered by the Tsar. But these mass shootings by the army also created the Duma. The Russian Constitution of 1906, also known as the Fundamental Laws, set up a multiparty system and a limited constitutional monarchy. The revolutionaries were apparently pacified and satisfied with the reforms, but I don't think they will be for long."

"You don't think anyone's going to murder Tsar Nicholas, do you?" asked Ethel.

"I have no idea. But I am rather glad we are about to return to good old England, home and beauty. Shall we go out on deck again? It's such a beautiful day."

CHAPTER 15

AND SO THE end of the visit arrived with no further opportunities of meeting with Tatiana. All I could do was wave forlornly to her from the deck of the *Lion* as the Tsar and the girls on board his royal yacht came to see us off. The squadron gave him a fine display of play-acting, weaving in and out of each other's coat-tails and churning up the waves before firing a thunderous salute and disappearing over the horizon at 25 knots like grey wolves over the Steppes—with little hope of their return.

One critic doubted "whether the orgiastic display by both hosts and visitors contributed anything to the preparation for war." Of course it helped. Thousands of Fritz would be tied up on the Eastern Front and not shooting Tommy, a happy state which lasted until Ivan ran out of ammo and boot leather and walked back home, picking up a red flag on the way.

Back in England, Beatty received his knighthood from King George, and Ethel became a Lady, which—being an American—gave her enormous pleasure. And on July 17th and 18th, "incomparably the greatest assemblage of naval power ever witnessed," as Churchill put it, took place at Spithead. Pity we didn't have very good movie cameras in those days; they made us look like rows of tombstones in a fog. But in fact, we were shining grey castles under blue skies, stretching out in parallel lines so long they were impossible to see from end to end. When the King came cruising by in the royal yacht, the lads roared and threw their hats in the air.

They would have been less pleased, as the fleet dispersed, to know that our war station was a cold and inclement hole punched out of the Orkneys called Scapa Flow. It may have commanded the North Sea, but its chilling seas and isolation didn't endear it to Jack Tars—just fifteen miles broad and eight miles across of turquoise ocean almost encircled by a flat landscape coloured grey, green, and ochre.

Look in vain for a Highland Fling or a Stag at Bay—this was a misplaced piece of Icelandic or Canadian tundra. The local towns of Kirkwall and Stromness were grey and dreek and, as the men found, were in practice off limits since trips ashore were short and largely involved supervised exercise on the boggy turf. As one rating memorably put it in a letter home: "I don't know where I am. But where I am, there are miles and miles of bugger all."

But we were in the designated place at the designated time. At 1 p.m. on August 4th, 1914, the signal was passed to all ships: "Commence hostilities against Germany." And from all vessels, the cheering could be heard. All ranks hugged each other, and the lower decks were allowed to splice the main brace—an extra tot of rum.

Not everyone thought we were ready for war. Old Percy Scott, constantly making himself unpopular, had quite a shopping list of things which were deficient: "No up-to-date mine layers, no efficient mine, no arrangements for guarding our ships against mines, no efficient method of using our guns at night, no anti-Zeppelin guns, no antisubmarine precautions, and only eight heavy ships fitted with director firing. And our torpedoes are so bad they will go under the German ships instead of hitting them."

Still, at least we did have a friendly and comfortable wardroom.

And London Dry of course.

Given the fact that the newly named Grand Fleet boasted about 150 ships to 100 in Germany's High Seas Fleet—as well as more of a punch in high-calibre guns—we didn't make a great start. And despite our great volunteer tradition, the German conscripts were better than we thought.

...ck-up came early in August just as the war was starting
The ...man battlecruiser *Goeben* and its light cruiser companion,
when ...into the Med, shelled Algerian ports, and outran our old
Bre... , *Indomitable* and *Indefatigable*. Finally, the *Goeben* was
...e 1st Cruiser Squadron of Admiral Troutbridge. His gunnery
...sed that they were outgunned and outranged, so they backed
...ridge might as well have consigned himself to a lead-lined box
...tom of the Med and thrown away the key—such was the odium
...at him for failing to fight, and he never went to sea again. If
...ight, he would certainly have lost but might at least have slowed
... enemy down. Suffice to say that Jacky Fisher, who returned as First
Sea Lord, thought that his commander-in-chief in the Med, Arky Barky
Milne, should have been shot. Prudence was not rewarded but nor was
risking a ship in the Royal Navy of the time. It was preferable to get blown
sky-high.

We did redress the balance nicely on August 14th with a neat little
operation hatched by Keyes and Tyrwhitt for attacking the German
destroyer patrols off Heligoland Bight, the strategically important North
Sea Island which protected the main ports used by the High Seas Fleet.

John Jellicoe, The Commander-in-Chief at Scapa, showed little interest
in the plan, helped by the discovery of the German's secret wireless codes.
For their part, the Admiralty said the battlecruisers could support "if
convenient." What wouldn't have been convenient—putting off a game
of golf?

By the time we got down there, some of the British ships were having
a tough time against the accurate light gunnery of the German flotillas.
Fog had conspired with the smoke and our sometimes-lethally-bad
communications to create confusion. Then the fog lifted, and *Lion*—
risking mines, torpedoes, and the sudden appearance of the High Seas
Fleet—led our charge at perfect shooting distance.

From the signal bridge, I could see it was a little one-sided: five
battlecruisers with 12-inch and 13.5-inch guns against assorted enemy
destroyers and light cruisers. In just 40 minutes of thunderclaps, three

German light cruisers light were at the bottom with probab

The only trouble was the successful British raid made the Ge~~ead.~~

more nervous about coming out.

But the Germans did have a weapon which made us nervou

submarine. Running slowly on electric motors underwater with

diesel engines on the surface, the early subs had to be carefully positic

for a kill, which was the case when U-9 found three of our outdated cruis

dawdling along at 10 knots off the Hook of Holland on September 22nd

One went down. The others crowded in to pick up survivors. But they were

live bait. The second took her final plunge, and the third followed—1,500

dead within an hour.

Then, at the end of October, Kit Craddock's two old armoured cruisers, *Good Hope* and *Monmouth*, had been sunk in the South Atlantic by *Scharnhorst* and *Gneisenau*, the crack ships of Admiral Von Spee. We dug around the whole affair in *Lion*'s wardroom. Poldhu, our wireless news service in Norfolk, reported that the Kaiser had awarded 300 Iron Crosses to the victorious German crews—characteristically over the top.

Highet was outraged. "We'd better avenge that," he said. "I'd go down there myself and blow the b-blighters out of the b-bloody water."

"I think we ought to detach two battlecruisers and destroy their whole squadron," said Trotter, a newcomer to *Lion*, with the soft lilt of the clever Edinburgh advocate about him.

Low was fiddling around with the "juice box." He glanced up. "Don't fancy Von Spee's chances. If Jacky Fisher catches him downwind, he's a dead duck."

"Dunno about that," said Highet. "First popgun goes off, and we all leg it to the far side of Ireland. I don't know why we don't all go to the far side of Greenland. At least we'd be safe there . . ."

"Waiting for the big fight," said Low, screwing in a new needle. "Anyone fancy anything on the juice box?"

"No!" we all shouted in unison. Low's ragtime records were already starting to get stale. We'd had just one one-sided fight since August. And now this massacre near the Falklands. Revenge was called for, but it wasn't going to be us as we moved to our new base at Rosyth near Edinburgh.

"Take two," thundered Jacky, and accordingly, the battlecruisers *Invincible* and *Inflexible* were detached from the squadron and sent charging south to wreak vengeance. They found Von Spee as they completed coaling in the Falkland Islands on December 8th. He must have known he was doomed when he saw their dreaded tripod masts appear on the horizon, coming out of Port Stanley at full steam ahead, and as shells from our old battleship *Canopus* grounded into the port with its 12-inch guns began to range. The British commander on the spot, Admiral Sir Doveton Sturdee, who had lunch served before the battle, was a "pedantic fool and ass" according to Jacky. Sturdee's own opinion of himself was indeed rather puffed up, but he could hardly fail. Three hours after coming within effective range of the 12-inch guns of *Inflexible* and *Invincible*—the German cruisers mounted 8-inchers—the *Scharnhorst* rolled over and sank. Three hours later, hit by fifty 12-inch shells, *Gneisenau* was scuttled and abandoned, with nearly 200 of her crew saved. "Excellent," said Jacky.

"Lucky buggers," said Highet in the wardroom as the news of the Falklands victory reached us. He smacked his lips and took another sip of gin. "To them, the glory in southern waters and showing the flag along the sunny South American coast. To us, the duty of tossing about in cold northern seas, waiting for nothing to happen but Sweet Fanny Adams."

"Ah, well," said Low, in a characteristically sentimental mood, "maybe one day good luck will find us." Surprisingly, he then recited a quote from Kipling, much loved, whose son was at the Western Front:

> "Roll down—roll down to Rio
> Roll really down to Rio!
> Oh, I'd love to roll to Rio
> Some day before I'm old."

There was silence for a moment.

"Thanks, Low. Whoever gets to Rio first, send a postcard," said Trotter, moved or slightly pissed or a bit of both. "And I hope I'm alive to receive it."

"This is 1914, Low," said Highet. "And you have as much chance of rolling to Rio as taking your decadent collection of jazz records to Berlin and having a dance with Kaiser Bill. Talking about the Kaiser, where's our Admiral? Since we moved to the mighty Firth of Forth, I haven't seen him for days."

"He's pacing," I said, "wondering, like all those clubbers in Pall Mall, what's happened to Rule, Britannia! According to Plunkett, who is of course very posh, one of the old devils got so upset about Kit Craddock that he knocked over his port and had a seizure. All at sea, eh? Or lured into inaction by a timorous enemy. And all because of those damned upsetting German mines, submarines, and airships. And if they're not enough, then there's Ethel."

"What about Lady Beatty?" asked Highet.

"Well, I don't think I need tell you, Highet, that Lady Beatty apparently hates Aberdour House over yonder and keeps popping off to London and enjoying the social whirl, which shows no sign of abating despite the huge casualty lists from France. They are still unaffected by the war in London, which of course is miles away from the fighting in France. If you live close to the coast, you can hear the gun over the channel, but really, they are miles away from the capital."

I started up the nearest stairway just as Beatty shot down it like a thoroughbred out of a starting gate. We collided, and I got knocked down.

"Oh, Tucker," he said, helping me to my feet. "Sorry about that, better come with me." He was obviously preoccupied and nearly cannoned into a clump of hammocks hanging like overripe banana skins from the ceiling. How sailors slept where they did—dotted around the ship—I couldn't imagine.

We finally arrived at the Signals Office.

"Fancy a guinea on the buggers coming out next week?" the Admiral asked Spick, striding into his office, brushing some raindrops off his cap, and running his fingers through his thick black hair.

"You're on, Sir," said Spick. And they shook on it.

"Well, take a break from this endless paperwork and come and have a slurp in my leaky stateroom. Tucker is included since I nearly wrote him off coming down rapidly from the deck a moment ago. Another quick downpour any minute now. Tailored uniform and shoes from Church's as well. I am going to send their next bill to the Admiralty." Beatty was meticulous about his clothes; he admired John Jellicoe but found risible his country-parson raincoats and the economical use of steel plates in the heels of his shoes.

Then the sun broke through, and we stepped back up to the windy upper deck for a moment.

"Fisher keeps writing." Beatty smiled, shouting to be heard in the wind. "And keeps saying in his usual capital letters, 'When they come out, Then we pounce. But meanwhile don't drop your guard for a second.' The cheeky old blighter. As if I needed telling. If this lot was just a war of words, I'd send him in alone—with his jar of red ink."

High above our heads, 100 feet up on the topmast, signal flags snapped in the wind. *Lion* swayed gently in her moorings to the west of the bridge, the last rays of the sun irradiating its lattice work and glancing off the ship's conning tower and the brass tampions capping the muzzles of its heavy guns. The ship, 675 feet long and 86 feet in the beam, was an endless source of fascination for the schoolboys who climbed high up the Forth rail bridge to get a better view. We stopped and waved at them.

Moored nearby were the other giants of the squadron—or Battlecruiser Fleet, as Beatty had started to call it—similarly sleek and purposeful: *Princess Royal, Queen Mary, Tiger,* and *New Zealand.* Small wonder that many of the schoolboys wanted to walk the decks of these sleek warships, possibly the most beautiful ever built and with guns which could each launch a one-ton shell—heavier than the entire broadside of *Victory*—over fifteen miles. But first, there had to be a target.

We ducked below again to escape another brief drubbing shower. The Admiral's ceiling had been patched up a bit but still leaked. You could see the tiny rivulets racing about and falling in droplets. Had Nelson's great stern cabin leaked?

Beatty called his steward to bring three gin and tonics. We clinked glasses.

"Any movies on in the wardroom this evening?" he asked. "I don't feel like writing letters all night, and despite its electric heaters, I can never get this bally place warm enough. God knows what it's going to be like when Edinburgh really turns into an iceberg after Christmas. I think the Scots say February is usually the worst. Anything on the screen with nice bosomy girls and all that?"

Ever efficient, Spick looked at his notepad doubtfully and coughed. "There will be an adventure picture showing tonight entitled *A Kentucky Romance* and a short film showing a race between a giant Russian plane and an express train."

Beatty was unimpressed. "Good Lord. Those blighters who run the fleet film club should be put in a funny farm. What's their strategy?"

"A bit of leg and heaps of novelty, sir," said Spick, smiling.

Beatty was still unimpressed. "Tell them to buck their ideas up. They must think we're all morons. By the way, who wins the race?"

"Well, I think in *A Kentucky Romance*, the cowboy gets the girl after rescuing her from a stagecoach, and in the race, the plane overtakes the train, then crashes into a snowdrift."

"Must see that," said the Admiral, whose strong destructive instincts were repressed beyond endurance. "Another snort?" He waved to the mess servant.

"Thank you, Sir," said Spick. He was trying to keep a straight face. "Oh, and there's a short item about the conversion of Lady Beatty's steam yacht into a hospital ship, your very own *Sheelagh*."

"Hum, all very well for Ethel to strut about in her Florence Nightingale kit, but it's costing a fortune, and hardly anyone's been scratched yet. And she wants to give every mess in the squadron a turkey for Christmas. That's 250, for God's sake. Think the lads would notice if we gave them goose?"

"Actually, we did lose a man today," I interjected about medical matters. "Stoker came up for a spot of air, leaned heavily against a rail which gave way. Down he went like a stone. We lowered a boat, but there was no sign."

"Wasn't stoker Williams, was it?"

"No, Sir."

"Poor bugger, don't we teach them all to swim?"

"Er, not quite, Sir. Jacky Fisher instituted a big swimming programme, but most of it was carried out indoors with men stretched out on stools doing the breaststroke in the air. Doesn't seem to work in water, Sir."

"Oh, well, anything to avoid getting wet. I am certain that most of the Navy avoid actual contact with the briny at all costs. Anyway, Tucker— hero of St Petersburg—hasten ye back to the wardroom. Spick and I have some serious business to discuss."

What business, I wondered? Still, I felt quite bucked, having had a drink in the Admiral's quarters and not altogether overjoyed to find Highet alone in the wardroom, indulging an evil mood. I called to the mess waiter for a pink 'un across the carpeted, wood-panelled expanse with its piano, Low's cherished electric gramophone his juice box, green baize games tables, and jolly hunting prints.

"Right you are, Sir," said the waiter. "Coming up."

Highet brightened, but not for long. "Splendid Cats, they call us—all tooth and claw. But when are we going to have a good scrap, Reg? Nelson would have said 'Enough' and sailed by now," he added with all the steel-bright certainty of a 21-year-old." A fresh downfall of rain fell on the skylight in torrents. He winced and continued.

"And what do we do?" He plucked a dog-eared publication from the mahogany table and flapped it about. "We sit around mauling old magazines and making feeble small talk. I've read this copy of *Punch* so many times I think I can quote it verbatim. The wit is waterlogged. And if I hear another of Lieutenant Low's ragtime records, I'm going to scream, load them into a torpedo tube with all our moth-eaten periodicals and witless movies, and fire them at the fucking fish. It'll be the brig for me, but at least there would be a few moments—an orgasm—of satisfaction." His chair wobbled dangerously as if on a mission of its own.

You can't pick your company in the Navy, but Highet was quite good value once he got the helm.

"Well," I said, trying to lure him off the tack, "if it's any consolation, Horatio's dead, so is his bookie, not to mention Lady Hamilton. Anyway, we can't just cast off and go, we steam. We may want a good scrap at the moment, but we're about as likely to attack someone as Brighton Pier. Even if Nelson had a fair wind, he'd need an Enemy in Sight."

There was a rumbling noise throughout the ship. *Lion* was coaling, a reminder that a steel battlecruiser ten times bigger than *Victory* needed more than a stiff breeze to make headway. It needed enough coal down the chutes and into the bunkers to keep the home fires burning in a small town for a month. And then it could chase anything afloat—that is, if there was anything afloat to chase.

Highet's frustration was understandable. Would the High Seas Fleet, Tirpitz's pride and glory, ever make a move?

"The Germans are quaking in their sea boots, waiting to come out and take a hammering. I know Jacky Fisher," I reminded Highet, "and he didn't build the most powerful fleet in the world so that his battlecruisers could rust away in the shadow of Edinburgh Castle."

Highet remained unimpressed. "But because of our superiority, the Germans will just rust away in Wilhelmshaven while we rust away here, just like a couple of Western gunfighters frozen in a photograph."

"Well, our Admiral just bet Spick a guinea that we'll see action within a week. Fancy a bet yourself?"

"Betting is for idiots," he said. And I knew Highet was careful with his money so didn't press the point and changed the subject.

"Anyway, I wonder what Poldhu is saying," I said, referring to our doubtfully accurate wireless press bureau as Low and Trotter entered the wardroom and put their feet up.

Poldhu's news bulletins were transcribed and posted around the ship and not treated with the respect their writers might have desired. "Is there really such a thing as Poldhu?" asked Trotter. "Sounds like a character from a fairy tale—Puck and Poldhu."

"Hold on, I have the latest headlines here." Low pretended to read from a mess menu card. "'The Germans are believed to be disguising their Zeppelins as enormous hens in order to terrify the population and confuse our gunners. Five Russian Divisions en route to the Austrian Front and thought to have been lost have turned up on the Isle of Wight and surrendered to the local postmistress. Ingenious Royal Navy experts say German flotillas have already succumbed to a new mine painted with the words *Lager Bier*. The enemy destroyer picks up the mine and, after an hour, can be boarded and captured without a struggle.' End of bulletin," he said to general laughter.

"You know, Low, you'd be quite a good fellow—if you weren't such an ass," said Trotter.

"And you'd be a passable imitation of a human being if you weren't from boring Edinburgh," said Low.

CHAPTER 16

GETTING HIS BIG Cats unscathed from their berths at Rosyth below the Forth Bridge twenty miles along the river was always a challenge, especially at night. But one thing that worried David Beatty more than navigation day or night was the chance that one of his £1 million vessels and their crews would fall victim to mines as they steamed out of the estuary into the North Sea.

Of all the naval weapons of the war, the most diabolical by far was the mine floating silent and almost invisible 10 feet below the surface. These marine bombs carrying more than 300 lbs of high explosive could rip open the hull of almost any vessel afloat. The Germans saw them from the very beginning as a way to "bring the war to the enemy coasts."

Specially adapted submarines and light cruisers laid their murderous cargoes all over the North Sea—including the Forth Estuary, where the battlecruisers would be vulnerable. Once the mines dropped to the seabed, the seawater dissolved salt plugs that held the retaining bars of the mine cradles in place, allowing them to rise to a predetermined level on their mooring cables. The horns on each mine triggered electrical devices sensitive to the slightest contact with a ship's hull.

Typically, some traditionalists in the service and the Admiralty regarded their use as rather underhanded and unsporting. But we weren't playing games and wanted to do something about the menace. Desperate for minesweepers, scores of fishing trawlers were fitted with devices to snare and cut mine mooring lines. It was dangerous work, and I was summoned to see Chatfield and Beatty about this after breakfast one morning.

"We are reliably informed that some German minelayers have been sowing their deadly contact mines around the estuary to the Firth of Forth," said Chatfield.

"And we've decided to send out a light cruiser to investigate the menace with you, Tucker, as *Lion*'s gunnery expert, going out with the ship to join some specially-equipped fishing trawlers to cut their cables and blow as many to buggery as we can," added Beatty. "And perhaps find some new tactic we can use against them."

"Sounds fun, sir," I said, trying to appeal to Beatty's enjoyment of danger.

"Well, I am glad you think so. No doubt it is fun unless you unexpectedly hit the bloody things. They could even blow a nasty hole in the underside of *Lion*. This is a real threat, Tucker, and I hope to see some initiative from you."

We chose a sparkling bright and calm early morning to steam past Edinburgh to the mouth of the estuary, meeting a squadron of six sweeping vessels dragging behind them a sweep 300 yards long. This had steel cutting jaws at intervals to cut the mooring cables, and we looked hard to see if we could spot the mines as they were swept and cut from their cables.

They were difficult to see as they only just revealed a gleam of their rounded shapes and their protruding horns as they bobbed just above the surface. And they were still very dangerous. Contact with a ship's hull could trigger an instant explosion. Sinking would be the inevitable outcome.

The traditional way of dealing with the mines once located was for them to be detonated by rifle shots from the deck. Enough bullets would puncture the chamber, and the mines would then harmlessly sink back to the ocean bed. But by far, the best result was when their horns were hit, allowing them to explode in a geyser of smoke and spray 300-400 feet high.

I was a good shot, as I'd already demonstrated to Jacky Fisher. And I accurately exploded three mines to gratifying applause from the surrounding seamen.

Then there was a shout from the lookout at the bows. Caught in the wash from one of the explosions, one of the freed mines was heading right for the stern of one of the trawlers. The helmsman clearly hadn't seen it, and I had only about ten seconds and one bullet left in the clip to hit it and had to make it count. I prayed and pulled the trigger. The result was another deafening explosion and another waterfall of spray, which drenched the crew of the trawler—who were lucky to be alive and quickly showed their appreciation.

But the trouble was, it was slow work, and I handed the .303 Enfield back to the officer in charge and suggested that a better way would be to use a machine gun spraying a large part of the mined area with bullets.

"A Vickers on a tripod or mounted on the bridge, shooting 600 rounds a minute, would clearly be more efficient," I said. It was the kind of solution that would appeal to Beatty.

"I think you might have something there," he said.

As it happens, my hunch was correct. We went out the next day with a Vickers, and the result was a veritable firework display of mines and oceans of spray as many of them were blown clear out of the water.

Word soon got back to Chatfield. "Good work, Tucker," he said. "Our shooting ace has done it again. 'And well done,' says the Admiral. And thanks for diminishing the problem. It's this kind of contribution that gets noticed."

CHAPTER 17

A ND SO IT went on. The next bit of excitement was steaming north to Muckle Flugga, a large rock, for some gunnery practice—more games. "We are as likely to find the enemy here as the *Titanic*," Beatty said. This became translated among the officers as "keep a good lookout for the *Titanic*."

Carelessly, one of our numbers, *Tiger*, got lost. "Your extraordinary bad lookout will cause a disaster," Beatty signalled the hapless ship by wireless. When found again, our newest battlecruiser wandered around like the *Marie Celeste*.

"If you don't get on with your practice, you'll be torpedoed," Beatty warned.

Up in the foretop, I helped our 13.5-inch guns hammer the rock several times while hoping for a better show from *Tiger*. In my inflated way, I now regarded myself as one of the proponents of the new central firing system. But someone on *Tiger* was turning the dials the wrong way. Had it been a game of cricket, its throws into wicket would have brained several fielders and possibly even reached the boundary. At worst, the system was seen to be imperfect; at best, it was attributed to "teething troubles."

"Well," asked Chatfield later when I saw him on the bridge, "what about your much-vaunted new gadgetry now, eh, Tucker?"

"The system does work, sir. It just needs practice."

"*Tiger* certainly needs practice. They were so far off the mark I was beginning to think they'd start firing at us."

Things began to happen when we returned to Rosyth after the target practice. It was before dawn. I was in a deep sleep, and Haddock was shaking me awake. There were times when I wished he'd do the right thing and jump overboard.

"You're wanted in the signals office as soon as you can possibly manage, sir." I got up, dressed, splashed my face with cold water, and stumbled out to report several minutes later, bracing myself against the pitching and the rolling of the ship.

Spick was looking his imperturbable self.

"Admiralty orders to sail at five," he said, his face alight with the prospect. "A German force left the Ems this morning, thought to be Admiral Hipper and his Scouting Group, our counterparts. Very big, juicy targets."

An officer arrived in "wavy navy" gear. Spick winced. It was Filson Young again. He was—thanks to Fisher—to report further about life aboard *Lion* with Beatty and Churchill's tacit permission. We all hung on to fixtures as *Lion* corkscrewed its way south. The weather was so appalling that the destroyers following us were forced to turn back, leaving ourselves and the 2nd Battle Squadron of battleships making headway. But *Lion* could sail in a typhoon. Guns loaded and the damage control parties with matting and tarpaulin ready to repair gaps in the hull caused by enemy fire, we were ready for anything.

"Can you find us some cocoa, Filson?" asked Spick. It duly arrived as thick as treacle, along with some welcome beef sandwiches.

Daylight found us running south-east, still in wild seas. At noon, we received a signal from the 2nd Battle Squadron under Vice Admiral Sir George Warrender that they suspected a raid on Harwich or the Humber.

Beatty paid one of his rare visits to the signals office.

"We want to hit them. And hit them hard!" he said. The prospect of action after the boredom of official visits and target practice appeared to electrify him.

By the early morning, we received signals—many of them scrambled by German radio interference—that several destroyers had been damaged by German ships. Then we intercepted an Admiralty signal to Jellicoe that Scarborough, a harmless northern resort of no strategic importance, was being shelled, a pointless yet murderous scheme.

Sir George promptly signalled Beatty: "Scarborough being shelled. I am proceeding towards Hull." Beatty's reply was a classic debunk: "Are you? I'm going to Scarborough."

Somewhere, between us and the coast, as invisible as ghosts, lay Hipper's main Scouting Force. Next, they bombarded Hartlepool, neatly avoiding an area sown with mines. By now on the signal bridge—with permission—I could barely make out our light cruisers through the worsening weather ahead of us.

Then houses in Whitby, a tiny fishing village and resort, came in for a hammering from the German battlecruisers' 12-inch guns.

Lion's bows dug into the North Sea, sending spray everywhere. Then, through the wind and wetness came a huge flash and the boom of heavy guns. We were very close. But then two of our light cruisers began going astray in the mist, and Beatty signalled them to resume station. Sadly, the signal was seen and misread by Goodenough, the light cruiser commander, who idiotically ordered all the light cruisers to break off pursuit of the retreating Germans.

And now we were now as blind as bats as the Germans escaped into the mist after causing considerable damage to innocent civilian targets. Inwardly, Beatty must have been seething but, characteristically, showed no signs of wanting a scapegoat—one of his few faults, in my book. Admirable it might have been, but I could never understand it.

For another four hours, we charged on through the mist and spray, hoping to find a lead. Wet and numb with cold, we could not find them. We fired a final defiant broadside then turned back to Scottish waters.

"Well, it might be a clear victory for the Germans," said Filson during the inevitable post-mortem in the wardroom. "But what they aim to prove by killing hundreds of innocent civilians and their children in northern seaside towns, I really can't see. They're shits."

"It can't be to challenge us, as such," said Trotter, "because as soon as we arrive on the scene, they leg it back to Germany."

"Cowardly shits," said Filson.

"At which point, we promptly lose them even though we're faster and can outrange their guns," scowled Highet. "One of these days we'll chase a squadron of so-called Germans to New York, shell Staten Island Ferry, and end up with the Americans putting us in chains."

We were back in harbour in late December, but we were not to have Christmas ashore because, as if to compensate for losing Hipper, 250 turkeys arrived on Christmas Eve and orders came for us to sail at 7 p.m. on December 24; and we came out from a snowbound landscape and an early morning fog into a brilliant Christmas sunrise in the North Sea to enjoy a cloudless sky and what would have been a perfect day for gunnery had there been anything to shoot at.

Instead, we met most of the Grand Fleet for some of John Jellico's much-prized gatherings: the cream of the Royal Navy showing off what it could do at high speed while keeping a careful eye out for anything that might be blown out of the water.

CHAPTER 18

CHRISTMAS DAY REMAINED sunny and sparkling. It was a good day to be alive. At sea, we were away from the sharp bite of the Scottish land wind which drives over hundreds of square miles of frost, including the snow-capped Pentland Hills of Robert Louis Stevenson's fond memory before he left for the tropics. Dying of tuberculosis in distant Samoa, would he remember some of Edinburgh's old pubs, the Royal Mile and Mons Meg, the monstrous cannon on the ramparts of Edinburgh Castle? I remembered Bidston Hill, Liverpool landing stage, and certainly Ma Boyle's and thought of my parents, their thoughts no doubt with me as they enjoyed Christmas at home. I even had fleeting thoughts of Margaret.

It was crisp on deck, but inside *Lion*, the generously dispersed electric radiators kept the temperature at around 70 degrees Fahrenheit. If it became too fuggy, you just bunged open a porthole.

As the enemy was at home and soaking up some festive schnapps, we joined the Grand Fleet, and the squadrons danced stately Scottish reels around each other, one battleship after another, turning cartwheels like large awkward girls at a country wedding. The light cruisers dashed around in all directions, looking for even a whiff of smoke from a potential enemy; they looked impressive with their creamy white bow waves but everyone knew it was just another exercise.

And then with bugles blaring the all-clear and bells ringing for the change of watch—in that sense, the routine of the ship remained the same—it was time for a selection of carols, sung to the dire accompaniment of the harmonium. One brave young midshipman stood up and gave a solo performance of the Coventry Carol, and the carols ended with a rousing rendition of Oh Come All Ye Faithful, which moved some of the sailors to tears. We were to read later with some satisfaction that there had been a brief Christmas truce in the trenches when our men and the Germans agreed to meet between the lines, sang carols, offered each other drinks and smokes. Few people on either side were killed on December 25, 1914.

Then the officers visited the men in their mess decks, receiving the prescribed amount of ribbing. Each mess table was decorated with Christmas cards, photographs from home, and in the air was a mood of brotherhood, although everyone knew we could have cleared for action quickly if demanded. Very popular with the ordinary seamen on *Lion*, Beatty was pressed with gifts of sweets, cakes, and cards, and we all had to have a good swig of their grog, which went down like liquid fire. Then the men the settled down to a gigantic feast of their own.

The wardroom had an enormous lunch which started in the late afternoon and lasted a couple of hours. Beatty was invited of course, and the feast ended with the usual friendly rag and violent arrangement of furniture. "What a day for a real scrap," said Seymour, a little carried away by Christmas port and then by a ferocious Beatty rugby tackle.

Bursting with food, wine, and good cheer, I slung on my coat to get some fresh air up on deck. It was dark now, as black as coal smoke, but as I passed one of the lifeboats, I was curious to see a dim light moving beneath the tarpaulin cover.

"Ding-dong, merrily on high" came a rather tuneless voice. I pulled back the cover to reveal an ordinary seaman waving a torch and clutching a pewter mug defensively.

"And what, pray, are you ding-donging about?" I inquired.

"Don't send for the guard, Sir," he said with a start. "I'm just drunk. Gave a big plug of tobacco to one of my mates for his rum ration, after I'd had mine, like, then swapped my Christmas pudding for another tot, then someone gave me another, so I thought I'd come up here and sleep it off. But I can't get to sleep, Sir. Angels keep appearing and singing carols: Ding-dong, ding-dong . . ."

"Well, you'll be frozen stiff if you try and sleep it off out here all night. How old are you, sailor?"

"Twenty-five, Sir."

"Well, keep your voice down, get out of that boat, and run along," I said, only slightly less drunk than the seaman.

He got up, fell down again with a clatter, tried again, and landed heavily on the deck, clutching my greatcoat to regain his balance.

"Steady on, sailor, or we'll both be over the rail in a minute," I said in a very loud whisper.

"Do you know what my Dad said, Sir? He said that working men are destined to be slaves all their lives to serve a horde of despicable tyrants. That's why we get pissed."

I half agreed with him, but never mind. "Everybody gets pissed," I said firmly, waving away the offer of a slug from the beaker. "Anyway, you're not a slave, you're a volunteer—a free Englishman rolling home."

"That's not how some people look at it, Sir, with respect. Have you ever heard of Ernest Jones, the poet of the people?"

"Can't say I have."

He swayed a little and walked unsteadily over to the rail.

> "We're low—we're low—our place we know,
> We're only the rank and file,
> We're not too low to kill the foe,
> But too low to touch the spoil."

I knew exactly what he meant. He could have been a docker in Liverpool, bullied to work one day and yelled at the next to return home to a starving family when there wasn't enough work to go around and where stray children were taken to a wash house and deloused.

"Perhaps we can talk about poetry when you're sober." I smiled. "Now where do you live, sailor?"

"Nowhere on land, Sir. My mother died in childbirth in Liverpool just after the war started—she was too old to try—and my Dad was so heartbroken he killed himself by drinking a bottle of carbolic in Sefton Park. Got in the *Liverpool Echo*, Sir. Here on *Lion*, I sling a hammock in the barber's shop."

"Well, the Navy's no substitute for a happy home." Nor was it, thought I—at least, not from where he stood.

"But it's a sight better than being down there, Sir." And he pointed down at the dark heaving sea.

"Agreed. Now I'm certainly not going to call out the guard because it's Christmas. Will you be all right, er . . . ?"

"Tomkinson, Sir." And he took a gulp from his beaker and knuckled his forehead.

"Don't knuckle your forehead," I said angrily. "You may be a slave, at least in your poet's imagination, but you are most certainly not mine. And you're not low either. Belay the bottle, rise up the ranks, and you could do all right. Raise your own family and even get prosperous. Nothing is predestined, Tomkinson. Understood?"

"Thanks for that, Sir. Many thanks." And then he saluted and made his way unsteadily towards the stern. I would have assisted him, but officers didn't help men into their hammocks in 1914.

Soon after midnight on Boxing Day, we were back close to the Forth Bridge again, the festive season continuing on its merry way without gunfire, and the New Year saw Beatty giving a tremendous party for all the officers—including warrant officers—in the ship. The best of about twenty short speeches was made by Highet. His stutter suited the schoolboyish atmosphere very well.

"What I m-mean to say is . . ."—boisterous applause—"g-give me a chance, you rotters. If the Huns caught some of you lot, they'd put you in a zoo, naming n-no n-names. Well, all I have to say is, they can't run away from us forever!" This splendid oration met resounding applause and some breaking of china.

"Capital!" shouted Beatty.

This all led to a heavy scrap in the wardroom in which the evolution "out-staff" was performed with some difficulty after prolonged and stubborn resistance and considerable splintering of furniture.

But dog days were to follow.

One thing that annoyed us were reports that HMS *Audacious*, one of the new super-dreadnought battleships with 15-inch guns, continued to serve with the Second Battle Squadron, although its loss to a mine in Lough Swilly, Ulster, had already been reported in the American papers. The Germans must have known about it, so why the news was withheld to us seemed yet another example of the Admiralty's perplexing wish to keep its mouth shut about everything.

Beatty got so bored he took the squadron out following a rumour about a Zeppelin, which we found. It was really too high for our guns to bear, but at my suggestion, we let fly with a 13.5 shrapnel, which punctured the fabric in some places and caused it to wobble entertainingly before heading for home. Beatty got ticked off for taking the ships out without permission. His way of venting his anger at the puppet masters of Whitehall was to take Filson on an epic fourteen-mile walk which nearly killed the journalist who was no match for him when it came to physical fitness.

Another Zeppelin droned into view some days later and dropped bombs, completely missing the ships—he may have feared our non-existent high-angle guns—and instead hitting a distillery, flooding the gutters with whisky, and causing a whole Edinburgh neighbourhood to get absolutely legless; one chap died of alcohol poisoning.

When I went down to the engine room to kill some time before my watch, one of the stokers asked: "Any chance of a scrap, Sir?"

"You never know," I replied.

CHAPTER 19

O N ONE OF those wintry afternoons, I persuaded Filson Young to come to Edinburgh for a few hours away from the ship, although the Athens of the North—damp, cold, windy, and with soot swirling from endless chimneys—had little to offer in the way of entertainment. The festive season was over. "If they're not careful, they might enjoy themselves," he said, looking at the grim faces and stout refusals to smile. After glancing at the Scotsman's list of entertainments, we agreed not to go to a cinema—even though they obligingly flashed a message when the battlecruiser men had to return to base—and finally Filson said: "Oh hell, let's have a drink," pointing out the Abbotsford at the end of Rose Street.

Imbibing in Edinburgh usually involved red-faced advocates and journalists getting slowly drunk, so we were quite pleased to be offered "a wee nippy sweetie"—whisky and a half of ale—by a couple of cheerful lads in the Highland Light Infantry, cheerful despite the fact they were en route to the Front.

"English, ye ken!" said one. "So to explain, we're just starting on the Rose Street Run. That's a pint in every pub doon the way there, fourteen in all. Then off to the station, to London, to the coast, over to France, and come back in wee bitty pieces if we're not careful."

"Good send-off, eh?" said his friend cheerfully. "Care to join us?"

"Love to," Filson said. "But we're on four hours' notice, and we've already had two."

"Aye, ye'll noo stand such a good watch after eight pints," said the first soldier.

"Watch out, more likely," I said.

"Mind you, you could chance it—those big boats of yours dinna seem to go anywhere. They just seem to sit there blowin' off steam, isn't that right, Jimmy?"

"Well, we don't just go charging around firing at thin air. The Germans are too cautious—we hardly ever see them."

"Och, I wish we'd joined the Navy—more chance of staying alive. From what it seems, in France all you have to do is take a peek out of your trench, and you'll get your head shot off." And refusing another drink, they barged off. And bloody good luck to them.

After this close encounter with temptation, we pressed cold noses against shop windows in Princes Street, went to the barbers, climbed up to the castle ramparts, and were about to slither down the icy Mound when, despite the sooty atmosphere, we noticed billows of black coal smoke coming from the general direction of the Big Cats. This started a buzz amongst ourselves and other officers ashore. By the time we reached Caledonian Station, the buzz was turning into a flap. Racing for the train, we just caught it, and once on board *Lion*, it was clear that this was not just an exercise but could be the battle we had all been waiting for.

I joined Spick in the Signals Office only a minute before Beatty clattered down the steel steps and joined us.

"Come on, what's up, Frank?" he said, nodding to me and Filson, who was tucked into a corner of the small space.

Spickernell tossed aside the brass case, which had rattled up the pneumatic tube from the transmitting station.

"Looks good, Sir. It says you are to 'steam at sufficient speed to be 220 miles south by daybreak tomorrow. The objective is to intercept and destroy Hipper's Scouting Group of four battlecruisers—*Derfflinger*, *Molke*, *Blucher*, and *Seydlitz* with light cruisers and destroyers on the Dogger Bank.'"

We had five battlecruisers available that day—*Lion*, *Princess Royal*, *Tiger*, *New Zealand*, and the slower *Indomitable* under the command of Sir Archibald Moore with numerous escorts. Almost an even scrap, but with one heavy ship in our favour—always a good thing to have the odds on your side even if one can't quite keep up.

"We're on our way," said Beatty. He was practically purring at the thought of a fight.

As the ships chased along the twenty miles of the Firth about midnight, Beatty again dropped in our office on his way to his sea cabin high up on the bridge.

He looked at the chart and spoke, in his sometimes-curiously-intense way, of his absolute conviction that we would corner the enemy this time and achieve a victory.

He had no love for Hipper but considered him a worthy opponent.

"It's about time the Battlecruiser Fleet showed what it can do," he told the crew over our loudspeaker system, raising a babble of excitement and speculation. "At action stations tomorrow, I want everyone alert. However long it takes, don't let your concentration betray you for a second. I want all four of them sunk!"

His face was a picture of resolution, of destiny. His cap was at an unusually rakish tilt. A man ready for battle.

For the moment, there was scarcely any wireless traffic, apart from the usual Admiralty rubbish—"Please account for Seaman Pickles missing socks." So I turned into my cabin, checking my lifesaver vest was within easy reach. And as *Lion* chased rounded the Forth into the North Sea and headed south, I slept.

CHAPTER 20

I T CLEARLY WAS the first battle of the new super ships as Churchill said, but the Battle of Dogger Bank was no duck shoot despite our material superiority. High up on the precarious foretop, Filson and I saw it all. Two hours after opening fire, *Lion* was lamed. Port engine gone, we quickly lagged behind our four sister ships, which continued to pound the crippled *Blucher* instead of chasing Hipper's three retreating battlecruisers.

And the gap between our ships which should have given chase widened with every minute that passed. Could Hipper's ships have been caught? It takes a long time, and a huge distance has to be covered before a difference in speed starts to tell. The stern chase of a ship steaming at 24 knots and twenty miles ahead by a ship going 28 knots would take hours before the range reduced sufficiently to allow effective gunnery. And I don't blame the Germans for their hasty retreat. For all they knew, Jellicoe's entire Grand Fleet, a forest of battleship masts and 150 big guns—some 15-inch—could have loomed on the horizon at any minute.

If I had been drifting under the strain of the constant shellfire, another call on the navy phone restored alertness.

"Yes," I shouted.

"Conning tower here. Afraid A turret magazine is on fire."

Sweet Jesus. Filson hadn't heard a thing of course, with the wind whipping round his head. I decided not to tell him that the whole ship probably had no more than two minutes left before being blown into a thousand pieces.

So this was it—the end of *Lion* and me. An uncontained fire in a magazine meant just that. I found myself praying. "Safe in your hands, Oh Lord," I muttered. And then came a strong impulse that it was time to jump. I shook Filson, but he just grinned as if I was giving him encouragement. Two minutes passed, and nothing happened. Another minute. I tried to make Filson understand, but it was no use, and I could hardly leap from the mast myself. In any case, the sea looked distinctly uninviting, pocked with shell splashes and hundreds of dead fish floating belly up.

Then the phone went again. "It's all right, the magazine's flooded." Probably the best words I have ever heard spoken. I don't think I have ever been so scared.

Lion was now listing ten degrees to port. Clearly, she was out of the fight. I wondered how many dead were on the tally, how many were now being patched up in the cramped sickbay.

Beatty wanted the other battlecruisers to attack the retreating German ships. But Seymour had only two remaining flag hoists. "Attack the rear of the enemy" was chosen. But almost certainly because of his blunder, the flag bearing NE was still flying when the halyards were hauled down for execution of the order. And the three remaining German battlecruisers were not going NE—they were legging it SE home. So the virtually beaten *Blucher*—which *was* bearing NE—was still being pounded by *Tiger* and *Princess Royal*, with the *New Zealand* and *Indomitable* following suit.

"Attack the rear of the enemy," *Lion* again signalled vainly by flag. But the signal was misunderstood or temporarily obscured by funnel smoke. What was quite clear is that captains—Admiral Moore on *Indomitable* now in temporary command—failed to use their common sense and continued to pound a beaten enemy.

By just after noon, it was all over. The *Blucher* capsized, and hundreds of men topped helplessly into the sea from her upturned hull. It is still a mystery why a Zeppelin suddenly hovered into view and began dropping bombs, frustrating and finally stopping the attempts at rescue. Hundreds more would have been saved but for the giant gasbag, which we machine-gunned to no apparent effect.

Those we did rescue were plied with warm clothes, sandwiches, cocoa, grog, and a warm bed if at all possible.

In an agony of frustration, Beatty tore off in a light cruiser at flank speed and boarded *Princess Royal*, vainly ordering the squadron by radio to chase the Germans—but they were now more than twelve miles away. One minute they were hull down on the horizon, then gone like pale ghosts. But the ghosts had spat real fire. And meanwhile, *Lion* was for the shipyard and some considerable repair work.

Clambering unsteadily with Filson down from the foretop to my cabin, I found my greatcoat, which I had left lying on a chair when I went for breakfast, looking as though it had been torn apart by a pack of hounds. A chest of drawers floated about in several inches of water. Letters were sea-stained. Our faces were black with cordite, and our ears were bleeding from the shock of the big guns.

Hammering noises came from below decks, where the carpenters were hard at work making temporary repairs. Remarkably, no one had been killed on *Lion*, but when I looked into the sickbay, full of blood and dirt and dimly lit by oil lamps, the moans of the injured provided ample proof that not everyone had got off lightly.

Beatty, in his vain attempts to pursue Hipper's ships, left us on *Lion* as, power gone, the cold North Sea brought down the ship's interior to near-freezing point. Huge steel cables securing *Lion* to *Indomitable* were being run in and secured, and she began the long job of hauling the wounded ship home, protected by a flotilla of destroyers.

On the bright side, Captain Chatfield's quarters had a coal fire; his galley and food in his pantry and he laid on a cheery meal for the officers, even managing to find several bottles of champagne.

"No longer at Action Stations, I think, gentlemen? Then drink up—and here's mud in your eye."

We were all pale, dishevelled, and half-crazed by the uproar of battle. The talk was sporadic, even a little hysterical.

"A b-bloody great chunk of armour plate missed me by a whisker," said Highet. "I hope to God I'm as lucky next time we meet the sods."

"Well, I'm quite lucky to have my head," said Filson. "Do you think the Admiralty will charge me for a new hat?"

"Well, I think we did damned well," said Plunkett, "considering that we appeared for some reason to be the main target. But I'm surprised our side armour didn't do better with those German shells. We need heavier plates."

"And then we'd go slower," said Seymour, dabbing a cut on his forehead, where he'd fallen against a rail.

But it doesn't take long in the Navy for humour to relieve the tension.

"I wonder what Madame Dubois will have to say about today's events," mused Spick, gazing at the bubbles rising in his champagne at which Chatfield tipped his finger to the side of his nose. It didn't take long for jokes to relieve the tension.

"No harm in it, surely," protested Spick, laughing. "Everyone knows our Admiral consults fortune tellers. Funnily enough, she answers to Josephine in correspondence. On David's recommendation, O. de B. on *Princess Royal* has been consulting her as well. She's in Edinburgh— Hanover Street—and a good deal of attention is paid to her predictions. So the fact that we are still alive was probably on the cards."

"Isn't it *in* the cards, sir?" I ventured to general laughter.

"Probably. All sounds a bit rum to me, but David has always been addicted to fortune tellers, and that's all right because he can do no wrong as far as I'm concerned . . ."

"Damned right," said Chatfield, enjoying the fun. "But I wonder what Ethel will think when she hears about today's events?"

"I don't know—Ethel has her own ideas. But the fact is that Beatty cares about things. He will now, unless I'm very mistaken, be berating himself for some of the crass mistakes made in the battle just fought." Spick grimaced at the thought.

"Lady Beatty would look jolly good in uniform," I said, trying to lighten the mood.

"Better than you at any rate, Tucker," said Spick. "You look like you've been coaling. Still, we've got off lightly. A big firefight, a big enemy ship at the bottom, another one out of action for months—and all we lot need is a damned good bath."

Which was one thing we could not have. We may have been sitting around Chatfield's warming fire. But the whole ship was as cold as ice.

Despite the loss of *Blucher* and nearly 1,000 men, the Germans drew some profit from Dogger Bank. The near-disaster to *Seydlitz* revealed a fault in her design. If a shell penetrated a gun turret, the flash of the explosion could travel down to the handling room below and into the neighbouring turret. Only immediate flooding of the magazine could stop a disastrous explosion, which would instantly sink the ship. To stop this from happening, they modified all their battlecruisers with extra bulkheads and decking. But the similar weakness in our ships remained undetected—and uncorrected.

But the immediate thing on everyone's mind was rest. And after dinner and a stiff brandy, the warmest place was bed and sleep and fitful dreams—about the boom of the guns, the mast swaying back and forth, screams of pain and panic, and a haze of coal smoke and cordite which still hung around many corridors like a mist.

There just remained with me and with others the nagging thought that had Beatty been able to remain in place with his instinctive genius, the squadron would have been able to prolong the chase for over an hour and destroy the enemy ships given our superior speed and the range of our guns. He must have known that and been grinding his teeth at the thought of the clear victory that had eluded him, as he handed the reins over to less competent colleagues.

CHAPTER 21

CONGRATULATIONS PURSUED US as we were towed into Rosyth for repairs. The day following the battle, King George signalled: "I most heartily congratulate you, the officers and ships' companies of your squadron on your splendid success."

We could hardly see them because of a thick fog, but throngs of people had gathered on the central island of the Forth Bridge to welcome the wounded *Lion* back to harbour. Our Marine Band responded to their cheers with Rule, Britannia! But there remained the question of the misread signal. Were some of our captains dunderheads? Fisher wanted to lay blame for an incomplete victory. While others waved and read laudatory newspaper accounts, he reached for his lash.

Moore's conduct in abandoning the chase had been "despicable," he thundered and he should be "hung, drawn, and quartered." And Pelly's conduct had been "inexcusable" in leaving *Moltke* to fire unmolested at *Lion*.

Beatty's conduct was characterised as "glorious" by the First Sea Lord. But Beatty was hard on himself. "I had made up my mind that we were going to get four, the lot, and four we ought to have got," he wrote in his diary, which I saw later.

He was hard on himself was our Admiral but not so hard on some of his wayward colleagues.

Once all our reports were written, I was asked to travel to London and deliver them personally to the man who would not be denied.

"You're for London, Tucker," Spick said with uncharacteristic solemnity. "He glanced at his wristwatch. "Just in time to catch the nine o'clock sleeper. Report to Fisher in the morning, and only open these sealed reports in his presence."

Most times you could josh with Spick. This was not one of them. I swallowed the tempting "Why me, Sir?" and tried to look pleased. Mind you, a trip to London might be full of pleasant surprises—dreamy-eyed girls instantly enraptured by the uniform, dancing at nightclubs and love-making in satin sheets at an upmarket hotel. Hardly likely, yet just the sort of things good old Vladimir must have had in mind when he bunged me that £10,000.

"I'll do my best, Sir," I said brightly.

"Just catch that damned train," said Spick, as severe as you'd like. "Fisher starts early—about 7.30 a.m.—and if you're not there, he's liable to wake up the whole Grand Fleet, let alone the battlecruisers."

So off I went. The tender whisked me over to Hawes Inn fast enough, but the damned taxicab got something stuck in its fuel pipe, and we jolted towards Edinburgh at little more than walking pace. I harried the driver to no avail, even offered him a fiver if he could perform some miracle of engineering and get it going.

"It'll go nae faster for love nor money," he said philosophically, looking over his shoulder as cyclists overtook us with ease. I was furious with the oaf, his lack of care, and his sing-song Scottish accent. "I am on important business of national importance," I cried.

"Aye," he responded, "try chalking the heid of the club, nothing will get this rig going faster unless ye have a keg of gunpowder handy."

"Right, laddie, I've just about had enough of you and your dismal attitude," I said. I pulled out my .38 which I had brought since going to see Jacky Fisher in the middle of a war might have had its dangerous moments. "If we're not underway in one minute, I'm going to fill this car full of lead - and you if you're not careful."

"So the English Navy are assassins, are they?" he said, stopping the car, lifting the bonnet, and muttering unspeakable things to himself. He gave something in the engine a few short sharp raps with a spanner, and then—a reminder that brute force is the only answer to some problems— the revs increased; and we were soon racing, if that's the word, towards the city and Haymarket Station.

Too late of course.

The stationmaster apologised profusely for the departure of the sleeper, but faced with more bluster from yours truly, his eyes suddenly lit up.

"Wait a minute, Sir. We have another engine in the sidings, Sir, with steam up and ready to go. If we fixed a wagon to it, and with authorisation, you'd be in London in no time."

"Will you accept my chit?" I asked, daring to involve the Admiralty in unnecessary expense. It was Jacky who started me on this chit business, so it was down to him. And of course it was Beatty who told me that one of Jack's chits could get you almost anywhere.

"Why of course, Sir."

So up puffed my special. I signed a chit and sped off into the night, clutching my report and several bottles of Scotch ale, flasks of coffee, and ham rolls provided by the station buffet. By some bureaucratic mystery, the £25 expenses which I had drawn from Spick remained untouched apart for the quid for the taxi driver, which was a bit rich. The remainder of the charges would come in later, including at least £250 for the special to London. But what was best—to abort the mission out of financial rectitude or to go hell for leather at the gate? Not for the first time I was aboard the twin-humped Admiralty camel. Choose either hump, and you get a rough ride. Still, I would rather be assaulted by an Admiralty accountant than by Jacky Fisher any day.

The wagon was first class and, more than that, had its own built-in sitting room with a comfortable armchair and a chaise longue. It had a small selection of books, including one fictional fantasy about the navy called *Dreadnoughts of the Dogger*, in which British ships were constantly gunning down and even ramming German navy boats in the North Sea. Disliking propaganda, I selected a slim volume which turned out to be the journal of Fanny Duberly, the remarkable woman who had gone galloping around the battlefields of the Crimean War.

I was drawn into her story as my special rattled south through the black night, hooting as it sped through some of the many small stations en route in a flash. Pulling only one wagon, the train must have been travelling at least 75 mph—the driver hardly needing the £5 I had pressed on him to do his best. I drank the strong Scotch ale and ate one of the ham rolls and went into a bit of a dream.

I could have been on a night train in Russia, rushing through endless dark forests to meet Tatiana in some secluded dacha faintly lit by moonlight and with a roaring fire in the hearth—the young English naval officer and the Russian princess meeting for a night away from prying eyes, enjoying every moment of their time together. A dream? But we were both very young. My eyes started closing, and I dimmed the lights in the wagon and made myself comfortable on the chaise longue. In no time at all, I was asleep.

Dawn had not yet brightened southern England, and I slept well enough until the train arrived at King's Cross Station. I very quickly shaved, paused to pass on my thanks to the driver and his fireman, then grabbed a quick coffee and a bacon sandwich at the station buffet. Stricken with conscience about my spendthrift ways, I then caught a taxi to the Admiralty.

CHAPTER 22

I T WAS EARLY morning and still dark, and the taxi driver was not quite sure where the Admiralty was. Manoeuvring my way down Whitehall in the Zeppelin blackout after the long journey from Rosyth, I became disorientated. I asked a policeman who was wheeling a bicycle: "Good morning, officer, is the Admiralty on my side?"

He copped my uniform and grinned. "I shouldn't think so, Sir."

It was suitable preparation for when I knocked on the door of Jacky's office a few minutes later. He threw it open and welcomed me with "Oh, it's you. And about time." He was obviously in his red ink and capital letters frame of mind.

He threw my papers about the battle on to his desk, riffled through the various documents and telegrams, read them for several minutes, and barked: "The Admiralty requires to know why the *Derfflinger* and *Seydlitz*, both on fire, were allowed to escape when both were in gun range of *Tiger* and *Princess Royal*."

He then turned his fire on Admiral Moore. "All signals made by Beatty had made it clear that Hipper's force was the objective . . . there is no doubt that he should have continued the action." His face started to purple. "It was inexcusable that *Moltke* was left unfired on and allowed to make target practice on *Lion*. And if he was a long way ahead, he ought to have gone on regardless of signals! Like Nelson at Copenhagen and St Vincent! In war, the first principle is to disobey orders. Any fool can obey orders!"

"Perhaps it takes exceptional courage, Sir, to ditch orders in a fast-moving action," I said cautiously. "One wrong move and, if it doesn't come off, you're damned."

"Yes, well, we all need a bit of luck from time to time, Tucker. But poor judgement will not be tolerated! You were there. What do you think?"

"My honest opinion, Sir?"

"It had better be."

"It was a complete cock-up. If a leader of Sir David's abilities has his wireless shot to pieces, it is up to Flags to point the way. And they messed it up. So the other captains, used to relying on his leadership, had no guide through the jungle."

"Except their own common sense."

"Precisely, Sir—in short supply, Sir."

"Seymour again, Beatty's Flag Lieutenant."

"Well . . ."

"Ha-hum. I must write a note to Beatty about him."

"And most of the ships are still wary about director firing, sir, just because the few that have it installed haven't practised enough. I think that ought to be remedied, sir. *Tiger* springs to mind."

"And it shall be! By jove, Tucker, you haven't lost your touch."

This idle flattery was leading somewhere. And I probably wasn't going to like it.

"Well now, I have a plan I want to tell you about."

At least Dogger Bank was put aside. So too for the moment was *Lion*—at least, that was what I thought.

"But let's leave that until lunchtime, shall we? In the meantime, I would very much like you to write down some of the things you told me about the action in clear English, including some of the faults you think could be corrected. This will be not an official report, but I like to keep a record of impressions. You can use a desk in a nearby office with a pen and paper, and then we can get it typed up by a secretary. Make a good job of it, then we'll meet again for a spot of lunch. All right with you?"

"Certainly, sir."

It seemed odd that I—a very junior officer on board *Lion*—was about to write a report about the action apparently for Jack's eyes only when he would very soon be getting an official report from Beatty, the man in charge of the battlecruiser squadron. As I had been when I first met him, I was being drawn into the old Admiral's world again, a world of high strategy well beyond my capacity to understand. Yet it was simple in the sense that our squadron had made a mess of the first action against heavy ships in the war. Heigh-ho, here I was, balancing on the camel's hump again.

This was the first report of its kind I had ever been invited to write. Where to begin? But I finally did, and the words started to flow. I could see the action in my mind's eye. The sheer terror of observing the action from the foretop, the superb confidence and coolness of Beatty, the unexpected accuracy of the German gunfire, the muddle over targeting which led to *Lion* taking more than her fair share of the damage, and the signalling failure and incompetence which allowed most of the German ships to escape. At least, if it was accurately reported, lessons might be learned for the next engagement.

I had pretty well completed my account when Jack's smiling face appeared around the door.

"Lunch?" he asked, and without waiting an answer, he ushered me along to the part of the old building which resembled a private club, except that nearly everyone was in uniform; and when Jacky appeared, everyone stood up and saluted. He had a favourite table—far enough from the next for secrets of state to remain unheard.

He ordered two whisky and sodas and leaned towards me, speaking quietly.

"From now until the conclusion of my plan, Tucker, you will have the honour of being a Special Envoy for the Royal Navy. We think you have leadership qualities, Tucker, and while getting shot up on *Lion* will continue to be your main business, there are other things you could be doing. I was going to send you among other lieutenants to the trenches on this new exchange programme—how to shoot a Lewis gun while covered in mud, that sort of thing. But now something's come up for which you'd be perfect."

"Not in the trenches, sir?"

"No, none of that. My plan doesn't actually include you getting killed, which might happen if we sent you to the front line—although you will have to keep your head down on occasions."

I might as well try it. "Well, I thought as *Lion* is going to be out of action for a few weeks, a spot of leave would be very welcome, Sir."

"Tucker, we are fighting for our lives!" And without any apparent sense of irony, he gestured towards the dining room, where two or three dozen top brass were stuffing themselves with Beef Wellington and House Claret while haw-hawing about this and that.

"Fighting for the country!" added Jacky, his voice rising. "And our English parish churches! And happy families gambolling beside the seaside in straw hats! That's why thousands of Tommies are up to their ears in mud at the moment, trying to reload their rifles as the thousands of Huns bear down on them with bombs and bayonets! And you talk of leave!" At this point, several old codgers gave me warning looks. Annoying the First Sea Lord could have dire consequences—a posting to Newfoundland, for instance.

Well, anything better than being in the trenches. I hope Highet didn't get picked. I'd grown rather fond of Highet even if he was a bombastic upstart who would try to upstage me at any opportunity.

Jacky's plan took all of a large sirloin steak to get through. First, you took the entire Grand Fleet to the Baltic through the Great Belt with thousands of Tommies and Russians in company and landed them on the unprotected north German coast of Pomerania, forcing the Germans to divert into a third front and destroying them—ending the war almost as fast as a shoot-out in Dodge City. This would be facilitated in part by the actions of a certain Reginald Tucker, I gathered.

Splashing about in his bath with his toy dreadnoughts, it might not have occurred at first to the great admiral that if you sealed the Baltic end of the Kiel Canal using the fleet, German ships could simply steam out of the southern—North Sea—end and reduce Britain's ports to rubble. Jacky's answer was to the problem was to sow mines in such unprecedented numbers that the High Seas Fleet could never use the North Sea exit. Had the Americans been in the show at the time, it might have worked, given their liking for gigantic projects, but we were still stopping and searching their merchant ships, which caused so much irritation it nearly brought them in on the German side.

To hell with all that. In a four-page paper aimed at the considerable number of critics of his latest inspiration, Jacky wielded his Napoleonic pen. "Risks must be taken to use our Command of the Seas with greater energy. Risks must be taken! Rashness in war is essential! Prudence in war is criminal!"

And so quartered in a nearby hotel, I found myself attached to Jacky's staff, awaiting his pleasure. There was a buzz of activity in his office and a steady blizzard of comments and criticisms about the scheme—some of them answered, most of them trashed. A man who got things done, Jacky had considerable heft. Cruisers with a shallow draught were ordered along with hundreds of landing craft. Thousands of mines were earmarked for his intended "total" blockade of Kiel. As Admiral Bacon recorded: "The conception is a bold one . . . a sign of genius and not of madness on Fisher's part." But madness was what Admiral of the Fleet Sir Henry Oliver and others thought of the scheme.

Whether my job was madness or the fruit of genius, I was not sure. But when my orders came, I found I had to go post-haste to St Petersburg, find the Tsar and his chief of staff, and persuade them to join in my employer's Pomeranian adventure to the tune of 50,000 troops, which were peanuts to them, and the offer of millions of allied roubles, which were definitely not. After their crushing defeat at Tannenberg early in the war when General Samsonov had shot himself in disgrace, they might be willing to try anything.

I saw Jacky in his office to get a fuller briefing. But it was actually more of a sketch. Unlike many generals and admirals of the time, he believed in setting objectives and then letting officers on the spot get on with it. Like

Beatty, he expected his officers to use their initiative rather than rely on detailed instructions.

"I don't think this should test your intellect too much," he said, his eyelid slightly drooping, betraying the strain of his workload. He was now over seventy, and the fabulous energy was waning; he sometimes took a short nap after lunch.

"You don't think it's more of a job for a senior diplomat, Sir?"

"Heaven forbid. The Ruskies don't want to see a slithering reptile from the Foreign Office. They want to see a young Naval officer with plenty of get-up-and-go: Fisher's envoy!"

He poured us both a nip of brandy.

"You may ask where Pomerania is. Well, I can point out the bloody place on a map. But basically, it's flat. Get a few German divisions diverted to that region, and we can start making headway on the Western Front. Because if we don't, Tucker—and this is the real point—Britain and its Empire are going to start owing so much to our cousins across the sea in America that we might as well become one of the United States, driving on the wrong side of the road, chewing gum, shooting anything that moves, and playing professional rounders . . ."

"Baseball, Sir," I said glumly. "Not much of a prospect."

"So my Baltic plan has an economical as well as humanitarian purpose—stop getting in hock to the Yanks and win the war as soon as possible. Now that's a target to hit! Think big, aim high. And cheer up!" At which point, some red-faced old duffer in the corner raised his glass and said: "That's the stuff, Jacky!"

Jacky gave the old boy a cheery wave.

"Darlington," he told me. "Used to be with me at Malta until he got the clap." He took a sip of brandy and began to shake with laughter.

"You like *Lion*, don't you, lieutenant?"

"I love the ship, Sir. Can't wait to get back."

"You will, you will. But haven't you ever wondered, Tucker, what it's like to be on board one of His Majesty's smaller ships? You're about to find out, and I think you'll find it great fun! Because of course we can't spare a battlecruiser to take you to Russia. It'll have to be something a good deal smaller, faster, and more manoeuvrable. God, I wish I was going with you. There will be someone waiting to liaise with you from Russian Naval Intelligence when you get there who has been told to give you all the help he can. And avoid Buchanan and the British Embassy crowd unless you are in dire peril. This is a secret mission, Tucker—not even Winston with his current Turkish obsession knows about it—and you are my envoy with my authority behind you to carry a message only to Tsar Nicholas.

"Anyway, Godspeed. Orders and my sealed letter to him are ready now, and a car will take you to your ship. And remember, Tucker, this is a vital mission which could change the direction and duration of the war! So try very hard. Keep your head. And remember, mad things have a habit of coming off!"

But why didn't the young First Lord know about it? I was to find out soon enough.

As I waited for the car outside the Admiralty, a group of very pretty young ladies distributing white feathers approached, clearly determined to get me within range of some German machine guns at short notice.

"Why are you here in London taking it easy when you should be at the front?" asked one of them. "Are you one of those shirkers with a cushy desk job here at home while others have to face going over the top every day?"

She stood right in my path, leaning on her parasol, a fetching straw hat with flowers on her head, her blonde hair tumbling below it. In her other hand, she clutched a quiver containing the feathers.

I decided to make the most of it.

"Good day to you, ladies, but you've got the wrong chap," said I with some relish and a winning smile. "I am a lieutenant in the Royal Navy and have been visiting the admiralty on a special assignment. And I have already been involved in one very large sea battle where I nearly got my head blown off and then nearly drowned. No, I am not going to the trenches, thank God, but that's as much as I am willing to tell you."

"Well, I just hope you're not fibbing because your conscience will get you in the end. But just in case you're not, good luck to you." And blow me down, she shook my hand, and she impulsively gave me a kiss on the cheek, which cheered me up no end because I had started to quake slightly about Jacky's latest assignment. For there would be no one I knew well— no Beatty, no Chatfield, not even my wardroom colleagues—to help if things went wrong.

CHAPTER 23

DAWN, AN L-CLASS destroyer, was sheer hell after the comforts of *Lion*. Two hundred feet long and only 27 feet in the beam, even in the Thames it plunged into the waves like an oversized bathtub and bobbed up again with the persistence of a duck. And as I knew already, it was quite a long haul to St Petersburg: all the way up the North Sea, round the top of Denmark, through the Great Belt, and into the Baltic proper. The Kiel Canal would have been manifestly quicker, which is why the Germans built it in the first place, but we had to do it the hard way.

I was welcomed by the captain, Commander May, who appeared stuffed to the gills with duty and determination but rather sombre, a pipe clamped in his mouth into which he mumbled, like someone with a sore throat. I was allotted a cabin little bigger than the cubicles in public lavatories with an undersized bunk. As we got going down the Thames and hit a fair chop, I discovered that to survive in a destroyer you had to be alternately mad or wet. In your cabin, anything moveable pitched to and fro as if possessed. Staying in this space was about the closest you could get to being an inmate of an asylum. But escaping on deck, you were guaranteed to be ready to face your cubicle again. After minutes in the open, you were soaked through and freezing. Compared, say, to the luxury of *Sheelagh*—even in her new hospital guise—*Dawn* was like being caught in a Viking longboat during a nasty hailstorm. On the plus side, she had three four-inch guns and four torpedoes, useful against

German destroyers, and went like a rocket—35 knots—which was indeed its "raison d'être."

The Germans had little to do in the Baltic except to keep the Russian Navy bottled up and to scare off any British which came to test the waters—like ourselves. So we had to keep our eyes peeled and spent most of the time on the bridge, scanning the horizon with our glasses. When May did spot smoke on the horizon, he tended to steer closer until he could satisfy himself that it was a harmless merchantman before resuming course. I found this a little illogical since if it turned out to be a German warship, it would then be in a position to identify us and possibly call out a flotilla.

Still, no one could accuse him of looking for a fight; he knew his main job was to avoid trouble and deliver Fisher's envoy to the land of the knout. Speed would work wonders in most situations, but we had to keep hoping the clear weather would continue. If it got misty, a German cruiser might loom up and blow us to atoms with one broadside. As a minnow amongst sharks, *Dawn*'s waterlogged crew couldn't afford to relax—and all for the sake of one uncomfortable passenger.

I said "Hello, chaps" a few times but got little response. Probably thought I was a spy. And nobody likes a spy skulking around with their secret codes and clandestine messages.

"Nice morning," I tried, tipping my cap, emerging on deck after breakfast one morning as the little ship tore on. And again, no one looked me in the eye. I might as well have been aboard the *Marie Celeste*.

But all things pass, and after churning up the Baltic in little time at all, I saw again St Petersburg and its port of Kronstadt without the crowds of 1914 and indeed with a neglected and embattled air about it.

I was greeted warmly at the dockside by Boris of Russian Naval Intelligence, who remembered me from our memorable battlecruiser visit in June. He took me for a vodka at his office as Captain May and company tied up and made ready for what might be a longish stay. I felt sorry for them, running a long and dangerous taxi service, but even in wartime St Petersburg, there were delights in store—if you knew where to look. And

British seamen had plenty of initiative when it came to looking for cheap booze and girls.

"As you know, I must see the Tsar," I told Boris. "An urgent message from Admiral Fisher. I can't tell you about it, so please don't even ask. My orders are that I must deliver the message in person even if the Tsar is in Vladivostok. No one else will do. I trust this has all been arranged."

Boris poured another Vodka. "Yes, but Tsar Nicholas is at the front," he said, "and is very occupied at a crucial stage with our armies. Couldn't you put it on paper? He's a voracious worker and would get to it within a day."

"Not a chance, Boris. What we are talking about is a plan devised at the highest levels and highly sensitive. It could shorten the war and save tens of thousands of Russian lives. It needs to be properly explained. That task has fallen to me, and I have just got as wet as a water rat coming here in person. Yes, it could have been sent in code or in a diplomatic bag. But my orders are to see the Tsar in person and answer any questions that might arise."

Drawing myself up to my full height, I added: "I am the Special Envoy to Fisher. If I can't see your Tsar for fifteen minutes, I might as well go straight back to England."

"Well, if what you say about your plan is true, it would be much welcomed—none more so than by the Tsar," said Boris, plainly impressed. "And you do well to trample over the usual diplomatic channels—they take so long. A train to the field headquarters leaves soon, at 6 p.m. I will escort you of course. Another vodka? And a spot of supper on the train? War hasn't trampled on our hospitality—yet. Meanwhile, it's still quite a consolation."

And so it was. Boris was a generous chap, and my head reeled from too many toasts as the train sped towards the Russian front. Supper was served, hot and quite delicious, to the accompaniment of further questions about the plan from my host.

"Can't you give me a hint?" He poured some more red wine.

"Nothing I would like better," I said. "But my express orders are to give a letter to the Tsar, get him to read it, discuss the plan involved, then wait for him to compose an answer, seal it, and give it back to me to return to the First Sea Lord in London."

"All right, you win, but you can't blame me for trying. Part of my job is to find out whether you are corruptible. It seems not. So you have just passed an important test. Now, shall we retire? It will be an early start in the morning."

I slept uneasily through the night—nerves, I suppose—and found myself in the morning approaching the distant rumble of heavy guns, constant and terrifying.

As the barrage grew in intensity, the train rolled up in a siding of the Moscow-Warsaw railway called Baranovichi which, Boris said, was midway between the German and Austrian fronts. The Germans, as he explained it, were most feared because they had a larger concentration of artillery and machine guns and well-trained troops, compared to which the Austrians were lightly equipped and had considerably less zeal. A dozen other army trains were surrounded by concentric rows of sentries mounting guard.

In one of them was the Tsar, presiding over tidal waves of troops, including the Cossack regiments, but without the fearful firepower possessed by the Germans. The strategy was to relieve pressure on the French after their gallant dashes to death on the Western Front and squeeze the German armies between two fronts. But after the disaster of Tannenberg, the French High Command was less convinced about the Bear.

And what if the Russians failed? It was unthinkable. Falkenhayn, the German Supreme Commander, would only then have the French and the still-comparatively-small British Expeditionary Force to deal with.

Boris, after showing endless papers and my own credentials, guided me to the right carriage guarded by Cossacks who stood with drawn swords, ready to sever hostile heads. I saluted them, received sidelong glances, and felt pleased that I had eventually reached my destination.

Last time I had seen Tsar Nicholas, he had appeared enervated, bored with an endless round of diplomatic visits and bombast. At our lunch aboard *Sheelagh*, Gwendoline Churchill had criticised him for being dim and retiring as the war clouds gathered last summer. But now he seemed in fine form; his face shone with rude health. He obviously relished being on firm ground among his troops, the sound of guns, and a daily round of life-or-death decisions. And he seemed pleased to see me, which augured well.

"Lieutenant Reginald Tucker of the Royal Navy reporting on behalf of the First Sea Lord, Admiral John Fisher," I said, saluting. "I have come directly from London, Your Highness, and ask for but a few moments of your time." At a glance, I took in my surroundings; they wouldn't have suited Jacky. The Lord of all the Russias favoured bearskins and oriental rugs. Inside the carriage were scores of icons which he must have venerated almost as much as life in the camp, which was called the Stavka, the ancient Russian name for the headquarters of the military chief.

"Welcome, lieutenant," said the Tsar. "You have come a long way at some risk to yourself. The least I can do is to listen to Lord Fisher's representative. Who would refuse to listen to the man who created the best Navy in the world? Coffee?"

I thanked him, handed over Jacky's letter, and explained the plan as best I could. The Grand Fleet would sail to the Baltic. Then 50,000 Russians would join 150,000 Tommies in a devastating attack on German's unprotected Pomeranian coast. Forced to reply, Germany would have to siphon off several divisions of her best troops, weakening their Eastern and Western fronts. I added that the element of surprise would be colossal. Did he agree?

"Impressive," said the Tsar, opening the envelope with the Admiralty seal and reading the letter carefully. "Fisher writes a good plan." Jacky had made sure it was typeset with lashing of capitals and red ink. "We appear to have everything to gain and little to lose. And we could possibly increase our own strength considerably. I have to tell you, Tucker, that sheer numbers of troops, while being carefully weighed in the balance, are of less importance to us than they are to your generals. I have millions at my command. And with your financial support, we could get more artillery and machine guns.

"Tell Lord Fisher that his plan meets with my approval, though I will of course have to let Grand Duke Nicholas, my Commander-in-Chief, have a look at the details. The Baltic being free of German warships as well as our troops fighting together in Pomerania? Excellent! Tell Lord Fisher my answer is a heartfelt Yes, with our thanks for his genius. I will draft a reply right away, though of course we could send it by wireless."

"If you don't mind, Your Highness, I believe I am expected to deliver a reply signed by you personally." The thought of further days and nights aboard *Dawn* so soon after arrival was appalling. "And I wondered first whether I might spend a day in St Petersburg, perhaps visiting your family, whom I met only last June?"

"Oh, yes, with Beatty, I remember. Quite a character. Tell me, why doesn't he wear his cap straight? A certain folie de grandeur, hum?" He smiled at his own perception.

"Oh, I'm afraid I haven't the faintest idea, Your Highness." He would hardly have expected a reply. I nearly said that Beatty at least looked distinctly more lifelike than some of his colleagues in the service, especially those at the Admiralty, who hadn't trodden a deck since 1900. Possibly reflecting on Tsarina Alexandra's unremitting manner, he did ask me about Ethel, who had certainly made an impression. I asked him about Tatiana who, it appears, was nursing the wounded at Tsarskoe Selo, converted into a hospital.

"What a life!" he said with feeling. "At her age, she should be going to balls and enjoying weekends in the country, the sort of life girls in Britain are still enjoying. If only you could take her back with you! But my dear wife would probably kill me for the very suggestion. And Tatiana would never go against her wishes. Nor would she entertain the idea of abandoning her duties. But perhaps after the war is won, as it must be." He beamed at the thought.

"So can I visit, Your Highness?" I was becoming understandably impressed with his vision, his humility, and his candour.

"Yes, and God go with you. I will allow you a day's rest. But I would like you back with your First Sea Lord as soon as you can. And now, lieutenant, we have a German army facing us, so if you'll excuse me, we have an attack to finesse, which may give them leave to doubt their ambitions."

"Good luck, Your Highness."

"Thank you, Tucker, for your brevity and wit and for undertaking a difficult journey with such potentially welcome news—I can see why Fisher reposes his trust in such a young officer. Just get safely back to London, that's all. There are plenty of Germans who'll try to stop you. And if they do, eat my reply!"

Escorted out to a waiting room in one of the other carriages, I had to wait not much more than an hour before an envelope with the royal seal was handed to me. A major part of the mission accomplished then. So far so good. But the train journey back to St Petersburg at noon seemed a lonely affair—until I heard a cough and a chink of glass from the service area, whereupon a distinguished gent entered my compartment and handed me a whisky.

"Thought you'd prefer this to vodka, lieutenant," he said amiably enough, introducing himself as General Sir Hanbury-Williams, Britain's military attaché to the Tsar.

"Nice to have company," he added. "And I thought you'd appreciate an escort back."

"Well, I hope you don't mind getting wet, Sir. My destroyer is like being in a permanent thunderstorm. Swimming might be preferable."

"I can imagine. No, sadly I am stuck in Russia for the duration. But every now and then, I break out of the headquarters, where the Tsar is as happy as a sandboy, and grab a few days in St Petersburg. Days off from school—remember that? Too much exposure to the Tsar and his staff can get you down, the prospects are not good."

"For the Russians, Sir?"

"Yes, they'd have had much better chances at Waterloo—cavalry in their thousands and old-fashioned rifles. This war is going to be fatal to

Russia. The best defence is this barbarous winter climate. And then there's the political instability which is mirrored in Germany but much nearer the surface here. Revolution everywhere from Liverpool to Chicago, the difference being that we and the Yanks are well on top of it with our police coshes. Here, things are more knife-edged."

"The Tsar wished I could take his daughter Tatiana back to London—perhaps to show off the more civilised side of Russian life," I blabbed.

"Well, the last I heard, she was up to her armpits in gore at the Tsarina's military hospital. Good luck." And he beamed with evident sincerity. He must have guessed I was on a mission of some importance but didn't press me.

Our servant arrived with the kind of lunch most ordinary Russians would have killed for: pickled herring, roast beef, Yorkshire pudding, potatoes, and a bottle of claret, the favourite of the Russian staff, after which Hanbury-Williams drifted into a long sleep, no doubt trying to forget his imminent return to the Russian HQ and the magnificent bravery and fatal lack of modern weaponry of its troops—that, or to avoid further conversation with a mere lieutenant.

And so I gazed out of the window at the unfolding vastness of Russia—mile after mile of snow-bound fields and copses with occasional signs of activity. Groups of soldiers were huddled around roaring fires, trying to keep warm, quite possibly lost—just a few out of five million poor, God-fearing souls now under arms in a world gone mad. Worse than being half-drowned on *Dawn*. I wondered what they were saying.

"If it gets any colder than this and we fall asleep, we might never wake up."

"Bloody good idea."

"Wish we had some fucking vodka."

"Only one clip of frozen bullets between me and Berlin. The bastards don't stand a chance."

I had another go at the claret, one too many. Certain headlines began to etch themselves on my mind, as though I was in the grip of narcotic chemicals or overweening bravado. In the style of the time, they were all triple-deckers.

NAVAL LIEUTENANT MEETS TSAR NICHOLAS AND EXPLAINS NEW THIRD FRONT
Mercy dash to Russia with new Fisher plan
pays off for young veteran of Dogger Bank
"Knew he was going to succeed," says First Sea Lord.

Possibly *The Times* and then the *Liverpool Daily Post*:

FISHER'S RUSSIAN ENVOY IS BIRKENHEAD MAN
Young lieutenant in Baltic destroyer visit Tsar's HQ
Mercy dash to visit Russian wounded before return to London

I could imagine Margaret agog over that one. Very few had a pair like Margaret, I reminded myself, even if they were as difficult to conquer as the peak of Everest. I shook myself and reached for the pot of coffee. I must stop thinking of myself as some kind of hero. At Dogger Bank, I'd simply been lucky. And now I was Fisher's envoy, cosseted, saluted, fed, watered, and even addressed by the Tsar of all the Russias, who—to the freezing soldiers out there in the bleak fields—loomed as large as God himself, even if they did hate the system. Entering an apparently endless pine forest, I drew a picture of *Lion* with its three funnels and eight guns in the condensation of the window, but it rapidly dribbled away into a wet smudge.

Who cared? The events of today would be forgotten a month hence; in due course, *Lion* would be melted down to make pots and pans, and dust would settle like the eternal Russian snows on biographies of Tsar Nicholas II. A photograph of yours truly would decorate the mantelpiece of new generations of Tuckers who would beam fondly at it in their ignorance and innocence, when Tucker's Sausages had become nationally famous and as relentlessly advertised as Pear's toilet soap. Margaret would grow wrinkled and grey, and Greta would go to the place where old prostitutes go—a bedsit overlooking the sea in Colwyn Bay. And what would become of Tatiana?

Fame would of course be pleasant, rather like old Vladimir's £10,000, but how long would either last? The onset of sleep would not provide the answer, but it provided some solace as the pines continued to whip by as numerous as the legions of Russian dead in East Prussia, their botched invasion in the first month of the war. No wonder Samsonov, their leader, had stolen away into the endless marshes and woods and blown his head off. All very tragic, but you shouldn't suicide because of the lack of Krupp guns. He should have changed his name, buggered off to America, and become a Mississippi gambler, ending up owning a big spread in Texas.

Could the Tsar really mean that he would like Tatiana to become a London debutante? Probably not—but by that time, I'd be back on *Lion*, exchanging insults with Highet, who was then, as I found out later, trying to carry out Sir John French's designs at Neuve Chapelle on the Western Front in Winston's jolly "exchange programme" between the army and the navy.

Meanwhile, was I on a wild goose chase? I wondered. As in the trenches, when a withering barrage lifted and the whistles blew, would my heart sing as I clambered out to advance, then be stitched in half by machine-gun bullets before I had gone the length of a cricket pitch? Between the generals and admirals of both sides, the only certainty was the impertinence of skylarks and seagulls on a clear, bright new day of battle. To fly, to sing was the answer. And let the devil take the hindmost.

"Tucker?" The voice of Hanbury-Williams brought me back to reality.

"Sorry," he said. "I was asleep myself. Jolly good lunch though, wasn't it? But it suddenly occurred to me, how are you going to get to the Catherine Palace to find the young grand duchess?"

"Well, last time I went with Admiral and some of his staff, all went for lunch in a horse-drawn gold carriage. This time I was just going to get a motor taxi from the train station."

"By jove, you're a bit wet behind the ears. It's a military hospital now. You're not in London now, Tucker, and you're not wounded. And there are guards all over the place."

"What are they going to do—shoot me? I would qualify to go to the hospital then, wouldn't I?"

I was actually extremely keen to see Tatiana. I had obtained her father's permission, and if anyone tried to stop me, woe betide them. Hanbury-Williams saw the dangerous gleam in my eyes.

"No, calm down, Lieutenant, but you will require clearance. You can't just bowl along there in a cab and knock on the door. You might well be arrested, and what would happen then?"

"Well, you better advise me what to do—which you're going to do anyway."

And so he did—which meant more infernal time. Arriving in St Petersburg, we stopped at his office, where he dictated a letter to his secretary, signed it with a flourish, put it in an envelope, and sealed it with wax. A taxi drew up outside as he was completing this business.

"And now you have proper clearance—stamped and sealed on behalf of His Majesty's British Government—which should get you through the entire Russian Army if necessary. Now, Godspeed, lieutenant."

CHAPTER 24

NOT MANY HEARTS were singing in the Catherine Palace which had been converted into a huge and draughty hospital, one of scores operated under the patronage of the Empress. From a palace devoted to aristocratic pleasures, it was now given over to pain. Every day trains full of the wounded—groaning, feverish, and facing amputations—arrived from the front. And somewhere among the army of helpers was Tatiana, the girl whose effect on me was a curious weakening of the knees and a light-headedness I couldn't quite fathom. Or was it that I simply liked her innocence and slightly dotty sense of humour? The latter could hardly be in evidence in this dreadful place, more like an abattoir than a hospital.

Up and down the alleyways between beds I went, from floor to floor, trying to find her. At last I did. She didn't see me at first; the grey eyes were kindly focussed on a standard bearer with smashed legs which she was attempting to bind up.

"Let me help you," I said. And I stretched the bandage, allowing her to bind it more tightly as the poor bastard howled in pain. "He'll be all right soon, with God's grace. Haven't you got any morphine?"

She looked up at me.

"If only. And who the devil are you?"

Oh well, nothing like making a lasting impression. "Your Royal Highness met me when some ships of the British fleet visited here last June. You took me to see Rasputin."

"Oh yes of course. Forgive me, but happy memories tend to evaporate in this hellhole."

"Will you do me the honour of dining with me tonight—forget this carnage for a few hours? I've just seen your father to discuss a new plan, and he said it would be all right if I saw you. Then I'm off back to England."

The moans and screams were rising as if from the gates of Bedlam. Tatiana looked around her in disbelief. She looked right on the edge of screaming herself, but the royal poise prevailed as she made her mind up.

"Very well, lieutenant. I would be delighted to join you. And you can tell me about this plan you've been seeing Papa about."

"It's top secret, Your Royal Highness."

"Not to me, it isn't. Have care, lieutenant, or I'll put you in one of these beds and cut your foot off. Then you'll know what it's like to fight in Russia." She giggled with a hint of hysteria. From one of the operating theatres came more screams.

"I have fought a major battle at Dogger Bank. So I don't think that would be very fair."

"How very odd. I think I have a bank myself in St Petersburg, don't you know? Never heard of Dogger Bank. Anyway, I thought the British Navy just went around getting everyone drunk and waving their guns at the nearest wireless station, then having races with each other."

She tittered again. "Sorry, but there's little chance of laughter here. Not very funny having half your head blown off."

"No. Actually, your Royal Highness, the Grand Fleet is extremely dangerous. We have races with the Germans, then when we get within range, we open fire and sink them, which stops them from making a mess of the Russian fleet."

"Have we not got a jolly good navy?"

"Up to a point, Your Highness."

"Well, they seem quite pleased with themselves."

That's because they're completely bottled up and never go to sea, I nearly said. It was plain that working in the slaughterhouse of the hospital had made her dottier than ever and, to me, oddly more attractive. Agreeing to pick her up later, I went to town to have a jar or two with Hanbury-Williams and asked if his man could dab the bloodstains off my jacket.

I picked her up in a cab at eight o'clock, noting the white dress with a black sash she had worn on our visit, which now, given the changed circumstances, seemed an age ago. She wore a silver and diamond tiara and an elaborate broach to denote her royal status—not that anyone would be in doubt of that. At Hanbury-Williams's suggestion, I had chosen The Contant, the heavily ornate restaurant with gilt everywhere where the squadron had been entertained on the first night of their visit. On the walls, famous battle scenes vied with waiters threading their way through the tables.

A string quartet played and sang. During their intervals, a young man of prodigious gifts played the piano. There was no sense that this was the swansong of Russian aristocracy and the upper class. But that is exactly what it was. Some of the regimental uniforms were theatrical to the point of absurdity, straight from Borodino.

"How nice you look," I said as we sat down.

"No, I don't. Working with people dying all around me for ten hours a day has made me feel pale and haggard. If I don't catch some fatal infection soon, it will be a miracle. And actually you, lieutenant, could look better if your uniform was properly pressed. Give your servant a good beating and put him on bread and water!"

"Too busy. Sorry, Your Highness—no reflection on you."

"Yes, too busy working. Clothes aren't everything. Just look at most of these preposterous pansies," she added, waving her arms around imperiously. "While I am bandaging up poor wretches from the front, they are sleeping off hangovers and making elaborate arrangements for lunch, where they meet their friends and gossip about how the war's going, blah, blah, blah, and much more importantly, who's been seen with who, and old so-and-sos gone bankrupt and shot himself in his hunting lodge and whether Spring will be earlier this year. If I had my way, some of them would be lucky to see the Spring."

She had grown even paler at the thought of the fate she would like to dole out to such miscreants. "Meanwhile, father is in a forest clearing, enduring the privations and dangers of the army. They make me sick." The latter sentiment was expressed with such vehemence that heads turned from several tables, bowing in recognition of the Tsar's spirited daughter—and receiving a knife-like glare in reply.

"It's just the same in London," I said in consolation, "all gossip and pigs in the trough," as our food arrived.

"Show the overdressed pansies and ladies of St Petersburg an ordinary soldier bleeding like a stuck pig, and they'd go into a permanent faint." She looked around the restaurant and pointed out some likely specimens.

"I wish you'd come to England with me—an emissary for Russia."

"What?"

"Your father said he thought it would be a good idea."

"Thank you, Reginald, but I must decline. It's nice of father, but I'm needed here. And I'm not a very good sailor. But when the war's over . . . who knows?" The time seemed to pass so quickly as we ate an excellent dinner and talked about everything under the sun. She pressed my hand and smiled, then looked over my shoulder. "Oh, dear, here comes that devious old attaché of yours, Handbury something. Hope it's not bad news for you."

Hanbury-Williams took his hat off as he approached with an aide.

"Revised orders, Tucker. You've got to leave right away. *Dawn* sails in less than an hour—Admiralty orders. So sorry."

"Good God, we haven't even had our coffee. You know who I am, don't you?" said Tatiana.

"Apologies, Your Royal Highness. But Tucker has vital information from your father for Admiral Fisher."

"Yes, and he hasn't told me what it is. What thieves in the night, daggers in the ribs! If you can't trust me, who can you trust?"

"Your Highness, it is more than my reputation is worth to divulge the barest outline of our plan to the Angel Gabriel. But we have a car waiting, plenty of room. I am sure Tucker would love you to come and wave him off."

"Yes, I would," I said. I'd half expected him to shorten the Tsar's grant of a day's leave to practically zero. Behind it all was undoubtedly Jacky's manic impatience and a large helping of politics.

"Oh, very well." Tatiana scowled. "But I must be back at the palace for the midnight shift."

"A driver and car will be at your disposal," said Hanbury-Williams.

Then we were bowling along towards the docks. We stopped, and I saw *Dawn* and Captain May on the bridge relighting his pipe; an icy Baltic wind was starting to blow along the quayside.

I turned to Tatiana. "If this plan comes off, I may see you sooner than you think. Sorry about dinner." The only thing I was pleased about in the circumstances is that the diplomatic corps was left having to pay the bill, including a particularly expensive bottle of vintage champagne.

She was looking at me closely. A car horn honked. Then she cupped my head in her hands and kissed me. Bliss . . .

But *Dawn* was ready to cast off. I opened the car door and jumped down on deck.

"Take care, Reginald" came the clear voice from the quayside as she waved me off.

I went down to the stern. "And you!" I shouted, my heart pounding, as we boiled away into the night.

I went to see May, who kindly gave me a large Scotch and saw me to my cubicle.

And at the same time, German Navy HQ received a wireless signal from a spy in St Petersburg that a British destroyer had just left St Petersburg heading south. Its course and speed, it was decided, indicated that an engagement by four light cruisers would be appropriate around 7 a.m. with almost certain success. The orders were duly wirelessed in code to the nearest light cruiser squadron.

I wasn't home yet.

CHAPTER 25

THE MORNING MIST had been nicely hiding us. Then it lifted. And from the deck, I saw our reception committee astern: four purposeful light cruisers flying their black-and-white flags. And they were legging it—you could tell from their high bow waves and the dense smoke billowing from their funnels. Commander May invited me on to the bridge, looking astern with his glasses. "Now what are they when push comes to shove? They look a bit dangerous for my liking." I hoisted up my own glasses and took a closer look.

"Bit new to me," I said, trying to sound unimpressed. "I think they're a new class with six inch guns and a dozen torpedoes. They outgun us, but we've got them on speed. Their maximum is 32 knots. We've got 35, but I bet you could run her up to 38 knots if you tried."

"Not for long," said May. "Burning out the engines would leave us a sitting duck."

"Flat out until we lose them," I said, getting quite anxious.

"Can't fault that," said the commander with a smile. "But let's see if we can disable at least one of them with a torpedo before we go. Okay with you?"

"Why not?" I said, hoping he knew what he was doing. And he barked a few orders down the speaking tubes. Seconds later, the helm was over, and the ship began to circle around towards the German vessels, which were travelling in line abreast. They started shooting; the shell splashes fifty yards short. We replied with the four-inchers, which didn't have the range. But now we were facing the flank of the nearest ship and in position for a good torpedo shot.

"Shoot!" bellowed May as we reached the optimum angle, and four tin fish—our full complement—dived in towards the German. And damn me if one of them didn't hit, causing a huge detonation and punching a fair-sized hole in her hull, just below the bridge. The ship took in water fast and—a bonus—the light cruiser on her beam had to peel off to rescue the crew also putting herself out of the race.

This left just two light cruisers still in pursuit. They were shooting well, but May knew what he was doing, swerving all over the sea like a madman. One German shell nearly sheared off our rudder, which would have made us totally defenceless. Another roared out and exploded close to the hull, nearly turning us over. I cannoned into the commander on the tiny bridge, and when the ship righted itself, May was shouting at a sailor clinging to the starboard rail.

"Any water getting in there?"

"No, sir—it was a lucky one" came the reply.

Our four-inchers, their crews highly exposed behind flimsy-looking gun shields, kept firing, and for a short time, they were getting the range—and some hits. Then some splinters took two of the crew down on the stern gun. The weapon was still working but was no longer being sighted.

"I'm supposed to be a gunnery expert—of sorts," I told May as I slid down, nearly losing my footing on the slippery deck, and took position at the gunsight, a single lens with cross hairs. Another shell was coming up the deck tube and was rammed in the breech. Aiming just over the bridge of the nearest German, I rapped out: "Shoot." The shell sailed over the ship, twenty feet too high. The gun crew knew what they were doing, but did I? "Ready," the man nearest me said as he closed the breech again.

"Down a bit. Steady. Shoot!" I repeated and was pleased to see a burst right at the stem of the forward six-inch gun, the crew scattered and out of action. Then one more, which fell short, demonstrating that in a stern chase, there is no defence better than superior speed. The ship we had hit fell back, and we were drawing away from the final opponent. Eventually, the gunfire died away. Thank God for a few extra knots when the chips are down.

Up on the bridge, May was on the navy phone. "Good shooting," he said with a smile. "And very good handling," I replied.

"Too early for the champagne though," he added. "The damage report isn't good. Few things wrong down below. I drove her flat out for too long. We won't last until England unless we put in somewhere, in Flanders, and botch up some repairs and appropriate some fuel. But I can't guarantee getting you all the way back home."

He thought for a moment. "If I was in a hurry, lieutenant, I'd contact the nearest aerodrome, say lots of mumbo jumbo about Lord Fisher, desperate mission, etc., and they'll give you a plane and pilot. These Flying Corps types are immune to discipline—they'll do anything for a laugh, officially or unofficially. Might cost you a case of Scotch, but I'm sure Jacky would sign with one of his famous chits."

I stared him up and down in admiration. "May, you are tremendously good value. You should have your own battleship."

"Thanks." And he disappeared below into the wireless hutch.

Meanwhile, we plunged on, seeing one German cruiser which gave us a couple of salvoes from his forward turret which fell short by 500 yards and then gave up. Thank God he didn't know about our limping engine.

Still, we were making headway and had been droning on for an hour or so when May eventually came back on deck. I guessed we were now just passing Belgian territorial waters—enemy waters—and opposite the fighting zone of northern France.

"Wireless had taken a bit of shaking—why are they such frail devices?—but I think it's sorted." We were moving towards the coast, evidently a friendly port. "There'll be one of these maniacs from the RFC waiting for you. So get ready—and good luck!"

All seemed ready for Fisher's envoy. A boat rowed out just beyond the quayside, and I clambered aboard, looking up at May. "Thanks for everything, commander. And get home safely. I don't want to have you on my conscience."

"Well, I just hope the fella knows how to fly." He smiled. "Or you'll be on mine. Good luck and clear skies be with you, lieutenant."

At the quayside, I was met by a representative of the new service, a knight errant in brown uniform, boots, and leather flying helmet called Lieutenant Barnsworth. At this stage of the war, fliers weren't regarded all that seriously since they couldn't inflict much damage—particularly on steel monsters like battlecruisers—but there was certainly something romantic about being a Knight of the Air.

"Climb aboard, admiral," he said, pointing to a waiting taxi. "We'll soon have you sorted out. Shouldn't take long to the airfield." He offered me a sip from his flask. "Glad you like a drink," he added. "We generally toss teetotallers out at 10,000 feet. Now, straight to the plane while we've still got a bit of light, then down for the night in a field and start first thing in the morning."

"Can't you fly at night?" I asked.

"No bloody fear. Can you? From what I know of the Senior Service, you chaps don't exactly like groping around in the dark either."

"You're right there."

"Just one thing," he said, fixing me with a stare and taking another swig. "Have you flown before?"

"Er, no. But it can't be worse than riding."

"Much worse! But seriously, if we meet opposition, I'll be all over the bloody place. So hang on." He grinned, but his hard eyes betrayed him. The RFC was not all fun—death or survival was measured in seconds. As in the trenches, the first two weeks could be fatal.

We entered the airfield, a fenced-off collection of sheds and tents with glum-looking French guards in their horizon-blue overcoats at the gates, then up to the plane, a Sopwith 1 1/2 Strutter painted in mid brown with the RFC roundels on the wings and fuselage. Barnsworth pointed up to the Lewis Gun in the observer's position. It was mounted to a tubular alloy ring—the Scarff Mounting Ring, I was to learn—which allowed it to be swung around ninety degrees.

"Can you use that thing?"

"Yes," I said—and I had, at Dartmouth. "A big drum lasts about 48 seconds. Can do."

Then we were aboard. The ground crew heaved the plane into position and rotated the prop, then stood away to avoid the wash of air as the engine came to life and the frail contraption of wood and canvas began to move. After a very short and bumpy ride, we were in the air. Barnsworth had lent me a sheepskin coat, but the air was ice-cold through the leather headgear as we climbed. Soaring upwards in the late afternoon sky, I saw the sea in the distance where *Dawn* was bashing on, trying to get home against the odds. May deserved a medal, and when—if?—I next saw Jacky, I would make sure he got one.

Hardly a bird was in the sky, let alone any squadrons of Jerries. Then thousands of feet below, a German spotter plane appeared, probably on some boring reconnaissance mission. I hoped Barnsworth would leave well alone, which he did, avoiding a possible call-up to the nearest fighter base. We still weren't using parachutes—unlike the Germans—because our generals believed it was better for outnumbered pilots to burn to death for three to four minutes or shoot themselves rather than live to fight another day. The offending brass should be landed behind enemy lines, then sprinkled with machine gun bullets as they ran for home.

Still, after another hour's flight, there was no danger as the sun set, and in the peace of a rising meadow, we landed and parked the plane beside some trees.

Barnsworth produced a picnic basket—bread, cooked meat, and red wine—and we ate heartily.

"And your opinion of flying, battleship man?"

"Love it," I said. "So far . . ."

"So far so good, eh? Well, let's hope our luck holds."

We then hauled a tarpaulin out of the plane and bunked down. I lay awake for a short time, going over events. Was there a distant rumble of guns? Probably, but in the First World War, you could never escape the guns. Crouching in some muddy hellhole fifty-odd miles away, some poor infantrymen, either our side or theirs, was being subjected to a routine night artillery "hate," which would certainly keep them awake and their nerves trembling nicely until the dawn attack. How fortunate to be away from that ten-mile-wide strip of lunacy called The Front.

The feeling of peace lasted as day broke, and Barnsworth brewed up some coffee and fried a couple of eggs each. Then we were up and away again. You can keep your gypsy caravans, motor cars, and the sea. Just float upwards, chase along at a hundred miles an hour, then flutter down anywhere.

We climbed high above the protective cumulus. And then it broke, leaving us perched in a blue sky and available for anyone to take a shufti— as they inevitably did.

Barnsworth turned to get my attention, then pointed down.

I felt a stab of abdominal pain—pure terror. Two Fokker Eindeckers, fast single-seat fighters, were climbing, hoping to fry us alive. One of them kept on steadily towards us, the other soared upwards, almost vertically. Barnsworth turned again; I could barely hear him through the noise of the engine and the wind howling through the struts and cables. "Watch that second bastard." I heard him test his forward gun, a Vickers mounted on the upper wing, its belt folded into a metal box.

My stomach heaved as he then executed a textbook loop and turn, fetching up below and just behind the first opponent. Then he moved in so close that you could have almost jumped from one plane to the other and gave it one long burst from the Vickers. The Fokker kept flying straight for a while, then began a shallow dive. As we moved alongside, I was relieved to see why—the pilot was slumped over his controls, either badly injured or dead. The other Fokker had disappeared.

I was lost; the horizon kept see-sawing. Giddy, I checked my safety harness. I had not, caught up in the excitement, learned the most important lesson of a Western Front flyer, which was to automatically keep quartering 360 degrees of the sky for trouble. Then suddenly, I became aware of chunks of leather being punched out of my seat surround. The rear leading edge of the upper wing was also being bitten away, fabric stretching in the 100 mph wind. You are very exposed in the observer's seat. Sure enough, a bullet nicked my neck; I could feel the warm blood running down below my collar.

It stung like hell. And then the second Fokker reared up right behind me. Feeling very exposed, stomach churning, I stood up, aimed, and fired—no deflection, just a long straight burst right into his engine. But he danced away sideways and upwards, giving me a burst as he went, which tore off some of the tailplane fabric.

Wrestling with the mounting ring, I gave him another long burst, which connected with his upper wing. Then—damn and blast—the ammo gave out, and I had to duck down and rummage in the unprotected cockpit for another drum. He was right behind me again. Praying I would avoid a chestful of bullets, I pulled the machine gun down towards me, snapped on the new drum, then popped up again like a jack-in-the-box, and fired about forty rounds into his engine and then above that to where the pilot was sitting. Glycol started pouring out of the engine; flames began licking around the cockpit. The fighter nosedived. Barnsworth gestured as it spun downwards, hit the ground, and burst into flames. He then gave me the thumbs up as he dived after the first German, which had landed in a field close to woodland.

"Got to get some evidence," he said as we touched down and switched off. "Bit cold-blooded, but otherwise, the kill won't count."

The downed pilot was still alive but in terrible shape, bleeding badly and in severe pain from hits in the shoulder, abdomen, and thigh. He wouldn't last. "Bitte," he pleaded, pointing his index and thumb, pistol fashion, at his forehead.

Barnsworth toyed with the toggle of his service revolver. "No," he said. "We can't go around killing helpless enemies."

"I thought we did that all the time," I said.

"Well, I know I did this to him—just like you put paid to the other fella—but I'm not up to giving him the coup de grâce. Nein." Barnsworth walked back to the Sopwith, returning with his flask of whisky.

"Drink," he said to the dying pilot.

"Danke," said the German, drinking deep, then trying to hand it back.

"Keep it," said Barnsworth. "Might keep you alive."

He then pulled out a knife and sliced off the fabric showing the Fokker's squadron number. Standing back as he took a few seconds to claim his trophy, I was suddenly aware of a faint noise, a tremor in the ground—and was that the neighing of a horse? Then I saw them, a group of riders with silver helmets—a German cavalry patrol less than a mile away and coming for us at a gallop. One or two of them were firing their carbines—wide, but not for long.

"Shit!" Barnsworth said. "Get the prop, quick."

I didn't need to be told; I cranked the propeller, scrambled into the back seat, cocked the Lewis, and fired a burst over the heads of the nearest riders. Given the Sopwith's not-altogether-racing start, some of the men pressed on very fast, coming almost alongside the plane. I'd seen enough human blood for one day, so I shot the horses and watched the riders tumble harmlessly on to the grass.

And then we were airborne and climbing into a sheltering bank of cloud.

"Good, eh?" I think Barnsworth said above the engine's roar. "Who'd be on a horse when you can be in one of these things?"

"I'll never ride a horse again," I shouted.

"Quite right. You'll never get to heaven on a horse. Got a chance in a Sopwith."

CHAPTER 26

WE FINALLY LANDED at 19th Squadron—no more lurking Germans, which was fortunate—with my rescue to celebrate. Any excuse would do in the RFC; the champagne was soon opened, and the first of many glasses drunk. In this respect, the camp was quite civilised even though it looked like a miniature of one of Russia's smelly, ramshackle villages. A medic thoughtfully produced a large sticking plaster for my neck, which staunched the bleeding and increased the impression of amateur heroics, which the chaps seemed to admire—full marks for downing a Fokker from the back seat with an ordinary Lewis.

But reality rapidly encroached. I was speedily handed a message from Jacky Fisher, which predictably urged me to proceed with all speed. How did he know where I was? But I could have bet on it really. Jacky was the boss; he would have found me under a haystack in Upper Silesia.

"Heard you took rather a nasty sting out of Barnsworth's tail," the Squadron Leader said. "I'm Captain Duff. Well done. Actually, we're one or two short at the moment—fancy a transfer?"

I took a long gulp of fizz. "Until you get your planes armour-plated, no thanks."

"Oh, dear—but you might change your mind after the lads have finished with you," he said, tapping the side of his nose and giving a sidelong glance at two chaps who seemed familiar.

"Aren't you supposed to be at Rosyth?" asked Chips. "Captain, this man's a deserter, miles from his post. He's got us all fooled."

"As he's from the Navy, would it be in order if we flog him round the squadron before we send him back under close guard?" said Ian.

"Captain Duff," said I, "I know these clowns are imposters. You might think otherwise, but they've never flown an hour in their lives. They're only here for the beer."

"And the wine," said Chips.

"And the girls," said Ian.

"Where are you staying? Want to share our tent, complete with home comforts like a paraffin heater?" Chips asked.

"I think not. Isn't there somewhere around here that's pest-free?"

"Well, if you survive the night's goings-on, I'll find you somewhere in squadron HQ," said Duff, pointing to a ramshackle wooden building which was straight out of Tom Sawyer. "Come on and have a clean-up. Drinks in the mess starting at 6.30 p.m., followed by dinner at eight. After that, we muster all the motor transport available and roar off to have some fun in the next village—keep forgetting the name of the place. Do you ever get that?"

I looked closely at him, the slight tick in his cheek. For all his apparent good humour, this was a man under considerable strain, possibly right on the edge.

I looked at Chips and Ian. They knew what I knew. And they shuffled around a bit. Then we parted, and I watched them return to their damp-looking tent, which looked dispiriting and uncomfortable. Those who daily courted danger deserved better.

My introduction to the pilots, full of juvenile jokes about the navy which I have mercifully forgotten and other schoolboy antics, went down famously. Then we all sat down at trestle tables and started throwing buns at each other in time-honoured fashion. It was a bit like *Lion*'s wardroom converted into a scout hut, but the food was better—fish soup, steak with all the trimmings, apple pies with cinnamon, about a litre of red wine each, then the port and brandy. By now things were getting out of hand, with pilots falling off their seats, saying "Happy landings" and "Going down—ladies' underwear!" And some ass kept leaning over to me and asking: "I say, do you have to be able to swim to join the Navy?"

Everyone then spilled out and clambered into cars—not that they were in any fit state to drive. I got into an old Citroen with Chips and Ian.

"Wait," said Chips, "until you see Madame Tilly's. It beats Maggie's in Liverpool into a cocked hat. Mind you, I'd give anything to see Greta's Kaiser Bill act again. Did she do that one for you? I forget."

"No, I got the 'Doctor's Careful Examination.' Felt quite restored afterwards."

"No doubt. But this place is in another league. Makes Maggie's look like a funeral parlour, which is oddly appropriate for pilots in this bloody show." He swerved to avoid a nocturnal fox, crashed the gears, and grazed a ditch.

"Have another drink," I said.

"Never kill anything if you can avoid it," he scolded. "I only fire at the Hun because he's trying to get me. We're worse than animals."

And then we were in the main square. "There," said Ian, pointing at a substantial stone-built house with red curtains across the windows which was almost opposite the local church. "Nearer, my God, to Thee," he added as we parked and marched inside.

It was complete bedlam. On a tiny stage, a fat accordion player was accompanying five comely girls with dresses cut to show a lot of leg and most of the bosom. Musically, it left a lot to be desired, but the girls bravely waded into the audience, sitting on laps and being as suggestive as you like. Everyone sat at huge round tables or simply milled around, with skimpily dressed waitresses taking orders. Everyone insisted on buying me drinks, which topped me up until, well, I was flying—or at least enjoying the earthbound RFC version of flying.

The accordion player then emitted his rendition of a fanfare, and Captain Duff tottered into the stage.

"In honour of our guest from the Senior Service, the 29th will now sing a musical tribute," he declared, slurring his words quite effectively. Some sheets were being passed around.

The accordion player let loose with the first few bars of La Marseillaise. Then the lads started to sing:

> "Let's say hooray for the Navy
> "Sailing up and down
> "What a sight to see is the Admiral
> "With his pants all falling down."

It got worse of course.

> "Oh the ship's going round in circles
> "But we're quite used to that
> "Hooray for the Navy
> "The ocean wave for me
> "Bonjour, monsieur
> "Je suis manure
> "Hooray for the Navy."

Huge applause followed this schoolboy effort, and I was then hoisted high and forced to drink a bottle of champagne at one go. With my head swimming, I thought it was very like a wardroom riot, except that Denise, one of the dancing girls, sat on my knee and started nibbling my ear.

Barnsworth was beside me, grinning like a polecat. "Better than the Navy, eh?" he said. Denise nibbled away. "I think you've got us in one important respect," I replied. Denise clamped my hand over her breasts and gave me a gentle tickle in the midriff.

He nodded. "Well, thank God for the Flying Corps. I suppose all this might seem excessive, but you can take a safe bet that one or two of us will fly through the Pearly Gates tomorrow morning. Good luck."

And then Chips came into view, grinning like a lunatic. "If I can find Ian . . ."

"He's under that table," I said.

"Well, it's dawn patrol for us tomorrow. Bit like school really—one minute you're ducking off and having a laugh, next you're chewing a pencil to shreds in some completely impossible exam."

"And tomorrow?"

"Artillery spotting—squirted at from the ground and liable to be jumped on by a Hun patrol."

"Take it easy."

"I used to," he said, taking a drink of whisky and looking me straight in the eye. "But then it's a good argument as to whether a careful pilot is in more danger than a reckless one. The newspapers have us flying winged steeds. The reality, as you now know, is that we are flying makeshift contraptions made by overworked girls in factories, which are difficult enough to get off the ground, let alone fly. Ah, well. See you for breakfast in the morning. And let's look forward to a pint at Ma Boyle's when the whole bloody circus is over."

We shook hands; he found Ian, and they staggered off into the French night.

The party was breaking up, and I would have gone too had Denise not continued to breathe "mon petit" into my ear. So I let her lead me upstairs into her bedroom. With probably three bottles of wine or more on board, I doubted that I could manage anything at all. But Denise had her ways; I was as randy as an alley cat, and in no time at all, she was on top of me. Funny, only eight hours or so ago, I'd been fighting for my life.

I must have slept until consciousness, marred by a monster hangover, burst in with the annoying fact that it was the cathedral quiet of 7 a.m. with no transport in sight. I kissed the slumbering Denise, tiptoed to the kitchen, pinched some croissants, and made a strong pot of coffee, then set off for the camp, not sorry for the walk of 2-3 kilometres. It was an ethereal morning, crisp and full of promise. I was still a bit pissed from the night before, which may have contributed to a carefree mood, a certain smugness, which—banishing my usual self-criticism—I allowed to linger. And the Tsar's letter still crackled in the inside breast pocket of my uniform.

My reverie didn't last long. From the next corner came a *toot-toot*, and Duff appeared in a nifty two-seater. I hopped aboard.

"Sorry to spoil your walk, but another Admiralty missive arrived in code. Here's the gist: 'Make utmost haste. If necessary, commandeer a Zeppelin. Speed is everything. Your report needed urgently—Fisher.'"

"Oh well, bang goes my weekend in the country."

"Have breakfast with us—starts 7.30 a.m. Chips and Ian should be back by eight. Then we'll sort out a car for you for the coast. By the way, jolly good show bagging Denise. She doesn't go with every Tom, Dick, or Harry."

"But she will entertain the Squadron Leader," I said, smiling.

"No comment."

Squadron HQ still looked as though a bomb had hit it after the previous night. A fair number of the red-eyed team were already tucking into bacon and eggs, ready to fly off after the dawn patrol had landed.

"How many back?" Duff asked the adjutant.

"Twelve, Sir. Just three more to go, including Chips and Ian."

A plane, burning, appeared over the hedge at the end of the field. It landed nose-heavy, the pilot popping out of his cockpit like a jack-in-the-box and landing on his head.

"Goner," said Duff, crossing it off his clipboard.

Another machine spluttered over the hedge, landed heavily, but taxied in without further ado.

"Ian," said the squadron leader, giving a broad tick to his clipboard. I could see Ian climbing out of his cockpit and coming towards us.

"I couldn't see Chips," he said, sipping a coffee. "Looked high and low. Then I ran out of ammo, and the fuel started to be a worry."

"We wait," said the Captain. "But let's have something to eat before it all runs out." And we lingered over our eggs until they congealed, drinking coffee, smoking cigarettes, and not for a moment taking our eyes off the end of the field.

"Bloody phone," said Duff as he was called into his office. It wasn't long before he returned.

"It's the worst, chaps. He was seen being chased by some Fokkers just behind the enemy lines. Then he was hit by some accurate flak and machine gun fire. He made it back to our trenches, then nosedived into a shell hole. Goner."

"Oh, shit," I said. Ian went pale and very quiet.

"I'm most sorry, but that's the reality here. We lose one or two pilots nearly every day. And in an hour, it starts all over again: a vicious circle of duty and death. I know it's a bit early, but I'm going to have a slug of brandy just to take the edge off. Anyone join me?"

We both nodded.

"That's the stuff." He swallowed a stiff one. "What a bloody awful war." He took another slug of brandy, and his hand shook as he poured it. He was obviously half-cracked.

"Damn," said Ian, gazing at the floor.

I felt dead. There was a *toot-toot* from a newly arrived car—my transport.

I was presented with a bottle of Scotch for the journey and a folded sheet of paper by Duff, who was now on his third brandy. "Take care," he said.

"Ian," I said to my friend. "This is no time for speeches . . ."

"No—let's you and I try to survive. I'll write to you on *Lion*. Au revoir, mate."

And so sitting in the open back seat as the car sped down the arrow-straight, tree-lined French roads, I took out of my pocket the sheet of song lyrics thoughtfully provided by the captain and sang out to the tune of My Bonnie Lies Over the Ocean—my own, and the RFC's, tribute to friends just gone.

> "Take the crankshaft out of my kidneys
> "Take the sparking plugs out of my brain
> "Take the tailplane out of my arsehole
> "And put me together again."

I took a big swig of Scotch, then another. And then I wept bitter tears for my lost friend. Gone for what? We were worse than animals, Chips had said. Too bloody right.

CHAPTER 27

THE REST OF the journey back to Blighty went quickly in a painful daze of grief and hangover. The drive to Calais, the Channel crossing, and the train trip up to London were a blur. Then, too soon for equilibrium to set in, I was in Fisher's office at the Admiralty, the brutality of destroyer action, airborne machine guns, and the loss of a friend receding and being insidiously replaced by the world of clicking typewriters, confidential memoranda, urgent phone calls, and barked instructions—strangely comforting after fending for myself.

Whether I was wholly safe under Jacky's wings, I would happily debate with anybody—in secret of course. But he greeted me like a long-lost son, then sat me down with an encouraging sherry and called in his private secretary to make notes.

I briefly explained the journey, the Tsar's pledge of support for the Baltic Plan, and his praise for Fisher himself. At this point, Jacky started swelling unduly with pride; I thought he'd burst. Then I handed over the Tsar's letter and said he thought the plan shouldn't wither on the vine.

"Does he, by Jove," said Jacky reading the letter and looking thoroughly pleased with himself.

"And he made a lot of the great togetherness and good, which would be achieved if our lads were fighting side by side with his chaps," I said.

"Could well be." But Fisher suddenly looked out of sorts. He shooed out his secretary and looked me straight in the eye.

"You don't seem very, er, confident, sir," I ventured.

"Nor am I. I'm very sorry, you done sterling work, but it looks at this moment that my Baltic Plan has about as much chance of getting off the ground as an ocean liner."

"Well, I expect the Pomeranians will be relieved, sir," I said foolishly.

"They would if they knew anything about it. Sometimes, Tucker, I think you're not quite there."

"Bit tired, sir."

"Phooey. The point is not about the people in Pomegranate Land—who gives a twopenny damn about them?—but about the powers that be here. And I am not relieved! I have Winston's half-hearted support. But Admiral Dewer is dead against and so is Oliver, the Chief of the Admiralty War Staff. Basically, they don't think you can cork up the Kiel Canal with mines. And they also think that the Grand Fleet and the armies involved would be too far from their bases. Admiral Bacon's in favour in a qualified sort of way—at least he thinks the idea shouldn't be shelved. But I've submitted the plan now to Prime Minister Asquith and haven't heard a peep—damned rude, if you ask me. He's kept it from the War Cabinet, and it looks to me that it has been well and truly sat upon."

"So my trip was a waste of time, sir?"

He stirred in his seat, the downward slope of his mouth hardening with determination. "I sincerely hope not. And your welcome news from the Tsar's woodland camp—showing his commitment—might well make all the difference." He didn't look very confident but was brightening all the same. "So right at this moment, we're off to see Winston. He must see this letter."

Then he grinned. "By the way, good show, Tucker. I hear you foolishly flew some of the way back with one of those lunatics from the RFC and downed an enemy plane. I think we're going to get you a medal for your troubles."

"Thank you, Sir. I'd be honoured."

"Precisely. And I bet you had a bit of fun with Princess Tatiana."

"Grand Duchess Tatiana. How did you know, sir?"

"Hanbury-Williams and I go back a long way. Sorry, but we had to get you back pronto. Now let's give the First Lord what for. And try and sound enthusiastic!"

We arrived at Winston's office to find him putting the stopper on a decanter of brandy. "Which way is the wind blowing, Bunty?" he asked keenly.

"Better, I think. In my mind, the Baltic Plan was being blown out of sight until Tucker here returned with a letter from the Tsar, saying his men couldn't wait to bowl down to Pomerania and help mow down some Huns," Jacky replied.

"Let's see then," Churchill said, taking the letter with its royal seal and reading attentively. "Excellent!" he said finally.

That made me feel a lot better, I can tell you. Jacky beamed. "So we go ahead, trample the critics, and prime the guns?"

Winston sipped his brandy and puffed contentedly on a newly lit cigar, deep in thought.

"Not precisely what I had in mind. What . . . er . . ."

"Tucker, sir."

"What Tucker enterprisingly obtained may be enough to do a considerable amount of damage without shipping thousands of Tommies out of the Western Front and committing the Navy to what one must describe as a risky adventure, to say the least."

"Oh, how so?" asked Jacky, bemused.

Winston pressed a buzzer on his desk. "Ask my Deputy Head of Naval Intelligence to step this way," he said into the intercom.

In less than a minute, there was a knock on the door. It opened, and there stood Colonel Rivington, eyes like gimlets, each hair on his moustache precision trimmed. He saluted.

"How difficult would it be to get a letter to somehow arrive at the door of the General Staff in Berlin?" Churchill asked.

"Well, we've got some very good agents in Berlin," said Rivington, "with immaculate cover. They have a much easier time than their German counterparts in London . . ."

"Ye-es. Make the mistake of reading a newspaper upside down on the Underground, and you're nicked within seconds."

"You're not thinking of blowing the whistle on the whole plan, surely?" said Fisher, horrified.

"Hold on, Bunty," said Winston, turning again to Rivington. "So placement of the letter in the right—or wrong—hands would be well-nigh 100 per cent certain?"

"That's the way I see it, sir." Rivington twigged me standing next to Jacky, and the corners of his mouth twitched a smile.

"And then, once the Hun calligraphers have compared the letter with others received from the Tsar and pronounced it genuine, Falkenhayn and company would have a genuine scare on their hands," said the First Lord, taking a swig of brandy, his eyes flashing with the speed of his remarkable insight. "The Kaiser would have to be consulted of course, and the whole snake pit of planners and strategists would expend huge amounts of useless staff time working everything out to the last redundant detail. There'd be considerable ship movements and a large holding force of troops diverted from the Western Front to defend the Fatherland—a victory for us and our phantom army without firing a shot."

He looked at Fisher, all smiles, and received a beam of approval. Then me. "Well, Lieutenant?"

"Brilliant, your Lordship," I said. "And brilliantly conceived and organised by Lord Fisher."

"Yes of course." And he eyed me closely for a few seconds.

"My orders, sir?" asked Rivington.

"Do it," commanded Churchill, handing over the letter. "Make a couple of very good facsimiles unless the original gets lost. Then do it as a matter of the highest priority with enough stealth to swat a fly. The pen mightier than the sword, eh, Bunty? And it's still your idea."

"Very good," said Jacky. "I usually prefer brute force, but if the Sausages get into a stew and divert major forces to fight a legion of ghosts, I can't say a word against it."

"What about telling the Tsar, sir?" I asked.

"Too risky," said Winston. "He's done his bit—though he doesn't know it. Besides, from what I know of it, Russian intelligence is as leaky as a sieve. His letter doesn't refer to timing or plans that could be tapped, but what it does do is indicate clear agreement. No, we keep the Bear in the dark."

And so it was done. When we got back to Jacky's office, he poured himself a Scotch and topped up my sherry. "Never give up, eh?" he said. But he was fretting. "That was a fair result and a very good one for Winston. With my Baltic Plan now sidelined but going ahead in theory, he can now return to beguiling everyone with his plans to force the Dardanelles and lay siege to Constantinople. And if I fight him over that—which I fully intend to—it will be seen as sour grapes from old Fisher. Still, brilliant idea to plant the letter. Didn't occur to me. Must be getting past it."

I laughed. "Actually, Tsar Nicholas told me to eat the letter rather than let it fall into German hands."

"Well, thank God you didn't."

Jacky looked as though he could use some encouragement.

"It all sounds like a good example of teamwork, sir."

"Teamwork!" he exclaimed. "Teamwork? You can't have teamwork with Winston. If he formed a soccer team, he would want to be goalkeeper, centre half, and centre forward! He rides, sometimes brilliantly—today's a good example—over anything that gets in his way. And now we are all to focus on the brilliant prospects unfolding in the Mediterranean. Still, anything that takes the pressure off the Western Front, I am bound to agree with."

"You seem to see eye to eye on most things, sir."

"Yes, but who gets the dirty work? Don't dare repeat this, but Beatty, for instance, will not take prisoners. After Dogger Bank—you were there— we had to do something about Moore. Beatty criticised but wouldn't touch him, nor that silly-ass Seymour, his Flag Lieutenant. Who acted? I did. Moore is now in charge of an ancient cruiser squadron off the west coast of Africa. Beatty is pleased. But it took me to do the dirty work. I've told you before, Tucker, if you find someone who's not up to it, sack 'em or at least put them out of harm's way. Better for everyone."

His Baltic Plan somewhat confounded, Jacky wasn't about to break into a dance, nor was I. Chips kept looming in my mind—Chips dead up in a stupid shell hole, his blonde hair bloodied, his body mangled. I had been lucky—surviving the battlecruisers' first encounters of the war, a destroyer action in the Baltic, a dogfight over France, and in my many encounters with Jacky, undoubtedly one of the most effective Sea Lords the Navy had ever produced. Love him—but don't ever cross him.

"Are you all right, Tucker?" he asked. "You seem to be in a dream."

"A friend of mine, sir, a pilot, took a fatal dive over the trenches."

"He's with God. And I think it's time that you forget all this, get your sea legs back, and make Beatty's acquaintance again before he forgets what you look like. And I think he's got something for you."

"Sounds good. Can I go right away, sir, if you don't mind?"

"Yes, lieutenant. I'll tell them you're on your way."

He got up, shook my hand, and put his arms round my shoulders.

"And one more thing, Tucker."

"Sir?"

"Keep driving forward! It's a mad war but it isn't half won yet, So full speed ahead, lieutenant, and keep me posted!"

And the old warrior opened his office door for me and even saluted as I started on the long journey back to *Lion*.

CHAPTER 28

A LONDON PEA-SOUPER. POLICE whistles and the cries of newsboys mingled with the honks of motor horns as a cold grey-brown London fog strangled London's traffic. "Get that bleedin' nag out of my way," roared my taxi driver, too old to serve but not too old to shout. Yet all this English madness was a homely contrast to the cruel blue horizons of St Petersburg and Northern France and even after Jacky's explosive last denial of my request for leave was extremely tempting.

But duty called; *Lion* awaited 400 miles north, and I was for King's Cross Station.

And from there to Scotland. Few cities can match the scything cold of Edinburgh in February. Wrapped in a roll-neck sweater, jacket, scarf, and greatcoat, I arrived in the late afternoon darkness, took a cab to South Queensferry, and as a chill westerly wind rippled the water around the squadron, climbed up the *Lion*'s companionway to the great teak main deck, sanded against the slippery frost. It was good to see Haddock waiting under the electric glare atop the steps. He took my luggage from the lighter man and smiled a greeting. But for some reason, he seemed agitated.

"Very good to see you, sir," he said a little breathlessly. "Welcome back. If we can hurry, Sir, your orders are to report at once to the Vice Admiral's stateroom in full dress uniform."

With no explanation for this tomfoolery, he then dashed aft to my cabin on Deck 2, where I found him solemnly brushing down my monkey jacket with its lieutenant's stripes.

I was irritated. After an interminable train journey from London, all I wanted was a hot bath, a few drinks, dinner, and an early night—in that order. Nothing else.

"Damn it, Haddock. What's this pantomime all about?"

"I don't know, Sir. But just as soon as you can."

Characteristic of Beatty, I thought as I struggled into the stiff formal attire. *He just liked things to happen now.*

But my nerves were starting their familiar hum. Could it be a full dress dressing down? Damn, it was probably that £250 railway special to London I'd signed for in Edinburgh and then conveniently forgot—enough to be cashiered and thrown into the brig.

Warmed up but with clammy hands and a sense of dread, I donned all the gear and marched right aft along the brightly lit main corridor of 2 deck, saluting the eternal Marine sentry guarding Beatty's cavernous quarters. He stood aside to let me pass, eyes straight ahead.

The waiting party looked up. With the great man were Secretary Frank Spickernell and Captain Chatfield. On the table between us lay not a court-martial sword pointing accusingly towards me but a dark-blue, gold-tasselled cushion and a medal. A sense of ceremony was in the air.

"Lieutenant Tucker," snapped Beatty in his official voice.

"Sir!" I said nervously as I wound up my best parade ground salute.

"It gives me great pleasure to present to you the Distinguished Service Cross for services to the Royal Navy, King, and Country and promote you to the rank of Lieutenant Commander, effective immediately." My heart was pounding with relief and shocked surprise.

Sometimes theatrical, Beatty was good at producing shocks; he certainly got me this time.

Spick and Chatfield were looking proudly at their pupil—I might just have rammed and sunk a submarine.

"Relax, Tucker," Beatty continued, sensing my discomfort. "You saved the life of that aristocrat in St Petersburg, making us the toast of the town, did some precarious spotting at Dogger Bank, visited the Tsar on a dangerous mission, helped sink a German light cruiser, and then, damn it, shot down a German fighter plane. You have served your country well. Now Captain Chatfield, please do the honours."

Chatfield pinned the medal to my breast and stepped back. Then he, Beatty, and Spick saluted.

"Champagne!" called out Beatty, his voice echoing round his great steel home at sea. All primed, his steward came in bearing a Jeroboam. "Thank you, sir, thank you, Captain, and thank you, Secretary," I said as we chinked glasses. *And thanks too*, I thought, *to Jacky Fisher*.

"At twenty-one . . ." began Chatfield a little stiffly, sounding like a headmaster.

"Twenty-two now, Sir."

"Very well. At twenty-two, Lieutenant Commander rank is very good going—and well deserved. I'm sure you'll cope with the extra responsibilities. And even if I and some of the older hands seem unreceptive at times, keep questioning the way we do things and looking ahead."

"Amen to that," said Beatty. He drained his glass and held it up for the steward to refill.

A question occurred to me, and I just couldn't help asking it, however naive and fatuous. "I should know, sir, but I've never been exactly sure what lieutenant commanders do."

Beatty's face twitched slightly. "Well, Captain?" he asked, looking a little puzzled himself.

"Well, they can con the ship, Sir, if the admiral, captain, and commander are all injured. And they can order more men about than a mere lieutenant. Instead of just a patrol, they can tell a whole company to go and get themselves killed or shin up something."

"There you are then," said the Admiral, having a good tug at his champagne. He smiled his film actor smile. "Don't worry, Tucker, it's just an amplification of where you've been before. Follow orders unless they're insane—in which case, you do the opposite. If successful, the Sea Lords will applaud your initiative. If not, prepare to be relegated to some dull training establishment on the Yorkshire Moors or even court-martialled for disobedience. Who said 'Any fool can obey orders'?"

"I think it was Lord Fisher, Sir. He said it to me on a train after we first met."

"Sounds like Jacky to me—always was one for ditching the rule book once out of sight of land." He looked knowingly at Chatfield. "Wonder what he thinks of Jellicoe's new Grand Fleet Battle Orders, which—if they grow much bigger—will be almost as long as the Old Testament. Anyway, Tucker, as you're under our command and brought us credit, he's mud in your eye. And now you'd better stand your colleagues a round or two in the wardroom. And keep that medal on—give 'em something to aim for!"

Everything was neatly in place in my cabin in contrast to the aftermath of Dogger Bank, when the floor had been inches deep in seawater and the scuttle cracked by shell bursts. Indeed, from the weather deck down to deck 7 well below the waterline, the whole of *Lion* gleamed after the extensive repair work and a repaint.

"Unless you'd like to change, sir," said Haddock, unpacking and putting things away. "I know Lieutenant Highet has asked if you would like to share a refreshment with him in the wardroom."

"Will do," I said, taking off the sword and scabbard. I'd grown to like Highet. Even if an aura of impending disaster did hang over him at times—like throwing up during banquets for instance—he was honest and not as daft as he looked.

And so, medal sparkling, I strolled into the wood-panelled wardroom with its cheery fire, piano, settees, and fox-hunting prints—all resembling the lounge of a country hotel, though on occasions, when late-night steeplechases were held over the furniture, a good deal noisier. Well, the war had to be won somehow. We had our moments of heart-stopping terror, but now at least I got to pull rank with Highet, fresh from his visit to the Front.

It was good to be back.

AUTHOR'S ACKNOWLEDGEMENTS

MY INTEREST IN the men and ships of the Grand Fleet began when I interviewed survivors of the Battle of Jutland in Edinburgh for Scottish Television. A number of them had served aboard the battlecruisers based at Rosyth. Inspiration and encouragement for the creation of a youthful character who would reflect the Royal Navy at that time was provided by George MacDonald Fraser, author of the Harry Flashman books, noted for their historical accuracy.

Apart from Lieutenant Tucker, some of the characters in this book are real, others are wholly fictional, and almost all of what occurs, at least in some form, actually happened in real life.

Insights into Sir David Beatty were provided by members of his family, including his grandson Nicholas, who invited me to visit their country house and showed me his personal museum with its models of *Lion* and *Tiger* and some of the other battlecruisers, his Splendid Cats. I later met and interviewed Lieutenant St John Fancourt, a midshipman who served in a 13.5-inch gun turret on one of *Lion*'s sister ships, *Princess Royal*.

My researches into the period were greatly assisted by the Historical Branch of the Royal Navy and the staff at the Imperial War Museum and Maritime Museum. Coincidentally, I was pleased to play a part in gaining recognition for the importance of the last remaining ship of the Grand Fleet, the light cruiser HMS *Caroline*, now restored and on show in Belfast.

Among the books which have provided invaluable help are Stephen Roskill's intimate biography published as *Admiral of the Fleet, Earl Beatty: The Last Naval Hero* by Collins in 1980; Rear Admiral W. S. Chalmers's *The Life and Letters of David, Earl Beatty, Admiral of the Fleet* by Hodder & Stoughton in 1950; Filson Young's marvellous account, *With the Battle Cruisers*, first published by Cassell and Company in 1921; and *The Dreadnoughts*, published by Time-Life Books in 1979.

With thanks to all those who have helped, this book is dedicated to the shipbuilders, stokers, gunners, admirals, captains, officers, and seamen in the Grand Fleet, who protected our shores during The Great War of 1914-1918.